THE DRAGONAXI CHALLENGE

THE HAKKAN SERIES: BOOK ONE

LESLIE E. HEATH

Dedication

For my dear friend Beth.
Your gentle encouragement gave me the push I needed to keep
plodding along even through the darkest times. Thank you.

ONE

Announcement

The bitter taste of failure burned in the back of Marella's throat. She gazed over the dozens of empty desks, spaced out to deter cheating, fighting the urge to close her earflaps and block out her instructor's gentle advice.

"Look, you're welcome to take the exam again next month, but my notes say this was your," the teacher checked the clipboard clasped to her chest, "ninth attempt. I think it's time you admit that a simpler subject might be a better fit." The teacher dipped her head to meet Marella's downturned gaze. Instead, Marella raised her eyes to the low ceiling of the classroom and examined all the protective runes carved in the corners. She'd rather look anywhere but at the pity she knew lurked in her teacher's eyes.

Tears stung her eyes as she swam away from the rows of desks set out for test day, unwilling to listen for another instant. She *would* be a biologist, she *would* spend her life studying whales, and this, this... *woman* wouldn't stop her.

Blinded by shame, Marella left the school without glancing back at the white building where she took her classes. It was one of a dozen nearly identical buildings all clustered together. All the youth in Endael City attended that school to determine their future career. Fuming, she kicked past the end of the school. She wouldn't let a few calculations keep her from her dream.

She needed to talk to Coline. Her tutor would have a plan for repeating the exam — again — and get her back on track. Coline had to have a plan. Marella couldn't accept anything less. She wouldn't. She had to study more, work harder, be better. Marella swore she'd spend every minute of every day working on the calculations she'd missed. She understood the biology and knew the ethology and how to predict the animals' behavior. The damned calculations stumped her time and time again.

Cursing under her breath, she bowed her head and shifted her direction enough that the current pulled her long green and purple hair forward to obscure her face. Afraid of meeting other students and having to reveal her failure, Marella swam as fast as she could between the single-story stone houses, ducking between buildings instead of using the open avenues leading toward the edge of town. She chose a route that avoided the bustling markets and open parks where her friends congregated after class. Marella was happy for their successes, she really was, but she couldn't face them just then.

The space between the houses grew as she reached the town's boundary, and Marella slowed and scanned the area before she ventured into the open waters beyond the last buildings. A school of silver fish danced overhead, casting shimmering light onto the flat, sandy ocean floor.

When the shifting mass of fish moved on, Marella swam out into the open, moving slowly toward the kidali with the smallest movements she could manage. She'd learned to swim that way as a small child since her grandma had said it made it harder for sharks and other predators to see her.

Half a dozen lengths away, the tall shapes of dark green kidali undulated with the current. The sight was almost enough to make her hungry. Kidali grew shorter and squatter than kelp but had a light, sweet flavor which had made it her favorite food since childhood. Maybe a snack could make her feel better.

A flicker at the edge of her vision caught her attention, and she gasped. A giant bultier dove toward the ground mere yards from her, its tentacles tucked behind it to allow a deadly speed. It pulled all ten of its long, curling legs out, flaring the skin between them when it caught the water. It turned an instant before colliding with the sand-covered stone and glided silently along the ocean floor. Light flashed over the pale gray patches on its skin, a warning to any nearby creature to stay away.

To anyone who hadn't encountered one before, it looked like an enormous blue octopus with pale gray geometric shapes over its body and legs, each outlined in deadly red. Its body stretched almost twice the size of her torso, its legs each more than double her length. This creature was anything but harmless. Despite its unwieldy size, it was one of the fastest animals in the sea. She'd only faced this deadly predator in her nightmares before and had hoped that status would never change.

Terror froze her limbs and made her long to swim as fast as she could at the same time. She gauged the distance to the nearest building. She'd never make it there before the bultier reached her. Silvery light flashed over its skin again, following the red lines and highlighting the pale gray patches along the tentacles.

A glittering sapphire eye regarded her across the empty

sea floor. She drifted toward the kidali field and tried to look as unthreatening — and unappetizing — as she could. A growing shadow above the bultier froze her in her tracks again. She didn't even breathe. She didn't dare look up, which would require her to take her eyes off the lethal cephalopod.

The shadow grew, and the bultier darted away into the town. Marella fought the urge to call a warning to the people nearby. That would only anger the beast and bring its attention back to her. She had to trust the watches would see it. Instead, she pressed herself low to the ground and breathed out to keep the sand out of her mouth as a massive blue marlin swooped over her. Its long spear nose rippled the water over her back as it pulled up to avoid colliding with the sea bed.

As soon as it moved back toward the surface, Marella leapt into motion and swam with every bit of strength she possessed, rushing toward the closest thing she could see: the shipwreck her parents had scolded her for exploring a dozen times over. Its half-rotted hull rose out of the sea floor like a ghostly beast, shifting and swaying with the current.

A vibration warned Marella she hadn't been fast enough, and she darted to her left and hid behind the sunken ship's mainmast, which lay across the bow and created a shadowed hiding place. She lay as still as she could, hoping against hope the bultier had gone elsewhere and the marlin pursued her. She could outwit a marlin. The vibration didn't slow, and Marella stayed frozen in place, sending a frantic prayer to Dalphein, god of the sea, the most powerful of the gods and protector of her people. While she waited, she prayed as fervently as she could.

"Please let it go away. There's plenty of fish for it to

eat." A shimmering above her announced the return of the silvery school of fish, punctuating her prayer.

Light flashed, giving Marella a heartbeat's warning before the bultier darted around the fallen mast less than a length away from her hiding place. She swam as hard as she could into the darkened hull, praying all the while that Dalphein would save her somehow.

Once inside the ship, she turned right, ducking behind toppled furniture to keep hidden and working her way toward the ornate staircase she'd explored so many times. Something behind her crashed, throwing up a cloud of sand and dirt and making it harder to see in the murky darkness.

It doesn't want to hurt me. It's just trying to get away. Marella repeated the words over and over in her mind, but they didn't allay her anxiety one bit. It hadn't chased her into the ship to escape the marlin, and a giant bultier could kill a supaerisi like her in mere moments. Others she'd known who had fallen prey to the beasts had been much stronger and faster than her, and she'd be a tasty meal for the animal if it could catch her. If. She drew a deep breath and kicked hard toward her only escape.

The bultier rounded the corner behind her, flashing eerie light over its skin every few heartbeats. The more rapid the lights, the more irritated the animal was, or so her teachers had always said.

In this case, it didn't bode well for her.

Marella shifted left and swam hard. She crossed her arms over her face before diving head-first into the only porthole that had cracked as the ship sank. Deep lines etched the window, and Marella slammed her elbow into the center of the spiderweb of cracks. The aged glass shattered, and she dashed through the opening, praying she could escape without cutting herself. It wouldn't do her any good to escape the bultier only to attract a swarm of sharks. Her flowing tunic snagged, stopping her cold for half a heartbeat.

One hard kick tore it free, ripping the garment down the side as she burst out into the open. The bright light of day blinded her, but Marella didn't pause. That porthole wouldn't slow the bultier for long, but it would take a minute or so to squeeze through the narrow opening. Unwilling to waste a second, she darted across the open sea floor and into the tall, waving fronds of seaweed. The kidali cast strange shadows all around her, but Marella kept going. She wove a pattern through the delicious field, moving as quickly as she dared toward its center.

"Oh, ye've got yerself in trouble again, eh? It's not those hunters from shore again, is it? You know to stay well clear of those sorts."

The gravelly voice startled Marella, and she let out a shriek. A heartbeat later, she recognized the voice and accent and spun to frown at the friendly farmer. "It's not my fault, Ms. Nazeli. I was just on my way to see you, and I got attacked by a marlin and a bultier."

Ms. Nazeli kept her faded blue hair in a tight knot at the back of her head. Her green skin showed all the wrinkles, marks, and scars of her many years, but her pale blue eyes shone with wisdom and humor.

"Attacked, you say? Let me see. Where are you hurt?" The old woman's piercing blue eyes squinted almost closed, and she leaned closer to examine Marella.

"I'm not hurt," Marella blurted out. "They didn't catch me. The marlin swam away to chase some fish, and I think I lost the bultier in the kidali."

She slowed enough to examine her arms and legs,

making sure she hadn't cut herself on the broken glass. She'd lost several scales but had no wounds deep enough to bleed.

"Now, that bultier's a sight smarter than any dumb fish, even a marlin." Ms. Nazeli pressed a bit of kidali between her hands and jerked her head toward the tiny stone cabin set among the waving seaweed. "Come inside and wait a bit to make sure it's gone. I've got something new for you to try."

Marella hurried into the little shack, eager to see what new kidali treats the old woman had cooked up this time.

~

An hour later, Marella slunk through the polished wood front door to her low-slung stone home. Warm wood planking lined the walls, reinforced with tiny runes to keep the seawater from destroying the deep gold shine. The large, central part of the house held well-worn furniture in a small square in the center of the room, with small tables between the two couches and beside the two matching chairs. All the furniture was upholstered with matching green daeko, a tough but comfortable fabric woven from the tough fibers in the center of the kidali plant.

She'd had to renew the strengthening runes near the floor only a month before, though she'd made them small enough to be almost invisible. The dining table and several ornate iron chairs occupied an open area on the left side with a small food prep area tucked into a corner beside the table. Five doors led from the main area to the bedrooms. No one entered the middle room since her brother had stormed out two years earlier. Her room sat between her parents' room and her brother's, and the other two were kept clean and fresh for guests.

The home wasn't large, but brightly colored tapestries on the floor and walls made it comfortable and inviting. Matching runes marked each of the pieces her father had bought from the land merchants, so they'd survive the sea. Cheerful yellow curtains fluttered in the window, an eccentricity her father had insisted on after a brief visit to the dry lands above the surface.

Marella sighed and swam toward the soft green sofa where her mother sat hunched over a creased document.

"Well? How'd it go?" Yeva flipped her shining cobalt hair out of her face without looking up from the heavy page in her slender, bronze hands. Marella had spent her whole life hearing how she'd be an exact copy of her mother if only she had blue hair. She had her mother's large yellow eyes, flat nose, and bronze coloring. They even had the same slender, almost pointy shape to their faces.

Marella fidgeted until her mother met her gaze. Forcing a cheerful tone, she said, "I failed the calculations again, but only by six points this time. I'm getting better. I just need one more try. Coline can help me study a bit more, right?"

Marella's father had grown soft around the middle though she still thought of him as the muscular man from her early childhood. His white hair fluttered around his worried bronze face, and he patted the empty chair beside his.

"Come sit down. We need to talk."

Her stomach dropped into her tail fins, but Marella did as she was told. Her mother's face crumpled, and she looked like she might cry. Marella longed to sit beside her mother, but she stayed put. Her father sighed and wiped a hand over his face.

"There's no easy way to say this, and I will not insult you by trying to soften it." Her father placed a hand over hers on the cushion. "You won't be taking the exam again, at least not anytime soon. We're moving to Pharlandzi."

The blood drained from Marella's face, and icy cold penetrated her skin. "Why? When? Why?" She paused to catch her breath. When her parents stayed quiet, she added, "Our home is here in Kaulo, and in Endael City. My home is here. My friends are here, and so is my future. Why can't you move and let me stay here with Uncle Maegar?"

Her mother glided across the room and settled onto the arm of Marella's chair. "I know this is a shock, dear, but you'll need to go with us. The king has chosen your father to represent Kaulo on the new Emissary Board in Pharlandzi. This might be our chance to do something about the Pharli turning their poor into slaves for the mines. If that's going to happen, your father needs his family to support him." She patted Marella's arm and continued, "Especially around people like the Pharli royals. We need to stick together and watch each other's backs. Your father's already sent a message to your brother. He'll follow as soon as he can."

"But I'm so close! I'll never pass that exam from so far away. I don't even know if they have it there, or if they'd even grade me fairly if they let me take it." Desperate, Marella grabbed her mother's arm. "Please don't make me—"

"I'm sorry, but this isn't up for discussion." Her father rose and swam to the other side of the room.

Marella searched her parents' faces for any hint of weakness but found none. After a long moment, she gave up and slunk off to her bedroom where she buried her face in her hands and wept. There had to be a way to change their minds. There just had to. She'd worked too hard to give up and move now.

She'd never be able to fit in with any group in Pharlandzi — the nation or the city — Marella was sure. She'd heard they killed Dalphein's creatures for food, a thought that made her stomach heave. And even her mother acknowledged that they enslaved their own people. How did they even rule there? She wasn't sure. Marella searched her memory for some scrap of information from her lessons, but nothing surfaced. She'd stayed so focused on the biology exam for so long that the rest, all the things she'd deemed unimportant, had faded from memory.

What was an "emissary board," anyway, and why should her father have to be on it? It sounded like a scam, a way to make the people of the outlying nations think they had a say in Pharlandzi's decisions. That had to be it. The king had heard the whisperings of the new coalition forming between Kaulo and its neighbors and wanted to make sure no one tried to attack them.

But even if that was the case, how could she convince her parents not to go? They'd already set their minds on the move. And once they decided on something, they didn't sway from it.

Her sobs grew louder until they drowned out every other sound, and Marella didn't hear her mother enter. She jumped when a gentle hand settled on her shoulder but didn't raise her head.

"It's not that bad." Her mother's voice was gentle, as if she were soothing a small child. "We won't be in Pharlandzi forever, and you can keep up with your studies while we're there. I'm sure you'll pass the exam when we return next year."

"A whole year?" Marella's voice pitched higher with every word. "I'll be a year behind everyone else. I'll never catch up! Why did you bother hiring tutors if you were just going to drag me off to the barbarians for a year, anyway? My future is over, and it never even started." The last came out in a wail loud enough to compete with the whales she'd dreamed of studying. She could feel that dream dying with every breath.

"That's enough. This isn't about you." All the gentleness had left her mother's voice, and the words cut like a knife. "Your life isn't over. You're only sixteen. You have your whole life ahead of you. For that matter, your education isn't over, either. And the Pharli are not barbarians."

"But you even said we have to watch our backs—"

Her mother shook her head, cutting Marella off mid-sentence. "Quite the opposite. They're genteel and sophisticated and conniving. They won't attack you outright. They'll discredit you with whispers instead."

"That's not the point! Why would I want to spend time around people like that?"

"The point is it's an honor for your father and an opportunity for you to see more of the world. When you pull yourself together, we'll go to the palace to accept your uncle's offer in person. And you'll be gracious and grateful."

The hand vanished from her shoulder, but Marella didn't raise her head. Instead, she sobbed even harder, though this time she kept it as quiet as she could. When she couldn't cry any more, she dragged a hand over her swollen eyes and swam to the window.

Surely her parents wouldn't really make her go. She

took a deep breath and sighed, welcoming the cool water on her hot throat. No, her parents wouldn't leave her behind. To do so would be a huge black mark on her father's honor, and they wouldn't allow that.

A quick glance in the mirror showed her large, yellow eyes rimmed with red, her green and purple hair knotted around her face, and scrapes and scratches along her arms and legs. She couldn't go to the palace looking like that.

She ran a brush through her tangled hair and smoothed a hand over the damaged scales on her legs. A line of large scales with small holes lined her right leg while the scales along her left leg each held a small peg that fit in the hole of the right scales. When engaged, they locked her legs together so she could swim or released them so she could walk on land — if she ever managed to see the surface. She'd heard her mother say that the land-walkers used similar devices to keep their clothing together but called them "snaps." Someday, she'd get to see all the things her mother had seen. At least, she hoped so.

A few of those locking scales had been pulled loose in her narrow escape, but she wouldn't be able to fix that in the time she had. Knowing she couldn't improve her appearance any more, she rubbed a hand over her tear-swollen eyes and swam out to meet her parents.

TWO

Palace

An hour later, Marella followed her father through the center of town. She kept her eyes glued to her mother's back when they passed the school. In single file, they swam through the carved double doors into the marble entryway of her uncle's palace and waited for the host to call them into the king's court. The stone sparkled in the light cast through the open doors, and Marella relaxed a tiny bit into the awe she always experienced in the palace.

She'd heard stories of grand palaces many floors tall in other kingdoms, but Kaulo had strong currents and what the professors at school called an "active ocean floor," which combined to mean that tall buildings wouldn't stand for long no matter how many runes they used. Flat, one-story structures with thick, angled walls lasted much longer. The palace blended into the landscape with its unobtrusive outer walls, but the inside had always taken Marella's breath away.

Intricate carvings decorated the glittering inner walls, and columns along the entrance set the palace apart. Glowing yellow orbs the size of Marella's head lit the hallways and the vast room where the king held court. Those had always intrigued her. She didn't know how they worked, but they'd captured her imagination since she'd been a small child. As she'd grown older, she'd learned that runes and crigoresi somehow made them glow, but she still didn't understand the mechanism. Much smaller, simpler versions of those lamps sat in the corners of her home to ward off the night's darkness.

"Vazken del Kapat, his wife, Yeva, and his daughter, Marella." The herald's voice rang out like a drum, sweeping through the area and silencing the murmuring crowd.

"Of course. Bring them in."

Marella maintained exactly two lengths' space between herself and her parents and followed them into the court. Supaerisi clad in their best court clothes bowed low on either side, offering a level of reverence usually reserved for the monarch and his wife and children. The extra attention made Marella a little uneasy, but she plastered a gracious smile on her face and completed the ceremonial swim to the front of the aisle without meeting any of those curious gazes.

I should have worn something nicer. She resisted the urge to tug at the ink-stained sleeves on the pale blue tunic she'd worn for the exam. The hole in the side that had seemed so small when she'd examined it in her room felt like a gaping window to her flesh now, and she couldn't stop the heat that moved into her cheeks. She did manage to keep her hands firmly at her sides, but it took all her concentration.

The king swam back and forth above the crowd, a gleaming line of silver encircling his head and a regal silvery-white tunic flowing around him as he moved. His hair had long since turned white, but that meant nothing to Marella. He kept himself as lean and muscled as his son, who was more than twenty years his junior, and the bronze skin of his arms shone in the waning afternoon light that filtered through the high, arched windows.

"Brother, I take it you have considered my offer? Will you represent your king and country in Pharlandzi?"

"I will," her father answered. "I'm honored to be chosen for such a role. Thank you."

"Excellent. You will need to leave as soon as possible, by next week at the latest. I shall send word of your acceptance, so they'll know to expect you. Will you stay for the evening meal?"

"We would be honored, brother."

Marella fought back a groan. She wasn't sure she'd be able to smile and make nice at the evening meal, especially since it would likely only be her family and the king — her uncle — and his wife. The king's son had recently left to explore the southern oceans in search of the elusive great whales, which left Marella green with envy. That was her dream. It had irked her when the prince had stepped into the role with only a fraction of the effort she'd put into it.

The king called an end to the formal court day and left by a side door, and all the guests and courtiers departed through the carved stone doors Marella had entered through. She remained in her spot and fidgeted with the webbing between her fingers, still fighting the urge to cover the hole in her tunic with her hand.

When the hall stood empty except for a few stragglers in close little groups, she followed her father out the main doors and around to a smaller entrance into the palace, where a girl with brilliant yellow hair and matching eyes met them. She couldn't have been more than a few years younger than Marella.

The girl flashed a bright smile and led the way down a long corridor and into a small dining nook.

"I hope this is all right." The king waved a hand toward the small oval table in the family apartment. The table and chairs were made of glittering stone, and paintings of past generations of royals decorated the walls. "I didn't want to put the staff to all the trouble of making up the grand dining parlor for just us."

"This is perfect," Yeva gushed, hurrying to her normal seat on the right side of the table and leaving one empty chair between herself and the king for her husband.

Marella said nothing and settled onto the carved stone chair across from her mother. When she'd been young, she had traced the fish and dolphins and kidali leaves that ran around the edge of the chair while the adults had talked, and she fought the urge to do the same now. Perhaps it would ease the fluttering anxiety in her stomach.

The servants brought out platter after platter of ornate dishes, each a combination of exotic seaweed, kidali, mushrooms, and fruits from the land up above. The brilliant red and orange land fruits made her wonder again what it must be like on the land above. She'd read stories and histories, of course, but how could anyone live without water? That subject distracted her until her uncle filled his plate and took his first bite: the signal that the others at the table could then begin their meal.

Maegar piled his plate high, but waited until everyone had been served before he took a bite. While he waited, he asked, "Vazken, what does Errebeld have to say about your appointment? Will he join you in Pharlandzi?"

"I don't know. I've sent him a letter, but he hasn't had time to reply, yet. I'm hoping he doesn't let his ideals get in the way of such a wonderful opportunity."

Maegar nodded. "Never understood what the boy had against the Pharli royals, myself. I don't think I'd make the same choices they did in that situation, but they did what they thought best to avoid a three-front war."

"You know how hotheaded young men can be," Yeva said between bites. "He'll settle down in time. Until then, I do hope he meets us there. I'd love to see him again." A sad look crossed her face, but Yeva smoothed it away as quickly as it appeared.

Marella listened to the conversation while she ate her fill and enjoyed all the flavors and textures she only got when dining with her uncle. Her gaze drifted to the empty chair beside her uncle's, where the prince would sit when he was home.

It must be lovely to be the child of the king, she mused. The prince and his sisters had all gotten to choose their careers and hadn't even had to take the exams to allow them into the specialized academies. And their parents had never forced them to leave everything they knew behind and move to the other side of the ocean.

A hint of an idea forced its way into her mind, and she blurted it out without even considering her words.

"Uncle, is there any way, I mean, would it be possible for me to stay here with you while my parents journey to Pharlandzi? I know it's a great honor and all, but I've been studying so hard..."

Her words trailed off at the thunderous scowl on her father's face and the shock on her uncle's.

"Marella!" Her mother was out of her chair and around the table so fast Marella didn't even see her move until an iron grip clamped down on her upper arm.

Her mother dragged her through the hall and deposited her in front of the outer door. "If you think for one second that you can override your father and I like that..." Her eyes narrowed. "Not everything is about you, Marella. This is so much bigger than that." Her mother shook her head and pressed her lips into a hard line. "Well, you'll have plenty of time to think about it. There will be no more clubs. No more parties. Go home. The guard will escort you home and stay until we get there."

Marella's stomach sank, and she blanched at each word her mother spoke. She'd known better. She'd already asked about staying. She glared at the guard assigned to babysit her for the evening and rushed out ahead of him. He followed a length behind, his face as expressionless as a parade guard's. Somehow his lack of emotion made everything even worse. He should be as annoyed as she was.

She shouldn't have to leave the palace with a guard anymore. She wasn't a child; she was nearly seventeen! The guard could at least have the decency to stay further back. Marella huffed and raced past clusters of people gathered in the markets between her home and the palace. She hoped no one recognized her. That thought brought her up short, and she slowed her pace and dropped her head, letting her hair swirl in a shining green and purple cascade around her face and making every effort to blend into the crowd.

It had been years since she'd been turned out of a royal meal — she'd been less than ten years old the last time — and the shame finally caught up to her. She wished she'd taken the time to consider her request before she'd said it out loud.

At home, she ignored the guard (who settled into one of the chairs in the sitting room) and swept into the privacy of her own room. She swam in circles for a while but soon tired of that and drifted toward the whale she'd been working on. It was nearly the length of her arm and was by far the largest piece she'd ever attempted. Sculpting always helped calm her nerves and center her mind, so she picked up her tools and set to work.

She stuffed the hurt and anger to the side. One strike with too much force would ruin the delicate piece, so she concentrated on her breathing and chipped one tiny sliver of marble away at a time. The soft rhythm soothed her and helped her think more clearly on the evening's events. Maybe she hadn't been fair to her parents. It had just been too much of a shock. She hadn't known how to handle it. Still, she was the king's niece and should be able to keep her cool no matter what challenges she faced.

Time faded into nothingness as Marella concentrated on the sculpture. She focused so hard she didn't hear her parents enter the house or swim into her room.

Movement by the door caught her attention, and she dropped the tools onto the low table.

"Before you say anything," Marella began. "I want to say I'm sorry. I know that's not enough. I knew better than to disrespect you by speaking to my uncle after you had already answered that question."

"Very well," her father said with a sigh. "Your punishment stands. No groups, no clubs, and no parties until we return from Pharlandzi. You won't have much time for those things, anyway. We leave in four days."

"Four days!" Marella couldn't stop the exclamation. "Why so soon?"

"The Pharli king has asked us to make haste, and so we will. I'm not sure what threat he's facing to bring all the ocean kingdoms together on such short notice, but it must be grave."

Her mother cut in, adding, "We'll travel light and buy any additional supplies when we get there, so don't pack too much." She smiled and added, "A day of shopping in the Pharli markets will do us both some good, and it'll help you feel better about moving, I'm sure."

Marella glanced at the sculpture. She'd have to finish it before she left and give it to Uncle Maegar as an apology. That would help soothe ruffled scales and ease any remaining tension in the family. Besides, that way, she wouldn't have to worry about dragging it to the other end of the ocean.

Her mind turned to more practical things. "What should I bring? I've never traveled so far before."

"Bring your clothes, your toiletries, your ceremonial garb. I'll figure out what else we need tomorrow and let you know." Her mother sighed and placed a hand on Marella's shoulder. "I know this is hard. It's hard for all of us. But it won't be forever. Before you know it, you'll be back and studying with your friends again."

Studying. Horror dropped her stomach to her toes.

"Is Coline coming?" Maybe if her tutor could go, she could keep up with her classmates and be ready to take the exam the day she returned, Marella reasoned.

"I–I don't know." Her father looked perplexed for the first time in Marella's memory. "I hadn't considered asking her. I guess it would be helpful to have her there. She can keep you from falling behind. I'll speak with her in the morning."

Marella nodded and yawned, exhausted by the day's events.

"Get some sleep. We'll talk more tomorrow." Her mother ran a hand over Marella's hair and pulled her in for a hug.

THREE

Goodbye

Brilliant turquoise light filtered through the window. Marella shoved the hair out of her eyes and sat up.

Morning.

The previous day's events flooded her memory, and a desolation she couldn't shove aside followed. Quiet sobs shook her, but she swam to the wardrobe and pulled out her favorite clothes and her most prized possessions. She draped a flowing green cape embroidered with her family's crest across her unmade bed. She set the thin, crystal-encrusted tiara that marked her as the king's niece atop the cape. The purple and green top that matched her hair and eyes and brought compliments whenever she wore it followed. At the end of the bed, she placed the bracers her father had given her when she reached the age to begin training for her required army service, and the bow and arrows she used for practice. Thick tears blurred her vision, and she wondered if she'd be back to join her friends in the same unit like they'd always planned.

She blinked her eyes clear and shook the thought away. She had so much to get done and very little time. Her first priority, she decided, was the sculpture. It would take the longest. She quickly folded all the things from her bed, set them into her trunk, and grabbed for her tools.

~

No matter how hard she tried, Marella couldn't keep her anxiety at bay. She moved in to carve a delicate pattern on the whale's dorsal fin and realized she might never get the chance to study the majestic beasts. An unexpected sob shook her shoulders at the same instant the chisel tapped the marble. A chunk of stone the size of her fist broke off, and Marella gaped in horror. Time slowed to a crawl as the stone drifted to the ground. How was she supposed to finish it now? Her chest clenched tight, and she struggled to draw a breath.

Her mind jumped to crigoresi, the mineral would let her use the power of the runes without depleting herself. A little stab of guilt shot through her at the idea of using the crig, since much of it was mined with Pharli slave labor, She soothed her conscience by reminding herself that her uncle refused to buy it from the Pharli royals. Many citizens had criticized him for that decision, since it meant the people in Endael and all of Kaulo paid a much higher price than other places.

Do I have any left? She struggled to remember the last time she'd used it. *I think I have one. Maybe two if I'm lucky.*

If so, maybe she could draw the runes to put the stone back on the sculpture and try again.

Frantic, she dug through the small trunk she kept beside her bed, tossing reinforced papyrus scrolls, cloaks, and archery targets over her shoulders, where they fluttered to the floor. In the very bottom, nestled among a bed of thick blankets, she spotted the crystal box she used to store the precious mineral. Two small yellow beads shone through the crystal, and Marella smiled. She only needed one.

Taking care not to agitate the water near the box and make the tiny beads float out of the chest, she reached down and pinched one between her fingers. The movement created enough of a current to bounce the other bead in its enclosure, and Marella slammed the lid shut before it could drift closer to the top. One dose of crigoresi cost more than she earned in a year of chores, so she had to treat it with care. She'd gotten the beads as gifts from her father and uncle when she'd turned sixteen.

She ignored the mess she'd made and returned to the sculpture, the bead held gingerly between her forefinger and thumb, and gave a silent thanks to the teachers who had insisted she learn at least the basic runes.

"You'd better be worth it when you're done," she muttered. Without another thought, she tossed the bead into her mouth and swallowed, grimacing at the foreign, slippery texture of the wax on her tongue. She fought the urge to gag and gulped in a mouthful of seawater to wash away the lingering taste.

Unable to help herself, she gagged once and settled in to wait for the familiar tightening in her gut, the slight quickening of her pulse, and the anxiety that came from ingesting the crig when she hadn't used the power. Her cheeks flushed with the rush, and Marella lifted the carving chisel to the whale. She poured every drop of concentration she had into drawing one perfectly vertical line the length of her index finger. That accomplished, she drew a line the exact same length that slashed down on the bias from the upper right and intersected the vertical line a finger's breadth beneath the top. She repeated the process two more times, each line parallel to the second one and intersecting the vertical line exactly one finger beneath the one above it.

When she finished the last line, the mark glowed with a deep violet light, and Marella rushed to press the jagged chunk of stone directly over the rune. A deep rumbling echoed through the room and Marella strained to hold the stone completely still. The light dimmed and faded away. Where it had been, the energy had repaired the damage without the slightest mark to show where she'd made her error.

Worried she might have used too much power, Marella settled onto her bed and waited for the fatigue and nausea that meant she needed to take the other crig bead. When it didn't materialize, she grinned and scooped up all the things she'd tossed onto the floor in her haste. That bead had been well used, she decided. She eyed the sculpture once more, picked up her tools, and set to work finishing the design on the dorsal fin.

~

The blue-green light shone directly overhead when Marella finally emerged with her masterpiece.

She protected the sculpture with her arms and body and eased her way past the bustling crowds in the market until she reached the glittering quartz palace wall. There she waited for an escort into her uncle's private meeting chamber with its imposing onyx desk and stark sapphire walls. Inside, she fought the urge to fidget while she waited some more for her uncle to take a break from the main court and come to see her.

Her nerves had frayed to the breaking point by the time the door opened. King Maegar swam into the room in all his grace and glory, and Marella shrank even smaller into her chair.

"Marella! I hadn't expected to see you so soon."

The warm welcome in her uncle's voice gave Marella the courage to meet his smiling gaze.

"I–I wanted to say I'm sorry. I shouldn't have said what I did last night, at supper. I'm sorry if I ruined your meal."

"You ruined nothing." The king laughed and settled into the imposing space behind the great black desk. "You certainly surprised me. I didn't expect you to come right out with it like that, but it's only natural for you to want to stay here where your friends are, where you've got your entire life planned out."

"So, you'll let me stay with you?" Marella cringed at the hesitance in her voice but couldn't make the words come out any stronger.

King Magar laughed again. "No, child. Go see some of the world before you lock yourself in here. Who knows, you may come to love it there."

Marella shook her head. She loved her home. She couldn't imagine loving anywhere else. Before she could say something she'd regret, she lifted the sculpture and set it on the desk.

"I made this for you. I've been working on it for a while now."

"I see." The king picked up the whale and turned it this way and that, examining all the marks and patterns she'd painstakingly carved into the marble. "Very well done. And it will fit perfectly here on my desk. Thank you."

He set it on the right corner of the desk nearest to Marella and swam over both desk and sculpture to envelop her in a crushing hug. "I know this is hard. Try to look at it as an extended vacation. See the sights, meet the people, try the food. They've got some interesting dishes there in Pharlandzi."

Marella smiled and wriggled out of her uncle's hold. "I'll try. Can I write to you? I mean, not as the king, but as my uncle?" she hesitated and flushed. "You've always given me such good advice, and I'm afraid I won't know how to act in a foreign city."

"I'd like that. And I'm sure you'll do just fine. Just be careful of their etiquette. It's a bit stricter than ours. Now, you'd better get going. You've got a lot to do and only three days until you leave." He rumpled her hair as he'd done since she was a tiny thing swimming circles around him and led the way to the door.

The light overhead had dimmed to the deep green of evening before Marella swam back into her home. She'd cried most of the afternoon after she'd told her friends and teachers about her father's assignment to Pharlandzi.

Her favorite professors had promised to put together some assignments for her to work on during her time away but most shook their heads and lamented the time she'd lose on her education.

Her shoulders drooped, and her eyes stung, but she held her head high when she entered the living area and faced her parents. She longed to hear good news about her tutor, her lessons, or anything, but after the sad replies she'd gotten from her teachers, she wasn't hopeful.

"Rough day? You look exhausted." Her mother swam

over and wrapped her in a warm hug, and Marella struggled to keep from crying again.

"Is Papa home? Do you know if Coline agreed to go with us?" Marella bit back a deluge of questions to let her mother answer the most important ones.

"I haven't seen him yet. He was headed to a briefing with the king and his advisers, but that was this morning."

Marella fidgeted with the webbing between her fingers. "I didn't see him at the palace, but I stayed away from the public halls."

"Oh? Why were you there?"

"I finished the whale and gave it to Uncle Maegar as an apology for my behavior last night."

Her mother squeezed Marella's hand. "That was nice of you. I don't think he was angry, though. From what he said after you left, I think he expected it."

"He said something like that to me, too." Marella smiled at the memory and pulled away from her mother. "I guess I should figure out what to pack. How much am I allowed to bring?"

"Your father has decided we can't be expected to move without the cart, so just pack your trunk. Bring whatever you think you'll want."

Marella nodded and swam to her room. She'd just tossed everything in her trunk that morning with no thought to saving space, so she'd have to empty it out and start over.

Night fell, and Marella barely noticed except when she

paused to light the small orb lamps in the corners of her room. They looked like miniatures of the ones in her uncle's palace, but these worked with simple runes and little enough energy that they didn't require any crig.

"Marella, supper," her mother called from the main part of the house.

Marella finished wrapping the crystal and silver bracelet in a blouse and set it on top of the pile in her trunk. She stretched and yawned, and her stomach growled out a loud complaint. Eager for food, she swam out to the main room and took her seat at the table.

Her mother set plates of simple sea plants and herbs she'd bought from the traveling merchants on the table. Before Marella could settle into her seat, the front door opened, and Marella's father and Coline entered, both grinning widely.

The middle-aged tutor's face lit with a brilliant smile and anticipation glittered in her pale green eyes.

"Are you coming with us?" Marella couldn't contain her excitement and rushed over to hug her.

Coline hugged back and laughed. "I am. I've always wanted to travel but never had the chance. I'm afraid I may slow you down, though. These old bones don't move as fast as they once did."

"Don't worry about that. You can ride in the cart if you get tired. We'll make sure there's a comfortable spot for you to sit in there." Marella's father said.

At the same time, Yeva blurted out, "You're not old by any means. You're about the same age as me, and I'm as youthful as ever."

Both women laughed, and Marella settled in to eat with a much lighter spirit.

Maybe, she thought, *with Coline's help and a year away,*

I'll come back smarter than ever and pass that exam with flying colors. Then no one will tell me I need to pick a different career ever again.

The evening passed in a flurry of joyful conversation and detailed planning. Marella let her attention wander when her parents discussed the route they'd travel and how they'd pack the cart. She had bigger things to plan, like how to fit all her scrolls into her chest. She'd have to start all over — again — after dinner. Since she'd have a tutor, she had to make sure she had the materials to study. Perhaps a year away would be enough to let her finally master those calculations without the pressure of another exam in a month.

FOUR

Letter

Errebeld del Kapat swung his spear and blocked the thrust aimed for his chest. He brought the spear's long haft around to pull his opponent off balance and moved in with a final jab. His spear's dull edge laid against Gallien's sapphire throat.

"I yield," Gallien said with a laugh. "Well fought."

Errebeld lowered his spear, and Gallien moved close. His lips closed tenderly on Errebeld's in a brief kiss, then again, and once more, until Errebeld couldn't hold onto the morning's anger any longer and leaned into the kiss. He grabbed Gallien's strong shoulders for balance as his mind fuzzed.

Gallien broke away a moment later. "Won't you go with me to Pharlandzi, though? Please? I really don't want to go alone." He pressed the argument they'd had all morning.

Errebeld dropped his hands, ran a hand through his unruly green hair, and swam across the open room for a snack. Once he'd caught his breath, he said, "No, I don't think so. Why would anyone want to go to a place like that?

I've heard the court is less friendly than a swarm of sharks when there's blood in the water. I'd rather stay here."

"Bah. It's not as bad as all that. You're reading too much into it. I've heard the old king's turned downright friendly as he's aged." Gallien La Roche settled in across from Errebeld, his arms folded across his bare chest.

"No, really, they're all corrupt. Every king everywhere. Even my uncle's not much better," Errebeld shoved a wad of kelp into his mouth and gulped it down. "He caved to the Pharli pressures years ago, didn't he? And crig prices shot to the surface as soon as he did. Now no one can afford the stuff."

"Did he cave, though? I though prices went up because he refused to sign the treaty." Gallien lifted a shrimp off the tray and eyed it for a moment before crunching it down. "And if they are all corrupt, what difference does it make?" He continued without waiting for an answer. "None at all. We're just as stuck as everyone else. Come with me. I've heard the city's amazing. I'd love to stroll the market with you in the mornings and try all the little eateries together in the afternoon."

"I don't know. I think—"

A knock at the door cut him short. Errebeld rose, but Gallien waved him back.

"Stay put. I'll get it." He yanked the door open, irritation painted across his features. "I didn't order anything."

"Forgive me, milord La Roche. I have an urgent letter for Mister del Kapat. I understand he's staying here?" The old man leaned left to peer over Gallien's shoulder. "Ah, there you are, sir. May I give this to you directly?"

Errebeld forced a smile to hide the sinking feeling in his gut. No one ever sent him letters. Ever. He took the waxed linen paper from the old messenger and tossed the man a silver coin. The messenger caught it, bowed, and swam off down the street.

As soon as he'd gone, Gallien pushed the door closed. "Well? Are you going to open it? Or just stare at it all day?"

"It's from my father." Errebeld flipped the letter over in his hands and drifted back to the chaise. "I haven't gotten so much as a note from him since I left two years ago."

"Well, then you should open it and see what it says." Gallien handed him a finely carved quartz letter opener that glittered in the afternoon light.

Errebeld cut the seal and unrolled the paper, unsure whether he wanted to know what the missive contained. Fears for his baby sister and his mother ran rampant through his imagination. Curiosity won over trepidation, and he scanned the letter.

To Errebeld del Kapat, my errant son, nephew to the venerable King Maegar,

Errebeld bristled at the opening but forced himself to keep reading.

I have been granted the honor of representing Kaulo in the new nation's council in Pharlandzi. Your mother, sister, and I are leaving at once for that nation's capital. It would be most indecorous for our eldest son to neglect to appear with us, and as such, I am expecting you to meet us there within a month's time. I trust that will give you adequate time to wrap up or hand off any projects which currently hold your attention. You will find us in the royal court, inside the palace at the center of Pharlandzi City, and I will ensure your name is on the list of expected guests.

I look forward to seeing you soon.

Safe Travels,

Your father, Vazken del Kapat, Regent Prince of Kaulo and Ambassador to Pharlandzi

P.S. I expect you to be on your best behavior while in the palace. I'll have none of your foolish talk of rebellion.

Errebeld crumpled the page in his hands and searched for a fitting means to destroy it. None presented themselves, so he dragged his worn travel pack out of the corner and stuffed the wadded letter in the outer pocket.

"Well? Aren't you going to tell me what it says? You look mad enough to spit. What's going on?"

Errebeld drew a deep breath, searching within himself for the pool of calm his father had taught him to rely on. It defied him at first, but soon enough he was in that placid lake where he could maintain control of even the strongest emotion. "It seems my father has accepted some sort of post in Pharlandzi, and he sent this to summon me to join the rest of the family there." Hearing the words out loud jerked him out of the calm and plunged him back into the icy fury. He yanked the laces tight, puckering the top of the pack closed before checking the buttons on the other pockets. "I won't go. I'm not some spoiled royal hound who comes running at the first summons with my hat in my hands."

"I don't know. Maybe you should reconsider. You've been on the fringes of the Society for a while now. This may be your shot to do something useful to them."

Errebeld's hands stilled. He considered the options but couldn't bring himself to answer his father's call, even for the Society.

"No. I won't come bounding in like some spoiled little royal ass looking for my next trust fund payment."

"What do you mean? You're not a spoiled royal ass? Color me shocked!" Gallien laughed at his own joke, and Errebeld couldn't help chuckling along.

"All right, maybe sometimes, but that doesn't mean I'm willing to jump at the chance to join the barracuda den that is the Pharlandzi court."

"I know your father probably worded that badly," he waved a hand toward the pack containing the crumpled note. "But think of how much you could learn! You'd be inside the royal court. The Society would pay you well for any information you could get from such a position, I have no doubt."

"I'm not going."

"But we could stay together, or at least see each other, if you go. And the Society—"

"I wouldn't even know who in the Society I could talk to about such a thing! They'd all think I'm crazy for even thinking that old king would let me within a league of any sensitive information."

"I don't know, I—"

"And they'd be right!" Errebeld flopped back onto the lounger. "I can't stay here, though. My father knows where I am, and he'll send his lackeys to look for me if I don't show. Or rather when."

"Stay here," Gallien said. "I'll be back in a few. There's more of your kelp in the pantry if you get hungry."

"Wait! Where are you going?" Errebeld trailed his friend to the front door.

"I just remembered an errand. It won't take me long."

"You haven't even—"

Gallien swung the door shut behind him, cutting off Errebeld's response.

Errebeld let out a string of expletives and yanked his pack up onto the closest chaise, pulling it open in the same movement. Whatever errand Gallien had remembered must have been important if he hadn't even bothered to change out of his padded leather sparring jerkin, but his sudden exit just frayed Errebeld's raw nerves even further.

Frustrated and angry, Errebeld turned his attention to his next move. He'd have to figure something out and be on his way by morning, though the thought of leaving Gallien behind left a hollow ache in his chest. Still, he had plenty of friends. Hopefully one would be willing to take him in for a while. It wasn't forever. Gallien would only be in Pharlandzi for a few months, and then they could pick up where they'd left off. Slowly, he picked up his clothes and belongings and tossed them into the pack.

He found the little crystal box where he'd hidden it under the chaise cushion and tucked the box containing his only crigoresi bead underneath all the clothes in his pack. Time lost all meaning as he hunted down his clothes and trinkets in the various rooms of the house.

"What do you think you're doing? You're not running off already, are you?" Gallien's voice froze him in the act of stuffing a carved whale from his sister into his already overfull pack.

Errebeld startled and hid a sheepish blush. "I have to. My father knows where I am," he repeated, "so if I don't leave, he'll send his lackeys to drag—"

"Why should he have to drag you anywhere?" Gallien closed the door behind him and swam further into the room. "You should just go. It's an opportunity you won't get again."

A knock at the door stilled Errebeld's hands.

"I'll get it." Gallien waved a hand toward Errebeld. "Put that thing away before anyone asks questions."

Heat flushed Errebeld's cheeks, but he hoped his bronze coloring would hide it. He stuffed the pack under the chaise a heartbeat before Gallien opened the door.

A young, slender woman with deep purple hair and matching eyes swam through the opening.

"Soraya! What are you doing here? Aren't you supposed to be in Ashmora somewhere?" Errebeld called. He hoped he sounded happy to see the woman.

"I was. I'm back." Soraya swam into the room with all the sinewy confidence of a shark. "What's this I hear about you refusing an assignment?" She shoved her shoulder-length violet hair behind her ears and stared hard at Errebeld.

"I know nothing about an assignment." Errebeld shook his head in genuine confusion. "My father summoned me, but that's nothing. I'm going south instead." He paused, struggling to find a reason to head that direction. "I need to see a friend in Talam."

"Is that so? Who?"

"I–I...a name?"

"I want a name. Who?"

Errebeld scrambled for some scrap of information that would put a friend in that area but came up blank.

"You're just running, aren't you?"

"No." He tried for indignant, but only managed a hoarse croak. "What do I have to run from?"

"You should go to Pharlandzi. We need someone there, and now that your family's happily ensconced in the palace, you're the best chance we've got to get some actual information."

"Who's we? And what information do you think I can get? I'm nothing." He threw his hands up. "Just the rebellious son of one of the most unimportant emissaries." Errebeld didn't realize he was backing away from Soraya until he hit something hard and warm. He checked behind him and Gallien's grin reassured him. Errebeld leaned into

Gallien's warmth and turned his attention back to the advancing woman.

"You know very well who we are. You've been begging for an important assignment for months, and now you have one. Will you take it? Or will you run?"

Errebeld eased away from Gallien and glanced between the two. He met Gallien's eyes and glared. "You told her. Why? Why would you do that? I told you over and over that I don't want to go to the city. I'm not some royal idiot who comes running every time my father calls, and I won't be forced into looking like one. Not by you. Not by her." He jerked his head toward Soraya.

"Of course he told me." Soraya barked a laugh. "Do you think this kind of opportunity comes along every day? You need to go. We need the information you could get from inside that palace."

"I'm not going, so you'll have to find another assignment for me." Errebeld fought the urge to cross his arms over his chest. Instead, he kept them loose at his sides, awkward and limp.

"Fine. I have a message you can take to my sister in Talam, since you're fleeing in that direction, anyway."

"I'm not fleeing." Errebeld despised the whiney sound of his voice, so he cleared his throat and tried again. "I'm not running. I'm going to visit a friend. And I can certainly carry a letter."

Soraya nodded. "All right. I'll have it for you at first light. You'll be ready to go by then, I trust?" She glanced over to the spot where he'd hidden his pack.

She didn't wait for a response but turned and swam out without closing the door behind her.

Gallien stared after her, and Errebeld lifted his pack off the floor.

"Well, I guess that's settled." Errebeld gave a tremulous smile, and Gallien swore and slammed the door.

FIVE

Presented

The morning of their departure, the faded, gray light matched Marella's somber mood. Her father had always told her the dim morning meant clouds covered the sun on the surface, but Marella had never been to the surface and had only seen sculptures and artists' renderings of the clouds and sun. Her lessons had taught her that Pharlandzi was near the coast, so the possibility of seeing the surface and maybe meeting a few land-walkers ignited her imagination and had her humming a cheerful tune while she swam.

"Do you think we'll see any sharks?" she asked her father.

"I don't know. Even if we do, they won't be very interested in us."

"I know, but I've always wanted to see one." Marella sighed and resumed her humming though she didn't stop scanning the waters for signs of exotic life.

After a week of northern travel, the water grew colder with every hour they traveled.

"How cold is it in Pharlandzi? I didn't think I'd have to

worry about freezing to death." She rubbed her hands along her chilled arms and kicked harder to pump warmth into her legs.

"It's not that cold. You'll get used to it in no time," her mother answered though Marella had seen her rubbing her arms, too.

"Haven't you been there before?" Marella decided a little conversation might distract her from the freezing water.

"I have when I was a little older than you."

Marella cocked her head, considering the timeline. "Were you and Papa already married? Did you both go?"

"Yes. And no. Your brother was small, and your father kept him home, so I could go to Pharlandzi and visit some of my family. I hadn't seen them since I was a small child."

"Oh. What's it like there? Is your family still there? I don't remember you talking about any relatives in Pharlandzi."

Her mother smiled, though it looked a little sad to Marella. "It's lovely. My family never lived there. It was just a good central place for us to meet. We may do something similar this time. As for the city, the palace doesn't sparkle like your uncle's, but that's because it's a different kind of stone. Still, the city is lovely and colorful and friendly. Since it's so near the port, all kinds of fabrics and gems are available, and people wear bright clothes and jewels they buy from the land merchants. The market there is unlike anything else I've ever seen."

They swam in silence for several minutes while Marella considered that. "And you didn't freeze? Really? That current's so cold!"

"Some of the currents are colder than the city. It's not

far from the mountains and the gorge, so the currents can be a little disorienting sometimes."

"Do you think we'll see any dragons? I heard they have dragons inside the city." Marella had gaped when her uncle had told her that and had insisted it couldn't be true. She still wasn't sure.

Her mother sighed and shrugged. "I'm not sure. If I remember it right, this is the time of year the dragons all take off into the gorge to breed. They'll come back in a month or so." She sighed again and arched her back in an exaggerated stretch. "You'll be fine, love. We'll never be far from you. I promise." She yawned. "I think I'm going to keep Coline company in the cart for a little while."

She swam back to the cart behind the hulking, yoked essek, and disappeared from view. Marella examined the creature pulling their loaded cart. Some people called it a sea ox, though the drawings she'd seen of land ox looked completely different.

The essek had a wide head, with dull black eyes that never wavered from its path. Monotonous brown scales covered its muscular body, and wide fins propelled it and the cart through the water. Marella had always thought its face looked like a blue whale's but without the intelligence she expected to find in the whale's eyes. A long moment passed, and Marella decided her mother wouldn't return.

Disappointed at the abrupt end of the conversation, Marella went back to scanning and searching for unfamiliar animals.

If it gets much colder, she thought, *I might even see some whales.* That idea set her heart to pounding and shoved all thoughts of the chill and her conversation with her mother out of her mind.

~

Visibility decreased with every day they traveled north, and Marella fought headaches from straining to see through the murk.

Another week of mind-numbing, monotonous, exhausting — and freezing cold — travel passed before the high walls of the city appeared through the cloudy water. Marella went still and drifted on the current, her arms and legs hanging limp at the sight of the grand wall. It rose so high, she couldn't see the top of it.

Her eyes stretched wide as the teacups her grandmother had displayed on her shelves, Marella followed her father around the wall and up to the tall metal gates set in the northern part of the towering behemoth.

"Are you ready?" her father asked when they approached the guards.

"I think so." Marella's voice turned up at the end, as if she'd asked a question, but she did want to see what that immense wall protected.

"Wait." Her mother's voice brought her up short. "Come here, Marella."

Confused, Marella did as she was told and circled around to the back of the cart.

Her mother had pulled her hair up in a simple topknot, and Coline's hair had been braided and twisted around itself. Both wore clothes suitable for her uncle's court." You can't enter the city like that. Come here and let's see what we can do to clean you up."

Strong hands gripped her shoulders and her mother shoved her down to sit on the floor of the cart. A great deal of tugging and pulling at her hair ensued, but Marella tried hard to trust her mother's experience in this strange new city. Besides, she wasn't in such a big hurry to see what lay beyond such a massive wall.

Several long minutes later, her mother released her to return to her father, who moved toward the gate even before she reached him.

She hovered close behind her father as he spoke with the guards, and her breath caught in her throat when the gate swung open. Marella had expected some kind of welcome and fought a wave of disappointment when two guards broke away from the group and led them toward the palace in a silent procession.

Brilliant colors and foreign scents swirled and bobbed around her, leaving Marella disoriented and confused. Her gaze wandered over the city's spires, curving alleys, and bright storefronts, and she struggled to keep up with her father as he swam toward the palace at the center of the city. Circular towers and spires sprouted around it, making it look like a foreign and colorless coral growth. A hollow pit of terror opened in Marella's gut, though she had no reason to fear the place.

None of the brightly dressed people in the markets or rushing along the packed alleys even glanced their way or gave any indication they noticed the newcomers. Loneliness and disappointment warred with wide-eyed wonder at the nonchalance of their welcome and the wild colors and tall peaks that marked the city.

Marella stared hard at a group of women dressed in brilliant pinks and yellows and swam into her father's back so hard her nose smarted and her eyes stung.

They passed through a narrow gate and stopped in a narrow green courtyard. Marella strained to see more, blinking against the pain.

"We'll wait here. The guards will announce our arrival,

and someone will come to welcome us. I expect you'll get some of that fanfare you've been looking forward to."

Marella perked up. "You think so?"

The brightly dressed women followed them into the courtyard and clustered off to one side, alternating between studiously ignoring Marella's group and overtly staring at them.

"Who do you think they are?" Marella asked, pointing to the group.

"Don't point, Marella." The sharpness in her mother's voice caught Marella by surprise. "You'll have to be very careful of your manners here. They're much more ceremonial than we are in Kaulo."

"Sorry." Marella lowered her hand and tried again. "Do you think they're ladies of the court? Do you think they'll show me around?"

"I don't—"

A drum beat strong enough to rattle in Marella's chest cut off her mother's answer, and a heartbeat later, trumpets joined the drums.

Marella grinned and grabbed her mother's hand. Her father's face was smooth and serious as if he'd come for a funeral, and her mother's was nearly an identical match. Shocked at her parents' somber expressions, Marella schooled her face into an impartial mask, or so she hoped.

The music grew until Marella struggled to keep from twitching with every drumbeat. Just when she thought she'd figured out the rhythm and flow, it cut off. The silence echoed through the open space and Marella held her breath.

The guard beside her father shouted, "Vazken del Kapat and his wife, Yeva del Kapat, Ambassadors from Kaulo, and their daughter, Marella del Kapat, arriving as requested, Your Grace."

The staccato words rang off the walls, but no one had entered the courtyard — at least not anyone who looked important, besides the women who'd been watching them.

A new current tugged at the braids at the back of Marella's head, and she closed her eyes in silent thanks to her mother for tying it back. When she opened them again, her mouth fell open in shock. The wall in front of the group had opened outward, two previously hidden doors as thick as her waist standing out from the wall. In the opening, a small group of people stood stock still, their eyes fixed on something over Marella's head.

At the left, a small woman stood unmoving. Her green skin glimmered in the turquoise light, and her dark hair coiled tightly against her head in a mass of braids and coils that shimmered and sparkled.

On her right, a young man who looked a year or two older than Marella waited with his hands clasped tightly behind his back. His skin was a shade lighter than his mother's, but his hair was the same dark onyx and clipped short, close to his scalp. He met her gaze with his violet eyes and lifted one eyebrow the faintest increment, and Marella flushed. She gave another silent thanks to her mother for making her clean up before entering the city. If she'd come in with her hair wild and clothes mussed, she would have looked like the barbarian she had accused these people of being.

Marella ripped her gaze away from the young man's and moved on to the last man in the line. He had a regal bearing that would have put her uncle to shame, though he was nowhere near as large. His hair had faded to pale blue, but he shared the same green skin color as the rest of his family. His bare chest showed a fitness that surprised her given his obvious years. He wore a wide, gleaming collar of overlapping bronze scales that draped over his shoulders and covered his upper chest and arms. Intricate patterns and designs covered every bit, catching the afternoon light and making it shine as if encrusted with gems. Like his wife, the king stared out at a point above Marella's head, making him appear aloof and more, well... kinglier, she supposed, than she'd imagined anyone could.

"Welcome, friends from Kaulo." The king's voice echoed off the walls, and Marella startled. "Please, come inside and make yourselves at home. You must have traveled hard to make such a journey so quickly, so I imagine you would like to rest and freshen up. We have rooms prepared for you, and I hope you will be comfortable here."

He didn't wait for a response but turned and swam into the cavernous opening behind the door. The rest of his group followed, and the guards ushered Marella and her family through the doors.

Marella fought the urge to stop and stare. The ceiling was higher than her uncle's palace roof with doorways wide enough to allow the entire group to go through at once.

Comfortable loungers dotted the room, separated by rugs large enough for... realization dawned, and her breath caught. They were big enough for a dragon. In all the bustle and fuss of the move, Marella hadn't considered that these people who befriended dragons might actually allow the animals to live inside with them.

"Are there dragons here?" Marella blurted out, not to anyone in particular. Excitement and fear mingled in her chest at the thought of seeing the beasts.

"I'm afraid not." A young girl stopped cleaning the rug nearest Marella and moved closer. "The dragons are all out at the breeding ground for another month. They'll be back soon enough, though. Then you won't be able to move anywhere in the palace without running into one." She smiled, gave a tiny bow, and returned to her work.

Marella stared after her for a moment, trying to reconcile the relief and disappointment, but her family had moved on without her. She swam hard to catch up, but her mind stayed on the encounter with the maid. The girl had her hair tied into tight braids against her head, just like the queen's.

Now that she thought of it, Marella hadn't seen a single woman in the city with her hair loose. She ran a hand over the braids her mother had placed in her hair, using her fingers to trace the intricate patterns. She'd have to find someone to teach her how to do her hair the way the local women did if she was going to have a chance of fitting in. Not that she'd ever blend in entirely. Everyone she'd seen had blue or green skin and scales. Her family would stand out with their bronze skin and golden scales.

The rest of the tour passed in a blur of rooms and furniture, each as ornate and elaborate as the next. By the time the queen pointed her to her own room, Marella thought she'd never find her way back out again. She hoped she'd have some kind of guide for the first day or so.

"Will you be all right here while we go find our rooms?" Her mother asked. She glanced toward the servant who'd replaced the queen as their guide. "Are you sure she can't stay in our rooms with us?" She didn't wait for an answer before turning back to Marella. "You're looking a bit tired and overwhelmed."

"I'm sorry, madam. Each adult gets their own rooms under our customs. Your rooms are just down the hall."

Marella's mother nodded. "I promise we won't leave you alone for long. And I'm never far away if you need me."

Marella laughed and pulled herself up straight. It

wouldn't do to have her hosts think she was too weak to handle a tour, especially if they considered her an adult here. "Am I that obvious? I'll be all right. I'm just going to rest a bit and try to figure out how to do my hair in those little braids all the ladies are wearing. You did an amazing job, but I can't expect you to fix my hair every day."

"Oh, I'll help you with that." A young girl ducked her head out of a side room. "I'm Feena. I hope you don't mind; I've just been putting away some of your things. The queen assigned me to be your helper while you're here in Pharlandzi. Your clothes are very different from what I'm used to, but they're so lovely."

Her bubbly chatter made Marella smile. "I don't mind at all. I'm glad I've got someone to help me. I was just thinking I'd be hopelessly lost for weeks." Excitement washed away her fatigue, and Marella smiled. She'd never had her own servant before. "I'm Marella. It's good to meet you."

Unsure whether to extend a hand as she'd seen some merchants do or spread her arms in a sign of welcome, as her family had always done, Marella waited for Feena to make the next move, but the girl simply bowed and vanished back into the side room.

The door to the hallway closed behind her parents, and loneliness more potent than any she'd ever known swept over Marella. Instead of letting it overwhelm her, she inhaled the strange scents of the palace and drifted over to rest on a lounger. She closed her eyes and let the day's events play in her mind's eye.

A heartbeat later, her eyes popped open. "Feena?" she called.

The girl appeared from the side room. "Yes, Miss Marella?"

"What happened to Coline? I haven't seen her since we arrived. Is she all right?"

"I... Well, I suppose she's been given a room in the servants' quarters. Is she your usual helper? I can teach her what she needs to know to help you if you'd prefer."

The disappointment in the girl's voice made Marella's heart ache, and she rushed to say, "No, she's my tutor. I was just worried because she was so nervous."

"Oh, well, that makes sense, I suppose. Why don't you rest while I finish putting your things away? This evening will be busy, but I can bring her to you in the morning, if that's all right."

Marella nodded and leaned back against the lounger. Everything else could wait, but her exhaustion wouldn't be put off another second.

～

"Excuse me, Miss Marella?"

A tap on her shoulder accompanied the question, and Marella groaned and opened her eyes, blinking a few times against the blur of sleep.

The young serving girl hovered by the lounger. Marella searched her memory for the girl's name.

Feena! Yes, I think it's Feena. I'll have to get better at names.

"Oh, good. You're awake. We need to get you ready for your presentation this evening."

"Presentation?" Marella struggled to make sense of the girl's urgency but let Feena grab her hand and drag her into the side room.

Now that she'd had a bit of rest, Marella's curiosity got the better of her, and she stared in wide-eyed wonder at the elaborate dressing chamber. The girl had hung all Marella's belongings on hooks lining the wall, and a massive vanity occupied the entire far wall. Brilliant yellow glowing orbs encircled a heavy-looking glass, casting brilliant light over the room and revealing Marella's disheveled state in painful detail. Her braids had worked loose while she slept, and her hair stuck up in random directions.

"Here, have a seat and let's see what we can do with your hair." Feena pressed Marella down onto the stool in the middle of the vanity, freed her gently removed the braids, and ran a brush through her long green and purple hair.

"Your hair is so long. Have you ever cut it?"

The girl spoke so quickly, it took her a moment to decipher the words. As soon as she did, Marella blanched and met the girl's eyes in the looking glass. She took a deep breath and worked to temper her reaction before she spoke. "Of course not. Why would I cut it?"

"I'm sorry. I know where you live women keep their hair long and free, but you don't have dragons, right?"

Marella shook her head and ran her hands through her hip-length hair, uneasy but sure she knew what Feena was about to say. "There won't be any dragons for a month or so, right?"

"No, but don't you want to wear one of the popular styles? You had it done up a bit when you arrived, but no one's worn that style around here in years."

Remembering her determination to try to fit in when she'd first arrived, Marella reluctantly shook her head. "My mother, what's she doing? She's letting them cut her hair, isn't she?"

Feena nodded and brushed through the area Marella had touched again.

Torn between the sense that she was somehow betraying her own culture by changing so quickly and the need to fit in to the court social scene in her new home, Marella fiddled with the webbing between her fingers. It didn't take her long to decide.

It's only hair, after all, she rationalized. *It'll grow back. I hope.*

"All right, go ahead. But you have to tell me everything else I need to know so I don't make a fool of myself tonight."

A dazzling smile lit Feena's lilac features, brightening her violet eyes and completely transforming her features. Marella couldn't help but smile back in the looking glass.

Feena chattered away, listing customs faster than Marella could memorize them and tugging gently at Marella's hair while she trimmed and braided and twisted it into a style more elaborate than any Marella had ever seen.

"Oh, dear, I'm not sure you've got any of that," Feena said after a while, her grin returning. "Don't worry, though, everyone here's friendly, and we're all so glad to have your family here that I'm sure no one will pay any attention if you make a little slip here or there."

Marella forced a grin and tried to push down the terror that had grown in her gut with every new rule Feena had mentioned. It seemed like far too much for one person to remember, and Marella wondered if she'd be able to keep Feena or Coline near her through the evening's events to help her.

The weight of Marella's hair piled atop her head felt strange, but not unmanageable. She stared at it in the mirror for a long moment until Feena turned her toward the line of clothes hung on pegs on the far wall, across from the ones Marella had brought with her.

"The king had these brought in for you to use until you have a chance to go shopping. What color do you like?" Feena kept up her conversational chatter, but her tone turned more questioning. "All your clothes are such pale colors; they simply won't do for your presentation. I've never seen anyone with quite your coloring before. It's so lovely and exotic. What colors look best on you?"

"I–I have no idea." Marella blinked at the rainbow of colors lining the wall. "I've never worn anything that bright before. What would you suggest?"

"Mmmm, let's see, well, this orange would look lovely against your skin." Feena draped an ornate gown over Marella's shoulder, shook her head, and hung it back on the wall. "That works with your skin beautifully, but clashes with your hair. It's such an unusual combination. Hummm, what else could we try? Ooh, I know, let's try this one." She pulled a deep blue gown down from the other end of the wall and draped it over Marella's shoulder. "Yes, I think that's perfect. Here, we need to get you dressed or you'll be late."

Feena positioned herself in front of Marella and held the gown open for her to slip her arms into. Marella hadn't seen a garment like it before and couldn't figure out how it was supposed to go on or close. Thankfully, Feena's competence saved the day — again. As soon as Marella slid her arms into the wide, flowing sleeves, Feena spun her around and tugged the garment tight around her waist and bosom.

Curious, Marella tried to see over her shoulder to what Feena had done at her back, but all she saw was a line of bronze glimmering in the light. Metallic threads had been woven into the blue fabric, and they caught the light whenever Marella moved. The effect took her breath away, and Marella froze to stare at her reflection in the looking glass.

"Oh, that looks lovely on you. Do you want me to line your eyes?"

Marella frowned, unsure what the question meant or how to answer.

"No, I think your eyes are perfect the way they are. Anything else will just be too much." Feena grinned at her handiwork. "You almost look like a Pharli native. You're going to do great. Just remember not to speak unless spoken to and everything else will be smooth as glass."

"Can you stay with me? Or Coline? I'm sure she knows the customs."

Feena grabbed Marella's hand and squeezed. "No, but you're going to do great. Don't worry."

Without another word, Feena swam to the door and led the way out into the corridor. It took a few tries for Marella to swim after her, since the gown weighed her down and flowed around her knees, tangling around her legs when she tried to kick against the water.

"Little kicks. Just glide and coast. You look lovely."

Marella spun, relief coursing through her at the sound of her mother's voice. The gown tangled around her legs again and Feena clucked and fussed, freeing the fabric and demonstrating the correct method of turning in the heavy garment.

"Ready?" Her father tucked her mother's arm through his and led the way down the hall at a pace Marella easily managed even in the gown.

"Don't forget to enjoy yourself!" Feena called after her.

White and yellow orbs lit the grand hall, with blue, purple, and green banners spaced between them. Multicolored crystal sculptures sat on tables around the edge of the room, and ropes of metal globes hung between the lights. The effect was a dazzling show of light and color that took

Marella's breath away. Her gaze alternated between the elaborate decorations and her parents so often she felt as if she were watching a game of kelpball. Still, she didn't want to let her parents get too far ahead of her. The mere thought of being lost and alone in such a place was enough to turn her stomach to stone.

Snippets of Feena's advice played through her mind, distracting her from the foreign scents and dazzling lights.

Her father led the way through the crowd which parted around them like a wave. He didn't slow or pause until he reached the far wall. Marella followed when he swam up, raising above the crowd until they hovered at the same level as the bright white orbs hanging from the ceiling. There, in front of them, the wall broke into a recessed box where the king, queen, and prince rested on bright orange loungers.

Don't speak unless spoken to. Keep your right hand behind your back and your left hand at your side. Don't make eye contact — it's considered rude.

Marella's mind raced leagues ahead of her body, and her stomach churned with anxiety. She had no idea how she'd manage to eat at the banquet following this ordeal and hoped desperately that no one would pay any attention to how much she ate.

The king rose to float in front of his family. "Welcome, Vazken del Kapat." His voice echoed off the cavernous walls, and Marella flinched. "We're pleased to have you and your family here to represent Kaulo on the new board. Will you introduce them?"

Marella's father bowed low. "We are pleased to be here, your majesty. This is my wife, Yeva. She has been presented here once before, nearly twenty years ago."

Yeva bowed, bending in half at the waist and drawing

her left arm across her chest. Marella watched carefully, prepared to copy the technique.

When her father waved her forward, Marella swam up to float between him and her mother.

Without thinking, she raised her eyes and made eye contact with the king. "Dalphein!" The curse escaped before she could clamp her lips shut.

A gasp erupted from every person in attendance, or so it seemed to Marella. The room fell into absolute silence.

"I–I'm so sorry. I didn't mean to—" her father grabbed her forearm and squeezed, and Marella bit her tongue. Right. She wasn't supposed to speak unless spoken to. She squeezed her eyes shut in a desperate attempt to escape the mortification.

Terrified tremors shook her so hard her dress quivered, but no one spoke. The silence stretched so long Marella wondered if everyone around her had left. She opened one eye halfway, just enough to see that, in fact, no one had left. Instead, the king had leaned forward and was staring at her as if she were a snail destroying his crops. Behind him, the queen wore an expression of shock and mortification, and the prince had his head cocked and a little smirk on his face.

Oh Dalphein! How am I supposed to fix this? Marella trembled but didn't dare speak.

The king let out a booming laugh, and Marella cowered behind her father. A heartbeat later, the rest of the attendees joined the king in a roar of laughter, and Marella's terror transformed to humiliation and shame.

When the hall fell quiet once more, the king waved Marella forward. "Vazken, it seems your daughter is still a touch impulsive. That is all right. You have not yet introduced her. May I have her name?"

"Your grace. She is Marella del Kapat, the younger of my two children."

The king raised an eyebrow. "Two children? I only saw one arrive with you. Have you left one behind in Kaulo?"

"No, your grace. My eldest is off in the arctic on a scientific excursion required for his education. I expect him to join us here as soon as he is able."

"Ah, how interesting. You must tell me more over the evening meal." The king waved a hand and Marella scampered back behind her parents determined not to embarrass them or herself any more that night — or ever — if she could help it.

Somewhere behind her, a drumbeat reverberated through the hall. The silence below shattered into a rush of conversation and laughter, and Marella's father drifted toward the floor and followed the rest of the guests out of the hall and into a long dining chamber.

SIX

Banquet

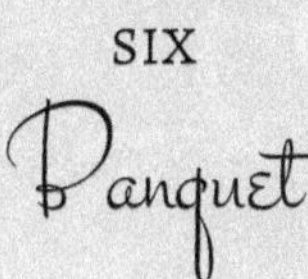

"I'm so sorry," Marella whispered when she thought no one else could hear.

Her mother put an arm around her shoulders and squeezed, but her father gave her a look that would have sent her into hiding if they'd been at home.

"Hold your tongue unless someone speaks to you directly," her mother murmured in her ear. "They won't forget that anytime soon."

Marella nodded and fidgeted with the heavy bronze bracelet Feena had chosen to complement her skin tone. Shame flooded her again, and she kept her eyes on her hands.

Her father led them to the middle of the table, where black leather markers engraved with silver letters announced their seats.

The men and women to either side of their seats bore deep bronze, gold, and green scales with brilliant colored skin and hair that marked them as the other emissaries. Marella sighed, relieved that her family wouldn't be the only bronze attendees. She only hoped they'd be friendly after her humiliating error in the grand hall.

When they'd settled into their high-backed chairs, her mother leaned over and whispered in Marella's ear. "Eat at least a few bites of everything. Anything less is an insult to the king and his chef, and you can't afford any more insults."

Marella nodded but reconsidered. She met her mother's gaze with one of concern. "But, Mama, don't they eat," she dropped her voice to a whisper, acutely aware of the proximity of the other emissaries, "don't they eat eels and fish and other living things?"

"They do, and you've left us all with no choice but to join them. If the presentation had gone smoothly, we could have excused ourselves from their traditional dishes, but not now."

"Oh." her stomach sank like a rock in the deepest parts of the sea. "I'm so sorry," Marella repeated.

Her mother shook her head and turned her attention to the conversation at the table. Most of the emissaries and their families were staring at Marella and whispering among themselves.

Marella's mother smiled her best royal court smile and asked loudly, "So, where's everyone from? It seems we're the last to arrive."

Her question broke the tension, and the emissaries nearest them introduced themselves.

"Not at all. There are still several groups expected, but I think tonight is something of a local custom. I'm Florence, from Linbaulta." The tall, stout woman beside Marella spread her hands in a traditional greeting. Her tan skin was a few shades lighter than Marella's but was a stark contrast from the blues and greens of the Pharli people. "That was quite an error, but you're from Kaulo, right? They're not known for strict society, so you should be all right. The king seemed rather entertained. I don't think I've seen him laugh before, and I've been here a fortnight already."

Marella forced a smile and returned the greeting. "I'm Marella. It's wonderful to meet you. I don't think I could be more embarrassed if I tried, but I'm hoping that's my one big disaster for the trip and everything else can go smoothly."

Florence raised her eyebrows. "Are you prone to disasters, then?"

Heat flushed Marella's face and neck. "No, not usually. I'm usually able to manage around the royal courts without embarrassing myself or my family."

The people seated within hearing distance laughed, and Marella chuckled along with them. She didn't particularly enjoy laughing at herself, but she didn't have any other choice that she could see.

Servants filled the dining hall in a parade of platters and dishes, saving Marella from further conversation. Feena entered carrying a platter half as large as she was, and she winked at Marella as she swam past.

Marella couldn't fight the wave of nausea that hit her when the nearest maid removed the cover from the platter and revealed an arrangement of dead sea life — eels on the bottom, piled high with shrimp, clams, oysters, and small fish. She searched the table for the vegetables, and found a platter of beautiful seaweeds, sponges, and coral one setting to her right.

I can do this. Just a few bites of each dish, with vegetables in between. That's not so bad. At least they're not asking me to kill it.

"Tell me, Miss Marella," the man across the table said.

"What was that you said to the king? It sounded like a curse, but it wasn't one I've heard before." He grabbed the tongs and piled shrimp and eels onto his plate. "I'm Roulf from Cascouran."

"Well, that explains why you haven't heard of our god," Florence interrupted. "She wasn't cursing, she was calling on the sea god to help her. Isn't that right, dear?"

"I–I, uh, of course." Marella jumped at that somewhat more respectable explanation. "My maid warned me not to make eye contact, but I accidentally met the king's eyes, and I prayed to Dalphein to help me fix my mistake, but that just made everything worse."

Roulf laughed at her explanation, and a few others within hearing distance joined in. Marella hoped that would be an acceptable excuse and could correct her mistake better than simple apologies ever could.

"They're still watching. You'll have to get at least a little. I'll eat some with you," her mother murmured.

True to her word, Yeva picked two shrimps and put one on her plate and one on Marella's. She found the smallest eel on the platter and split it between her plate and Marella's. That finished, she piled greens and land fruits on both plates.

"Just try to swallow it whole. Chewing will just make it worse," Florence whispered. "I know you're probably vegetarians. I am, too. After this banquet, we can go back to eating our own preferences."

Marella nodded and swallowed hard. She could do this. She speared the shrimp with her fork, popped it in her mouth without thinking, and gulped hard, forcing the little dead creature down her throat through sheer force of will. She chased it with her favorite mushrooms, which helped stave off the gag that threatened. She repeated the process until she'd eaten a satisfactory number of dishes and finished the meal with a heaping plate of kelp.

When all the guests had finished eating, the king and queen rose and led the group back to the grand hall. Marella waited until her father rose and stayed close to him as the group swept her along.

In the main hall, Marella stopped to get her bearings near the edge of the room and hovered close to a crystal statue of a giant squid. She thought she'd successfully blended into the wall, when a voice near her ear startled her and she nearly knocked into the statue.

"You're not planning to hide over here all night, are you?" The prince drifted out of a nearby doorway, a warm smile on his face. "I've been looking forward to getting to know you."

"I—" Marella bit her cheek, unsure what she was allowed to say or when. She searched for her mother, and found her halfway across the room.

"Don't worry. I don't stand on ceremony as much as my father. I'd rather get to know people the way they are." He bowed low and added, "My name is Avak. I think my father's going to make an announcement, and then there'll be dancing. I'd be very pleased if you'd open the night with me."

Heat flooded Marella's cheeks again, but this time with excitement. "I'd love to." A horrible image flashed through her mind. What kind of music and dancing did they have in Pharlandzi? "I–Er...if I know the dance."

Prince Avak chuckled. "That's fair. Do you know how to waltz?"

Excitement again replaced trepidation. "I do. It's one of my favorites."

"Excellent. I'll let the musicians know to open with a

waltz." The prince bowed again and vanished into the crowd.

Marella scanned the room for her parents again, but they'd vanished into the crowd. She sighed and drifted into the mass of people, wishing she had someone to talk to about the prince's offer. Images of humiliation flashed through her mind though she'd always been a graceful dancer. But she'd never tried to dance in this kind of heavy, flowing gown, and she didn't know how to move her head so her hair wouldn't topple out of its pins. Or injure her neck. It had gotten heavier and heavier through the meal.

A drum sounded the rhythm she was starting to recognize as the king's introduction. The prince had said the dancing would start after the king's announcement. The thought made her stomach flutter, and she wished again that she had a friend she could confide in.

Relief and horror flooded her at the same instant. Her parents had risen to the announcement height with the king and the royal family — and all the other emissaries and their families. As far as she could tell, she was the only guest missing from the group. She hovered in place, uncertain whether to stay put or try to catch up to them.

The prince met her terrified gaze and gave her a smile that made her cheeks burn and her stomach flutter. He motioned for her to join them with a tiny movement of one hand, and she moved as quickly and as gracefully as she could to do just that. She took up a spot behind her parents, where she hoped she'd mostly be hidden from the guests below.

"Welcome friends. I want to officially welcome all of our new ambassadors to Pharlandzi. I promise, our time together won't be nearly as formal as our meetings thus far.

All the ambassadors and their families, please come forward and take a bow.

You've come to help keep us all as free as we are right now, and all of Pharlandzi thanks you. Of course we're all aware of the factions of rebels sprouting up throughout all our nations, and together, we will find a way to quiet that unrest and maintain a lasting peace."

The newcomers moved together like a school of feeder fish, each trying to blend with the crowd and not stand out. As one, they bowed to the crowd below, and retreated behind the royal family.

"This ball also serves another, more traditional, time-honored purpose. It's time for our citizens to enter this year's Dragonaxi Challenge. This is the event many of our young men and women have trained for since they first learned to swim without their mothers' support. This is a challenge where our young men and women will brave the gorge, where the dragons go each year to breed, and attempt to team up with a young dragonet. Those who succeed will become part of our elite force of dragon riders."

The men and women below let out a loud cheer. "Those who wish to enter will need to see Queen Sona before the end of the fifth dance. The selected challengers will be announced before the end of the evening."

Another cheer rose, this one louder than any that had preceded it. The king waved a hand, and the drums beat twice in perfect synchrony before melding into a delicate waltz.

Before Marella even registered what was happening, the prince moved through the group of ambassadors and took her hand in his.

"I hope you haven't changed your mind." He gave her

another one of those soul-melting smiles and bowed low over her hand.

"Of course not." She hoped he didn't notice the quiver in her voice.

He didn't give her another chance to back out but pressed a hand to her back and ushered her into the middle of the now-empty dance area. The drumbeat picked up the tempo, and he spun and twirled her around the dance area in a more graceful and breathtaking waltz than any she'd known before. By the time the music stopped, her cheeks blazed with heat, and her breath came in shallow gasps. The prince gave one final bow and vanished into the crowded room.

Marella tried to see where he went, but he was too quick, and she lost sight of him within a few heartbeats. The drums beat out a new rhythm, one she didn't recognize, and Marella hurried away from the dance area before she embarrassed herself.

"That was unexpected. When did you meet the prince?" Her father's voice behind her brought Marella to a dead stop.

She turned slowly, unsure how her father would react to another surprise. "After supper. He found me trying to stick to the edge of the crowd to watch and asked me to start the dancing by waltzing with him."

Her father smiled the first genuine smile she'd seen on his face since he'd announced the move to Pharlandzi. "Well, you looked wonderful, and certainly made up for any embarrassment earlier in the evening." He kissed her cheek and nodded to her mother. "I think we're going to try this one."

Marella smiled and waited until they'd vanished into the

press of bodies in the dance area before she wandered off in search of people closer to her own age.

It took longer than she expected, because people stopped her every few feet to welcome her to Pharlandzi. Several also reassured her that the little slip at her presentation wouldn't be remembered beyond the end of the evening.

Finally, a nice older woman pointed Marella toward a sitting room at the edge of the great hall. That was where the Dragonaxi entrants would be waiting, and there weren't many young people at the ball who hadn't planned to enter, or so the woman told her.

Marella thanked her and drifted off in the direction she'd pointed, unsure how to begin a conversation when she arrived. If all the people her age had spent their lives training for a dragon challenge, would she have anything in common with them at all?

Since her only other option was to hang around the edges of the dance hall alone, Marella braved the sitting room. Somewhere around thirty teens lounged on chairs, chatted, or played at one of the four stones tables set up in the room. When she entered the room, two young men and a young woman stopped their conversation and rushed over to greet her.

"You're Marella, right?" The girl asked. "Did your parents arrange for your dance with the prince? It looked absolutely perfect. I'd kill for that kind of opportunity."

"I—"

"Oh, I didn't introduce myself. I'm Taline." She bowed low, and Marella returned the gesture.

When the girl straightened, their eyes met, and Marella had to work to hide her shock. The girl's brilliant yellow eyes were a shock of color against her dark green skin and deep purple hair.

She realized she was staring and dropped her gaze to the marble floor. "I'm Marella. It's good to meet you."

"Well? Did your parents set up your dance? How was it? It looked like the dance of a lifetime."

Marella chuckled. "No, my parents didn't know until the music started. He, the prince, I mean, he found me hiding before the king's announcement and asked me." She didn't want to answer that last question, so she hesitated. It had been amazing, but she didn't know this girl enough to confide in her.

"All right, fine, you don't have to tell me all the details. Come sit with us. Do you play stones? We could use another player."

Relieved, Marella smiled and followed the girl to the table. "Doesn't everyone play?"

"I think so. But you're not from here, so I didn't want to assume."

"Can you just run through your rules with me so we can make sure we play the same way?" Marella asked.

"Of course!"

They passed the next three hours in cheerful conversation and a competitive game of stones which had very few differences from the way she'd learned it. Marella finally felt like she might actually fit in and relaxed into the easy chatter in the room. The music streamed in through the open door but wasn't loud enough to impede conversation.

SEVEN

Travel

Worn from three days' lonely travel, Errebeld perked up at the sight of a small village along the southern pass. After two nights of sleeping in caves and huddled under scrubby seaweed, hope for good food and a comfortable place to rest rose in him. Even the smallest villages along the currents usually had an inn, so he shifted his course and moved closer to the cluster of low stone buildings.

A sign over the door of a long, squat structure announced it as The Wayward Traveler. The scent of food and bodies wafted through an open window. He swam through the half-corroded iron door and let it drift closed behind him. The common room held a dozen tables, and patrons filled half of those. Errebeld found an empty table and sought the server.

A young man with brilliant green skin and hair and matching scales swam to Errebeld, who'd rested his back against the wall to scan for an empty table. "What can I get for you, sir?"

"What kind of seaweed platters do you have?"

The server shook his head. "Only kelp and kidali, I'm afraid. The merchants haven't been through in a while. We do have an assortment of shrimp and eel caught today, though."

"Kelp and kidali will do just fine. I'll have a bit of both. Do you have any rooms available for the night?"

"Of course. Is it just you?"

Errebeld nodded.

The young server hovered, waiting, and Errebeld pulled a copper out of his pouch to pay for the meal, considered, and brought out a silver for the room. It had been too long since he'd traveled, he thought. He should have known he'd have to pay in advance.

While he waited for his food, he let his gaze wander over the room. Most of the patrons looked like simple travelers with skins of every color from bronze to green to the deepest purple. Those two had to hail from the far north, since the offspring of any who relocated south tended closer to lavender. One man huddled with a young woman across the room caught his attention, and Errebeld studied the man's manner and features as well as he could from that distance.

"Here you are, sir." The server plunked a porcelain dish down onto the heavy wooden table, and Errebeld glanced from the dish to the server, startled.

"Thank you." It only took a moment for him to regain his composure and flash a smile. He pulled another copper from his pocket and tossed it to the man. "For your speed. That was impressively fast."

"Of course, sir." The server pressed the coin into a pocket on his belt and swam away to check on other diners.

Errebeld inhaled the delicious greens and leaned back against his chair. Without thinking, he scanned the room and straightened his back. A sender man with pale green skin, scales of a darker green, and shimmering purple hair swam toward him from the other side of the common room. He barely had enough time to regain his composure before his friend reached him.

"Errebeld! I not expect you here, and alone! How's Gallien?" The man held out a scarred green arm and grabbed Errebeld's shoulder in a friendly greeting.

"He was well enough when I saw him." Errebeld struggled to keep his tone cheerful. "He's headed to Pharlandzi to visit friends. It's good to see you, Keird. I didn't expect to find you in a place like this, either. You're getting better with the common tongue, too."

"Well, we stop where there is meal and chaise when traveling, yes? And thank you. I try to learn."

Errebeld smiled and nibbled at the scraps of his meal. "Have you eaten?"

"I have. Share a bead?" Keird waved a server over before Errebeld could refuse. "Two bowls daquiona." He plunked three coppers on the table.

Across the room, something clattered, followed by a shout. Two men faced each other, each with a curved blade in his hand.

"I warned you to leave it alone," the taller man said through gritted teeth. He wobbled left, but held the knife steady.

The server approached with two bowls of colorful beads, and Errebeld gave him an uneasy smile. "I think that's our cue to leave. Is my room ready? We can enjoy those away from the excitement," he added with a wave toward the bowls.

"Yes, sir. Follow me." He swam off toward the opening in the back wall and Errebeld followed. Behind them, chaos erupted as other patrons chose sides and joined the fight. He swung the door open into a small room and pointed down the hall. "Your room is number twelve. Two doors down and across the hall."

"Thank you." Keird took the bowls from the server and followed Errebeld into his room.

Once the server had backed out and closed the door, Keird asked, "Now, why you're here and Gallien not?"

Instead of answering, Errebeld removed the porcelain lid from his bowl and examined one of the bite-sized beads inside. The little rune stamped in the top said it had been made in Zegela. It had traveled a long way to the little inn. He popped it in his mouth and bit down to break the wax open, and the peppery-flavored liquor warmed his tongue and slid down his throat. Once he'd sucked all the liquid out, he spit the wax into his hand and dropped it beside the table.

Keird laughed. "You don't eat casing? Some say it the best part."

"Some have no taste, apparently. That stuff's awful, but the daquiona's quite good."

"Why are you not with Gallien? You stayed together always this last two year."

Errebeld winced at the question and its implications. "I don't have to go everywhere he goes." The sulky tone of his voice irritated Errebeld, and he started over. "He had an errand to run in Pharlandzi, and Soraya asked me to carry a letter to her sister in Talam, so here we are."

"I go that way, too. We travel together?" Keird smiled.

"Absolutely. That's way better than going alone. Can you leave at first light? I promised Soraya I'd be quick."

Keird dumped the bowl of beads into his pack. "Yes, but not drunk. We save it."

"Good idea. Got a bit more room? I can't fit one single bead in my bag." He handed his bowl to Keird, who emptied it into his pack and pulled the strings tight.

An hour into the journey, Keird dropped his pack on a rock beside the well-traveled route. "Are you all right? You jumping at every fish."

"I don't know. I just can't shake it. It's like someone's watching me, and it makes my shoulders itch."

A group of supaerisi swam past, and Keird stayed quiet until they moved out of earshot. "This is popular route. That not mean they following you."

Errebeld pressed his lips into a line and searched for whatever had raised his hackles. Another laughing group swam by, and he shrugged. "Maybe you're right. Let's go."

The two enjoyed a comfortable conversation about mutual friends for the rest of the morning. When nothing happened, Errebeld finally relaxed. They swam through midday, passing and being passed again by the same groups of swimmers they'd seen earlier in the day.

"Should we stop?" Keird asked as they passed a little inn beside the route.

"Nah, we're almost to Belzon." Errebeld picked up his pace. He wanted to reach their waypoint before darkness fell.

They passed another building, and something shot out from behind it. A powerful arm grabbed Errebeld around his upper arms, and another closed around his throat. Keird shouted, and someone grunted.

Errebeld struggled against the iron grip. His fingers reached for the knife strapped onto his belt, but he didn't have much leverage with his arms pinned. Inch by inch, he pressed closer to the handle until he finally slid it free.

"Now, don' be doin' that," a gravelly voice said in Errebeld's ear. "We don' mean ya no harm. Jest—"

Errebeld slammed his elbow into the man's gut, unwilling to listen to his demands. The man loosened his grip just enough, and Errebeld twisted free, yanking his knife up in the same movement. He tried to ignore the trembling in his fingers and hoped he wouldn't have to use the blade.

"Who are you and what do you want?" He asked. The attacker wore his purple hair close cropped around his clean-shaven face. He was dressed in a fine, embroidered linen tunic in a distinctive style Errebeld recognized as Wiktawan.

A shout and a groan brought him around to face Keird. He held one attacker off at knifepoint while another lay wounded and bleeding on the ocean floor. A cloud of red wafted up from his position, and Errebeld's stomach sank.

"Let's go," he called. "No time to chat." He swam with all his strength for Keird's position, his knife still ready.

Overhead, something large blocked the light for the briefest moment, and Errebeld's heart kicked into high gear. He and Keird swam back into the current — and away from the bleeding man — with all their strength.

Errebeld checked to see if the men had followed and winced when a shark took the bleeding man's arm off. That spurred him faster, and he gave thanks to Dalphein that neither he nor Keird had been wounded enough to bleed.

Side by side, the two men raced for the next town. Errebeld hoped he'd find safety and a fresh meal there. They hadn't stopped at midday, and his empty belly rumbled its complaint as soon as the terror of the attack wore off.

The dimness of twilight had deepened almost to the night's blackness when the inn's lights glinted off Keird's still-exposed blade. He sheathed it a heartbeat before he swung the heavy iron door inward.

Laughter, the buzz of conversation, and the clink of dishes greeted them, and Errebeld relaxed and swam past his friend toward one of only three empty tables. It sat just left of center of the crowded room, but Errebeld didn't have the energy left to wait for anything near the door. Before he and Keird had even settled into the chairs, Keird had his hand in the air to summon a server. Errebeld drifted into the chair and kept his still-trembling hands knotted beneath the table.

They ordered their food and made small talk until they could retreat to their shared room without drawing attention.

"Who were they?" Keird exclaimed as the door clicked shut.

Errebeld shrugged. "Not bandits."

"Why not?" Keird settled down on one of the two loungers and dropped his pack to the floor.

"Did you see their clothes?"

"Yeah, look Wiktawan. What's it mean?"

"I don't know. Where were you last week?" Errebeld scratched his forehead and struggled to make sense of the attack. He and Keird had both dressed in plain traveling clothes and wore no jewelry or bright colors that might attract attention — a decision they'd made specifically to avoid bandits.

"Pharlandzi, why?"

"I don't know. I thought maybe they'd followed you, but they weren't Pharli." His voice drifted as his mind wandered.

A heavy silence fell, and Errebeld relived those last awful moments before the sharks arrived. "Did I—" He choked on the words and cleared his throat. "Did I break my vow?"

"Stop it. You can not save them."

Errebeld shook his head and whispered, "I should have tried."

"If you try, you die with them."

Deflated, Errebeld settled onto the farthest lounger. "You're probably right. Maybe one of them got away, right?"

"Maybe." Keird shrugged and pulled out the daquiona beads he'd saved. "Here. Have one. They help."

Errebeld opened his mouth to refuse but thought better of it and grabbed a handful. "No more than this. We have to leave at first light if we're going to make it to Talam on time."

EIGHT

Honored

"Now, why are you hiding in here?" Prince Avak swept through the door and sidled up to Marella. "Your parents have been looking everywhere."

Marella couldn't help but smile up at him and drifted up to his eye level. She met his violet gaze for a heartbeat but remembered too late that people in the city considered eye contact rude and dropped her chin to her chest. When she wasn't looking directly at him, she found she could think clearer.

"Why are they looking for me? Is something wrong?"

"I don't think so." He cocked his head to the side. His gaze burned into her forehead, but she refused to raise her head. "I think they're just worried about you getting lost in a strange new place."

"That makes sense, I guess." She started to wave to her new friends, thought better of it, and bowed instead. "It was lovely to meet you all."

The prince drifted out the door, and Marella followed. She expected to find her parents floating above the party, searching the fray as they'd done when she was small, but the space above the dance area held nothing but lights and crystal beads.

Confused, Marella turned to find Prince Avak much closer than she'd expected. She hopped backward and bumped into a table holding one of the elaborate crystal statues. It wobbled, but the prince reached over and steadied it before it could fall.

"I'm so sorry. I didn't mean to startle you. I believe they're playing another waltz. Dance with me again?"

The pleading in his eyes nearly made her forget why she'd left the game.

"I should find my parents. They're probably worried." She leaned right and gave a tiny flutter of her flipper, but the prince darted into her path and they nearly collided.

"They're fine. They're having a snack with my parents and the other emissaries. I just wanted to dance with you one more time before my father makes the announcements and everyone leaves."

Marella cocked her head, struggling to make out the prince's motives. She filtered a dozen questions through her mind but discarded each. She finally settled on a single word. "Why?"

"You look cute when you're flustered." The prince shrugged. "And you're interesting."

Heat flooded her cheeks, but she set her hand in his and let him lead her to the dance area. Once more, he set his hand on her waist and swept her into the dance, twirling and twisting to the song's syncopated rhythm.

Within seconds, her heart fluttered in time with the music and her breathing quickened.

In the middle of the song, with no warning at all, the music cut off, and a frantic drumbeat exploded into the hall.

The dancers around Marella grumbled and left the dance area, and Prince Avak dropped her hand and swam off into the crowd. Bereft and alone, Marella drifted along with the crowd and searched for her parents. The frantic beat stopped, and Marella swam toward the room where she'd played stones with the other teens. Before she reached it, Taline called Marella's name. Marella scanned the room and found her new friend waving an arm over her head.

"Hey!" Marella rushed over to the group. "What's going on? What do the drums mean?"

Taline grinned and grabbed her hand. "They're about to make the announcement. They're going to tell us who they've chosen for the Dragonaxi Challenge this year."

"So, everyone who signs up doesn't get to do it?" Marella tried to understand the process but kept her eye on the crowd, searching for her parents.

"No, only twelve get to participate each year."

"If you don't get in, how many times can you try?" Marella asked.

"You're allowed to enter twice. If you don't get picked either year then you're out of luck."

"Shush! They're about to start!" The young man standing beside Marella covered his mouth with his hand to emphasize his point.

Heat rushed into her cheeks. Had she been blushing all night? She had no idea what would happen during the ceremony. *Is it a ceremony? Or just an announcement?*

Marella spotted her mother's bronze skin and purple gown through the crowd and drifted off in that direction. She'd be able to follow her mother's lead on expected behavior.

Marella reached her parents at the same time the drums

cut off. Her mother grabbed her hand and squeezed, and they turned together to watch the ceremony.

"We had more entrants than usual this year, and a few that we did not expect. Congratulations to all the young men and women who found the courage to attempt the Dragonaxi Challenge. Those who succeed will have a friend for life and the honor of belonging to our elite force of Dragoni."

A gong sounded, rattling beads near the ceiling and drawing Marella's attention higher, past the spot halfway up where the king and his family presided over the party.

A group of three dragons and their riders circled the hall near the ceiling. Each dragon was different, one green and one blue and one purple with shining black spots, but the riders all wore the same brilliant red uniforms with matching tight caps covering their heads. Marella gasped. She hadn't expected to see dragons so soon based on what the maid had said that morning.

"They're yearlings," her mother murmured in her ear. "Too young to breed, so they stay here when the others go to the gorge."

"Unfortunately, we had more applicants this year than we have available spots in the Dragoni, so not everyone will compete. It was not an easy decision, and I have spent the entire evening discussing the choice with the highest-ranking officers in the Dragoni.

"This night has gone later than expected, so please hold your cheers until all twelve names have been called. Challengers, when I call your name, please make your way to Admiral Vitelio Ferroa."

The king pointed to a man dressed in scarlet and swimming back and forth at the center of the ceiling. The dragons circled him slowly, but the man did not acknowledge either the dragons or the people gathered in the bottom of the hall.

"Now, if we're ready." The king pulled an etched leather scroll out of a pocket and glanced out over the crowd.

"Dyfan Bainum." The yellow-haired young man she'd teamed with on the game of stones grinned and darted up to the admiral.

"Lilit Rodnoian." A muscular young woman with a grave expression lined up beside the admiral.

Marella struggled to pay attention as the king called name after name of people she either didn't know at all or had barely met. She lost count of how many he'd called and was halfway through counting the people in the line when the king called a name she knew.

"Taline Avaliani." Marella smiled and fought back a cheer for her new friend. She'd wanted this so badly. Marella couldn't help but be happy for her.

"And last, the one we had so much trouble deciding on, as her entry was quite unexpected and unorthodox. Still, it seems wrong to deny her the opportunity to become truly one of us if that is her wish. Miss Marella del Kapat."

The hall exploded in a cacophony of cheers and exclamations of dismay. Marella felt as if she'd turned to stone. She couldn't find the muscles to make her legs swim up to the line with the others.

"Why would you do such a thing?" Her mother's incredulous expression brought back the ability to move.

Marella shook her head, her eyes wide as dinner plates. "I–I didn't. I don't even know what it is."

Her mother looked as if she were about to say more, but the king called Marella's name again.

"Please join Admiral Ferroa and the others for your

briefing."

She did as she was told and swam slowly toward the group at the ceiling. As she passed, Marella couldn't help but notice Prince Avak's expression of surprise and admiration. She didn't know how this had happened, but he seemed to think it was a good and brave thing to do, so she'd play along. She'd never seen a dragon before, but she'd spent her whole life studying the ocean and its creatures, so it shouldn't be that hard to make friends with a baby.

I hope. A pang of dread shot through her at the shocked and dismayed expressions on the other challengers' faces. The admiral wore a thunderous expression that made it clear she was not his pick for the last spot.

"Follow me," Admiral Ferroa barked.

Marella gulped and followed the line of challengers toward a broad door set into the wall near the ceiling. The soft flapping of the dragons swimming toward her shook her nerves, but she reminded herself that they were her potential teammates and wouldn't hurt her.

They wound through unadorned halls above the main areas she'd seen before, and Marella fought back alternating waves of terror and elation.

How did I get a spot in such an elite challenge? Who put my name in? Why? Why would anyone do such a thing?

It was either an enormous compliment or deliberate sabotage, depending on who had done it and why. Did they expect her to make a fool of herself as she'd done at her presentation?

"You don't have much time. The currents are already changing, so you'll have eight days to prepare for the gorge and then sixteen days to return with a dragon. If you succeed, you become one of us — a part of the most elite dragon force in the oceans and on land. If you fail, you'll either be dead before two weeks are up or you'll be exiled. Failed challengers are not allowed back into the city." The admiral met Marella's eyes. "With no exceptions. You have one day to decide if you wish to accept this challenge. If you decide it's too great a risk, you will be escorted out of the city as a failed challenger." He swam in a circle, staring each person in the face for an instant before moving to the next. "Any questions?"

No one spoke. Fear and dread felt like stones in Marella's stomach.

"Very well then. We will meet in the main hall below at sunrise eight days from now. You are free to go."

The teens clambered for the door, and Marella found herself alone with the dour admiral. "I'd advise you to strongly consider exile as your better choice. You and your parents can leave the city in peace." He swam out the door before she could react, and Marella wound through the corridors for an hour or more, until she finally found the hall of etched and inlaid portraits she'd seen on the tour that morning. She followed that corridor until she ran into Feena.

"Oh, miss! I'm so glad I found you. Here, let's get you cleaned up. I think your tutor wants to meet with you before you go to sleep. I can't believe how brave you are to put your name in for the challenge! It's got to be the hardest thing ever. People here train for it from childhood."

The maid chattered on and led her to her room, where she swiftly undid the ties on the back of the gown and swept the heavy garment over Marella's head. She replaced it with something soft and fluffy that somehow held off the chill of the foreign castle and made Marella feel warm and sleepy. Before she could doze off, Feena pushed her down onto the stool and picked all the pins and clips out of her hair. When it was all free, Feena ran a brush through it and braided it loosely on one side.

Marella yawned. "Why doesn't anyone here wear their hair down?"

"The dragons and their riders don't take kindly to tangles of hair in their way," Feena answered. "Better to wear it up than get it tangled in a dragon's tail.

"I guess that makes sense."

"Is she back yet?" Coline poked her head through the dressing room door. "Oh good. Marella, dear, we have to talk about this."

The older woman brushed Feena aside and pressed her hands on Marella's shoulders, her face less than a hand's breadth from Marella's face.

In a hoarse whisper, she choked out, "What in Dalphein's blue sea were you thinking, signing up for such a thing?"

"I didn't! I swear I didn't. I never went anywhere near the queen all night. I stayed in the room with the others my age."

Coline cocked her head, her eyebrows drawn so close in the middle they almost met.

Marella shook her head again and shouted, "I swear it! On Dalphein's lamp, I swear it. I never put my name on that scroll. I can't even find my way around this castle, let alone the city. Why would I sign up for some challenge outside of either?"

"Are you sure?" Coline raked Marella's face with her narrowed gaze, and Marella squirmed like a child caught telling falsehoods.

"I am." Marella sighed. "I don't know who put my name in or why, but I don't think I have any choice but to go through with it."

"What would make you think that? Of course you don't have to do it. From what I've read, you have three days to back out."

Marella hung her head. "I have one day, but if I decline the challenge, I'm exiled from the city forever."

"So that's why you did this!" Her mother's sharp tone brought Marella's head up in confusion. When had she come in? "You found a perfect way to get back to Kaulo, didn't you?"

"No! I swear I didn't put my name on that scroll!" Rage filled Marella at starting the conversation over again, but she refused to let it cloud her head. She inhaled slowly and gritted her teeth. "I already said I have no choice but to go through with it. I can't get myself exiled and have Papa lose his position. We just got here. I won't leave in shame. Not now, not ever."

Shame. Oh, no. She couldn't shake the awful thought away, so she voiced it. "Oh, Dalphein. Do you think someone did this because of my miserable failure at the presentation?" She dropped her head into her hands and felt the heat fill her cheeks at the remembered shame.

"Is everyone decent?" Her father's voice echoed through the chamber. "I couldn't wait any longer. What have we found out?"

Marella swam out of the dressing room to find her father hovering by the open outer door.

"Everyone's dressed. You can close the door," her mother said in the same sharp tone she'd used toward Marella.

Her father shot his wife a long-suffering gaze and turned his attention back to Marella. "Now, what made you think to put your name in for this thing?"

"Dalphein!" Marella paused to regain her composure. "I

swear I didn't, just like I told everyone else. I never went anywhere near the room where they were taking names. I stayed at the other end of the hall, playing stones in full sight of a room full of people." She settled onto the lounger and made a show of getting comfortable.

For a long moment, no one spoke. Her father broke the silence just when Marella started to nod off. "Well, what do we do now?"

"Now, I'm going to go to sleep. This has been one of the worst days of my life, and I'm ready for it to be over." Marella answered, her words clipped more than she'd intended. She focused on calm and continued. "Tomorrow, I'm going to seek out someone who can teach me what I need to know to survive this challenge. Once I know how not to get killed, I'll worry about how to succeed at it." Was it something she could succeed at? Or was it a win/lose challenge? She had no idea. She just knew the cost of failure was death or exile. "Ugh. I don't even know what it is yet. I guess I'll have to figure that out tomorrow, too."

"That's not a bad plan," Coline said, "but I think we should start with Dalphein's temple. You need a blessing more than anyone I've ever known. I'll come with you and make sure you have everything you need."

A knock on the door brought Marella up off the lounger. Everyone she knew was already in the room.

"Enter," her mother called.

The door swung inward, and Feena swam in, her hands held behind her back. Marella blinked. When had the serving girl snuck out?

"Sorry to bother you, miss." She held out both hands and presented Marella with an intricate yellow flower. "It's from Prince Avak. He sends his congratulations on your selection for the Dragonaxi Challenge, and his thanks for keeping him company at the ball."

Marella had no idea how she was supposed to respond, so she smiled and glanced over at her mother and Coline.

"She's very pleased to receive such a gift," Coline said, smiling back at Marella. "Please let the prince know his gift is well-received, and that Miss Marella is very touched that he thought of her."

Feena smiled and bowed out of the room.

"Well, you certainly seem to have caught the prince's attention." Her father grinned. "That can't be a bad thing. I've always said you were princess material."

"Thanks, Papa." Marella gave a little kick and raised up to kiss his cheek. "I need to get some sleep now. It's been a long day, and I'm afraid the next week is going to be full of even longer days."

"Of course." Her father wrapped her in a hug and squeezed once then released her and swam to the door. "Your mother and Coline will have to help you prepare. They're starting the emissary board meetings tomorrow morning first thing."

"Sleep well," Marella called, an instant before the door closed behind the trio.

Alone at last, Marella sank onto the lounger and considered what the next weeks would hold. She didn't know much about the challenge, except that the other people chosen had trained for years for it and that not everyone survived it.

Can I do it? Should I? What if I fail? The two options for failure didn't bear consideration. She'd have to find and befriend a dragon. *But how? And how in Dalphein's great name did I get into the challenge without entering?*

NINE

Preparation

"Miss Marella, it's time to get up."

Cold fingers closed around Marella's shoulder and shook her gently.

"Miss Marella?"

Marella opened her eyes and yawned. "I'm awake." She yawned again and rose off the lounger. "Can you teach me how to put my hair up? It doesn't look like I'll have much time to learn, so just show me the simple styles for now. We'll work on the more complicated things after the challenge."

Feena smiled. "That confidence is good. It'll get you through."

They fell into an easy conversation as Feena walked her through a simple pattern of braids and loops that would keep her hair from escaping during the busy day ahead.

"How do you know what time it is in here?" Marella searched again for a window, but there weren't any in her rooms.

"Here." Feena pulled out a wax stick and drew a complicated rune on the wall. A circle glowed off the wall, the rune in the center. "That's sunrise." Feena pointed to a point at the top of the circle. "And that's sunset. This one's dinner. And that's the morning meal."

Marella pushed aside the shock of such casual use of the power and struggled to keep up. She couldn't afford to get distracted by the awful truth of how that crig was mined. "How long will that stay there?"

"Until you wipe it away. See this little blue dot?" Feena pointed to a little spot inside the circle. "That's where we are right now, so it's almost sunrise."

"Oh. Then my mother and Coline should be here any minute. Where can we get something to eat before the morning meal? I'm sure they don't want to wait that long before we leave."

The door swung open without a sound. "You're absolutely right. We're not waiting for the morning meal. Good, you're already dressed." Marella's mother scanned her appearance, nodded, and turned back to the door. "Come along. You don't have much time. We need to find out as much as we can."

Her mother grabbed her arm and dragged her toward the door, but Marella cast a warm smile toward Feena. "Thank you for all your help."

Feena bowed low, and Marella allowed her mother to pull her out the door and down the hall.

"Where's Coline?" Marella asked when they'd made it halfway to the front entrance.

"She went ahead to find Dalphein's temple. She'll meet us at the front courtyard and show us the way."

Marella nodded and let her mother drag her along. It wasn't worth the energy to fight her when they both had the same goal, anyway.

"What about food? I'm starving." Marella's stomach rumbled and punctuated her statement.

"There's always food at the temple. We'll eat there. Temple food will more likely appeal to our tastes, so we can wait a little while. You want more eel and shrimp?"

Marella grimaced and fought a gag. "No." She'd happily wait to eat something more palatable than the slimy dead animals served at the banquet the night before. The corridor ended into a wide, open space. Her stomach rumbled again, but she ignored it and raised her eyes to the massive walls surrounding the cavernous entry hall.

She hadn't noticed the etchings and crystal inlays that sparkled along every section of the wall the day before, but now she had time to examine them. She swam up the wall, tracing the intricate dragons and ferns and kelp images with her index finger. The light from dozens of orbs and lanterns reflected off the inlays and cast the etchings into stark relief.

A tiny creaking sound echoed through the chamber, and the faintest morning light filtered through the new gap between the doors.

As soon as the doors had opened enough to fit through, her mother rushed out into the early morning. Coline greeted them with a smile and held out an arm, ushering Marella and her mother through the smaller gate and into the city. Lights flickered on in scattered windows as the city's workers began their day. Coline moved swiftly through the alleys and rows, not pausing to allow Marella to enjoy the enormity and beauty of the city. She'd barely noticed any of it the day before and yearned to explore, but of course there wasn't time for that. Coline was on a mission and wouldn't stop until she'd completed her goal.

The tutor finally slowed in a narrow alley and came to a

stop in front of a massive stone building with spires and towers protruding from every section of roof. No windows allowed a peek inside, but breathtaking murals depicting Dalphein's life and lamp had been inlaid into the stone walls.

Her eyes traced the delicate lines, wondering at the opalescence of the piece, until the awful reality struck her. Mother of pearl. The only thing that shone like that was mother of pearl. The inlays were all skeletons of sea creatures who had once lived. A wave of nausea struck her, and Marella choked it back.

Surely, they didn't kill any creatures for this. They used shells they found. They wouldn't kill for Dalphein's temple.

The thought soothed her conscience enough to allow her to enter the building without guilt.

"Ah, back already?" a shriveled old woman greeted Coline. Long years had bleached her hair white, and Marella struggled to tell what color her skin and scales had once been. Both had the look of aged daeko, faded, worn, and wrinkled from years of life and activity. Not unlike the sofa in their living room back in Kaulo, Marella thought.

The woman met Marella's stare with a surprisingly sharp blue gaze. "You're the one everyone's talking about, yes? Well, come in, and let's see what we can do for you."

The woman closed the door behind them and Marella gazed around the room. Brightly painted fabrics covered the stone walls, and a pile of cushions sat in the center of the otherwise bare floor. A tray of seaweed and vegetables sat beside the cushions.

"I was just getting ready for my breakfast, but something told me I'd need extra today. Join me? I have plenty."

"Thank you. We haven't eaten yet." Marella's mother settled onto the cushions beside the old woman and beckoned Marella and Coline to join her.

"I've met Coline but not you two." The old woman bowed to Yeva and Marella. "I'm Porzia, Dalphein's high priestess. And you are?"

"I'm Yeva, wife of Vazken, ambassador from Kaulo and brother of king Magar. This is my daughter, Marella."

"Your choice of words says much about you. Welcome, Yeva, wife of Vazken, and Marella, daughter of Yeva."

Marella sat beside her mother and wondered at Porzia's words. What could she tell from a customary introduction?

"You're here for a blessing, yes? Worried about the dragon rites? Eat child. You'll need your strength." Porzia shoved a hefty bit of kelp toward Marella and popped a smaller one in her own mouth.

"Yes," Yeva said between bites. "We need any help or information you can give us. We didn't have any other idea where to begin to prepare for such a thing."

"Well, of course not." Porzia smiled and gulped down some bit of brown seaweed Marella couldn't identify. "Now, I can't do much for you in the gorge. That's outside Dalphein's realm. He rules over everything from the surface to the ocean floor, but that gorge doesn't have a floor. It just goes down forever. Nope, even Dalphein himself doesn't want anything to do with it, lamp or no lamp."

Marella shook her head, confused. "I never heard of any part of the ocean Dalphein didn't rule over."

"Of course not. You're from the flats, aren't you? Wide open expanses, kidali farms, bright turquoise waters, yes?"

Marella nodded.

"Dalphein's strength is best in places like that, and of course in the reefs and mountains. But no, he won't go in the gorge. That's Ikeshal's realm. Only the underworld lord has control of places that deep."

"What am I supposed to do? I need his help." A deep

pit of despair opened in Marella's gut and she set down the kelp. "The others all trained for years, and I've never even visited a reef. I don't know what to avoid or where to go for safety."

"Don't fret, young one. I'll direct you to the places to find that information. Besides, you won't go in alone. The challengers go into the gorge in teams of three. Usually, all three come out together or none do. Here's hoping you have some strong team members. Now, what strengths do you bring to the team? What can you do to help?"

"Well," Marella wracked her mind for something helpful. "I'm a good shot with a bow and arrow. That might be helpful."

The old woman cocked her head and regarded Marella with an inscrutable expression. "What would someone like you be doing with a bow and arrow? You eat plants, yes? What would you have to shoot at?"

Marella chuckled. "I mainly shoot at targets, but I've been training for the day when I had to join the Kaulo army. Everyone has to. We each serve three years and then we're free to pursue our chosen careers."

"I think I understand." Porzia tipped her head back and stared up into the peaked ceiling. She sat that way until Marella thought she'd either gone to sleep or forgotten her visitors.

"Ah, of course," the old woman said at last, lowering her chin and staring hard at Yeva and Coline. "I need a moment alone with the girl. What she needs to hear is not for anyone else."

Yeva's brows drew together. "I'm her mother. Whatever you have to say to her, you can say to me."

"No. Dalphein says this is for the girl alone."

Coline rose and swam toward the door they'd entered

through, but Porzia called her back. "There's a little private room at the end of that hall. You'll find food and comfortable seats in there."

Yeva and Coline left the room the way Porzia directed, and Marella debated whether to rise or stay sitting.

"Listen girl, your only chance at surviving this challenge is to rely on the team they give you." The old woman closed her eyes, and her face went blank. When she spoke again, her voice had a strange accent and foreign tone that made the small hairs at the back of Marella's neck stand up. "Be wary... of your treatment of others. Whatever you do... will return to you four times over. You give kindness, you'll get kindness in return. You give cruelty, well... let's just say I won't envy your reward. Kindness... is the only way to survive."

Silence fell, and Marella shifted uncomfortably. A heartbeat later, Porzia opened her eyes and blinked a few times.

"I hate when he does that. No respect for a body's own control." Her voice and accent had returned to the slow drawl Marella associated with the city. "Did you get the information you were looking for?"

"Not exactly. You said to always be kind, but I try to do that, anyway."

"Trying isn't enough now. In every interaction, show kindness. A moment's lapse could cost you everything."

Marella picked up a bit of red seaweed and nibbled at it. It had a light peppery flavor that made her stomach growl, and she ate the rest in one bite.

"Go get your mother. We're just about finished here, and you have a busy day ahead of you."

Marella rose to obey, but before she reached the corridor, her mother's voice echoed into the main room.

"Your maid told us to come back now, is that all right, Porzia?"

"Of course, dear," Porzia answered, smiling. "Dalphein's servants will never lead you astray."

She spent the next ten minutes drawing a map on the floor with a shining red wax stick and directing Marella on what to ask for in the specific shops. Armed with a plan, Marella, her mother, and Coline headed out into the city.

The week flew by in a flurry of shopping, studying, and searching out dragon riders willing to talk to a selected challenger. There weren't many, and of those, only one, who introduced himself as Cedomir, was willing to talk to her specifically. The others said the challenge should be reserved for natives who understood how important it was to their culture and society.

She'd spent three hours each afternoon with Cedomir, learning as much as she could about how to identify a safe cave for sleeping and finding the dragon nests and identifying a potential dragonet friend.

He also spent many hours lecturing her on the dangers of the gorge, including eels that could blend in with the surrounding rock and had a lethal sting. Marella recited the important points back to him at the end of each session and repeated them to herself throughout each evening. Her family dined in solitude in their chambers for the entirety of that week, unwilling to sacrifice a moment of study even for meals.

Marella had to practice swimming in the heavy garments they had bought to protect her from the cold in the gorge, and the heavy belted-on pockets she could use to carry a knife and food.

By the time the week ended, Marella didn't think she could learn another thing if her life depended on it.

She double checked her pack and prepared to get some sleep before the challenge began the next morning. A knock at the door made her pause, though she didn't stop her work and let Feena answer the door. She didn't need any distractions. Her mother's voice brought her up short, and when her father entered behind his wife, Marella set down the pack and gave her parents her attention.

Her father took a deep breath, and his words came out in a rush, stumbling over each other so Marella had to pay close attention to catch what he meant. "I've spent the past several days in negotiations with the royal family, and they've finally agreed to give you safe passage back to Kaulo if you choose not to do this fool challenge. And they'll let me keep my position, so you don't have to do this for me. Should I let him know to have a carriage ready for you in the morning?"

Marella took a long moment to try to piece together what her father had said but ultimately answered, "What? I'm not sure I understand." Shook her head, trying to fit all the pieces together in her mind. "If I leave, it discredits the entire family. Even if you keep your position, you'll lose the respect of the rest of the people here."

"There might be a little adjustment period where we have to figure out how I fit in again, but no one would blame you for staying alive instead of dying in a challenge that kills people who have trained for it for over a decade." Her father put a hand on her shoulder. "I just want to see you safe. If that means living with your uncle in Kaulo while your mother and I fulfill our obligations here, then so be it."

"Can I have a bit to think?"

Her mother frowned. "What is there to think about? You get to do what you wanted in the beginning and stay with your uncle and continue your studies with your friends instead of trying to survive in the gorge. Everything we've heard and read this week makes me even more sure you don't want to go to that place."

Marella blinked, still somewhat stunned. "You're probably right, but I've spent the past week thinking of nothing but this challenge, and I need a minute. You just dumped all this on me without any warning, and the challenge starts tomorrow morning."

"Very well." Her mother set her hand on the door. " We'll leave you to think on it. Feena can let us know when you've decided. Don't wait too late, though. I'll need time to let the king know to have the carriage ready and your things packed before the challenge starts."

Once the door closed behind them, Marella settled onto the chaise to consider her options. A strange sense of disappointment settled in her stomach when she considered leaving, but that wasn't enough to make a decision.

"Should I start packing your things, Miss Marella?" Feena hovered near the dressing room, a look of uncertainty on her face.

"Not yet. Can you help me talk this through?" She swung her legs over the side and patted the empty spot on the chaise. "I don't know what the right thing is."

"I suppose, Miss, but it's your decision. Don't you want to go home? Your mother said you didn't want to come here in the first place."

"It's not that I didn't want to come here. I was nervous about leaving my friends and family and everyone I know behind and going to a place where I didn't know if I could fit in. But now I'm here, and while I don't exactly fit in, I think I want a little more time in the city. It's so beautiful here, and most of the people have been kind."

"But Miss Marella, we're not talking about spending time strolling the markets. We're talking about the *Challenge*. Lots of people who grew up here and train and practice for years don't succeed."

She was right. Marella searched her mind, trying to figure out why she felt like she had to do this and why she genuinely wanted to, though that second part was a little easier. How many biologists would give their right arm to have the opportunity to locate a dragon den and befriend a dragonet? She could learn so much about a species that for some reason no one had included in any of her studies.

Marella drew a deep breath. "Right, so it doesn't seem like that training makes that much difference, does it? Besides, there's the *dragons*! I didn't know they were even real animals, and now I have the chance to get to know one. I always said I wanted to study whales, but dragons are amazing, too, and I could contribute to the textbooks since no one else has."

Feena let out a sad sigh. "You're going to do this, aren't you. Is there anything can say to change your mind?"

Startled, Marella sat back. She hadn't realized she'd made up her mind, but Feena was right. She had. "No, I don't think so. I have to at least try."

"Should I tell your parents, then?"

"No. Not yet. If you tell them now, they'll be in here all night trying to change my mind, and I need to get some rest if I'm going to have a chance."

"Very well, miss. If you're sure, we should check your pack one more time."

Marella nodded and dumped the pack on the table to sort and repack. Again.

TEN

Dragonaxi

She rose well before dawn on the appointed day and spent an hour meditating and praying to both Dalphein and Ikeshal — which felt foreign and blasphemous. She'd never dreamed she'd pray to the lord of the underworld at any time besides a funeral.

Feena packed extra food in her bag while Marella tied her hair up and dressed.

"I'm putting your crig in the bottom of your pack," Feena called through the open door. "Are you sure you have enough?"

"I'm sure," Marella answered. Her parents had bought her one more bead of the precious mineral, so she had two to help her in the gorge. She couldn't imagine needing them both, but she'd rather have extra, just in case.

As soon as she'd finished dressing, she left for the grand hall before her parents could check on her and asked Feena to let them know she'd decided to go through with the challenge.

When she reached the great hall, the sounds of her movement echoed off the walls. Not a soul moved in the vast, empty room, until Admiral Ferroa swam through the door at the ceiling. He nodded in her direction but stayed near the ceiling at the end of the room — as far away from Marella as he could possibly get. She sat on one of the benches along the ornately carved wall and waited. According to Feena's time charm, she had a little over an hour until the challenge began.

The others didn't take long. Within twenty minutes, Taline swam in with three more challengers close on her heels. None of the challengers spoke to each other or even acknowledged that the others were in the room, and Marella took her cues from them and kept her eyes down.

A gong sounded at the appointed time, and Marella startled at the sound reverberating through the space.

The admiral swam up to the line of challengers. "All right, anyone want to take this last opportunity to leave in safety and peace?" No one moved, even to breathe, or so it seemed to Marella. "Very well. Follow me."

He led them through a narrow doorway set beneath the king's box and along a labyrinth of winding passageways that spiraled down into the depths of the castle. Marella hadn't realized before that moment that anything existed beneath the palace's ground floor, but they continued down at least three more floors before the passage leveled out into a straight, narrow corridor.

The admiral waved them all into a small room and closed a heavy stone door behind him.

"You'll be divided into teams of three, and you'll swim to the gorge in two groups."

A few of the challengers rearranged themselves to hover near their friends, but the admiral ignored them and continued his speech. "My top officers and I have spent the past week dividing you into teams based on your individual strengths and weaknesses. We've given you team members who complement your abilities and can shore up your weak spots. I warn you not to attempt to rearrange the teams once you get into the gorge. Many have tried it before. Precious few have lived to tell the tale, and even fewer have successfully paired with a dragon."

Marella tried to ignore the empty space surrounding her, as all the other challengers clustered close to each other. They'd spent years training together. Of course they wanted to complete the challenge with people they knew and trusted. She wondered if her decision to study and prepare instead of socializing had been misplaced, but it was too late to change it now.

"Line up along the wall when I call your name. Group one, team one, Dyfan Bainum, Hasmig Khederian, Kasbar Naroyan. Team two, Lilit Rodnoin, Takvor Pilosyan, Marella del Kapat. Follow me." He didn't give them any time to greet one another but led the six terrified teens out the door opposite the one they'd entered and down another, narrower hall.

He swam swiftly and never looked back to make sure the challengers were behind him. Something scraped the wall behind her, and Marella glanced back. Two well-muscled soldiers dressed in the same scarlet uniform as the admiral swam side by side behind the group.

The corridor drew narrower and darker until it ended at a heavy steel door just large enough for one person to fit through. Admiral Ferroa didn't look back but threw the door open and darted out into the open water beyond the city.

No one spoke except for the occasional polite comment when one swam too close or bumped into another, and Marella wondered how far they had to travel. That was the only question she hadn't thought to ask. At least, she hoped she'd thought of everything else.

Instead of worrying, Marella turned her attention to the landscape. She'd never seen anything like it. Rocky crags alternated with narrow stretches of flats covered in a dense carpet of multicolored seaweeds.

The admiral swam around the rocky outcrops, rather than raise up to swim over their tops. Marella longed to ask why, but no one was close enough to hear or answer her without raising her voice, and she didn't want to draw the admiral's attention. They swam in silence past rocks and fields and hills.

Marella grew so used to the quiet that her thoughts almost completely drowned out any exterior sounds.

"Hey. I'm Lilit. I guess we're teammates."

Marella startled. The other girl in the group had swum up beside her and smiled cheerfully.

"I'm Marella. It's good to meet you." She couldn't think of anything else to say. Small talk seemed out of place in such a setting, and Marella didn't know enough of the place or culture to make an effort at anything deeper.

"So, what skills do you have to help us?" Lilit kept her smile, but her voice had hardened.

"Well, I've spent the past several years studying oceanography and biology, so I'm skilled at identifying edible plants and animals. And I'm pretty good with a bow and arrow, so I can help us catch food and defend ourselves."

The girl nodded and her smile warmed a little. "That's a relief. I was really afraid you'd be useless." She laughed, and Marella joined in, though it felt a bit forced.

Before they could say more, the admiral stopped in

front of a huge boulder. Marella and the others clustered near him.

"This is your final chance to back out." The admiral swam back and forth in front of the small group of teens. "If you pass this rock, you will not be able to stop without a dragon to help you on your way. No one will judge you for choosing to stay safe and alive. Only one in three who enter the gorge ever come out again. The nearest village is a three-hour swim that way." He pointed to his left.

One in three didn't sound like very good odds to Marella, but she couldn't back out without dishonoring her father, so she'd continue.

"I'd like to leave." A soft voice spoke behind her. "I'm sorry sir, but I think I'd rather live in exile than die in there."

The young man named Takvor swam forward and bowed low in front of the admiral. He eyed the guards with a wary expression, but they made no move toward him.

"Very well. You may go in peace." Admiral Ferroa bowed.

When he straightened, the young man swam back the way they'd come until he disappeared beyond a cluster of rocks.

"Anyone else?" The admiral met the eyes of each challenger as if willing them to back out. He waited so long the challengers began to fidget, and Marella shifted her pack on her shoulders.

"Very well," he said at last. The two guards swam around the group and stopped beside the admiral.

"You'll come through when I call your name, and not a moment sooner. Your team won't descend into the gorge until all members are through. Dyfan, you're first."

The slim young man took a deep breath, adjusted his

pack, and followed the admiral around the boulder. A heartbeat later, a shout of pain punctuated the silence.

Someone asked, "What's happening," but no one answered.

Each of the four remaining youths wore expressions of fear.

"Hasmig," the admiral called.

The intense young man with the brilliant purple hair shrugged his shoulders and disappeared beyond the boulder. Marella waited for a shout like before, but nothing happened.

"Kasbar," the admiral's voice bounced off the surrounding rocks and echoed in the silence.

Only Marella and Lilit remained, and Marella didn't know if she dreaded the sound of her name more, or the thought of being alone among the crags. For an instant, she wondered if she shouldn't turn and leave. Her father had given her permission to do just that, right? But what would happen to Lilit if both her teammates backed out?

"Marella."

Time's up. Marella squared her shoulders and lifted her chin, determined to face whatever lay beyond that rock with all the bravery she possessed.

She moved slowly, trying to get a peek at her surroundings before she left the protection of the boulder, but something stabbed her left forearm and pain shot through her like lightning. Somehow, she kept from crying out, but thick tears stung her eyes and blurred her vision. The pain dulled to an aching burn after a moment but didn't go away.

The admiral leaned against the boulder with his arms out stiffly in front of him. He wore a pair of heavy gloves that covered everything up to his elbows and held a wicked-looking animal between his protected hands. The creature was long and slender, like an eel, and shiny black. Red needle-like spikes grew from its hide, forming a ridge down its back and matching rows down either side. Hateful yellow eyes bored into hers and when it hissed, it displayed a mouth full of sharp teeth.

"What is that?" Marella whispered.

"It's a dragonaxi. You have sixteen days until the poison kills you, and your crigoresi won't cure it, no matter how skilled you are with runes. Save it. You might need it later." The admiral murmured in the even tones that said he'd repeated it many times before. "You'll find the antidote growing inside a broken dragon egg, but only one that has birthed a dragonet. Without the help of a young dragon, you will not survive. Good luck. Wait here for your teammate." He pointed to a spot out of sight of the boulder.

Marella did as she was told, fighting the urge to rub her aching arm. She finally decided it would be wise to at least make sure she wasn't bleeding. Blood in the ocean was like a beacon, calling all sorts of dangerous creatures to your location and advertising your injury. She rubbed a hand over the spot and watched for a telltale puff of red in the water. It didn't come.

Good. At least I have that going for me.

Lilit cried out, and Marella winced. She wondered if the others had known about that part of the challenge.

"You two may go to the right." The admiral had put down the creature and pulled off one glove at a time. "A soldier will be waiting to show you where to enter the gorge."

"Let's go," Lilit said. "The sooner we get started, the sooner we find the antidote and stop the burning."

ELEVEN

The Gorge

Lilit took off to the right, as the admiral had directed, and Marella followed close behind. She searched the landscape for any sign of the other team but saw only a small school of brilliant yellow fish darting back and forth between the boulders.

Marella sped up and came alongside her teammate. "Did you know about the dragonaxi? I've studied oceanic biology my entire life and have never seen or heard of such a creature."

"No. I thought they were children's stories. Legends the old folks use to scare the young. In the four years I've spent preparing for this challenge, no one mentioned that." Lilit rubbed her left arm, where a series of scarlet splotches marred her blue skin.

Marella lifted her arm and examined the spot where the dragonaxi had speared her. Like Lilit's arm, angry red marks covered her forearm.

They swam in a straight line for another hour. The daylight had begun to fade before two dragon guard members in scarlet coats swam out to meet them.

"You'll enter here," the shorter of the two said. He pointed to a narrow crack in the ground that led up to a yawning black crevice in the ocean floor. "Good luck. Stay together if you want to have a chance at survival."

The two soldiers stayed still, watching Marella and Lilit. A tense moment passed, and Marella gathered what remained of her courage and swam down into the dark crack, moving slowly toward the gorge.

She'd never felt smaller than she did the moment her head dropped below the top of the rocky walls. Even in the palaces, she'd known that the ocean floor lay somewhere below her. The awful blackness beneath her fins opened like a mouth ready to swallow her up. Glowing eyes blinked at her from hollows in the rock, and Marella kept a safe distance between herself and the rocky ledge.

"Well, what now?" Marella asked when Lilit swam up to her. "I guess we need to find somewhere to spend the night, but when do we start looking for the dragons?"

Lilit just shook her head and pushed past Marella. "Safety first. We have to find a safe place to retreat to if we're threatened or chased."

"Of course." Marella shook her head, feeling foolish. Cedomir had said that repeatedly, and she'd forgotten it as soon as she'd descended into the gorge. She hoped that wasn't an omen of things to come. She said a silent prayer to Dalphein, added one to Ikeshal, and swam harder to keep up with Lilit's rapid pace.

Something massive cut off the light from above, and Marella froze.

"You have that bow ready?" Lilit whispered.

Marella swung her pack off her back and pulled her bow free from its side. She checked the string and, when it was firm and ready, pulled an arrow from the quiver around her waist.

When she was ready to shoot, she turned in a slow circle, searching high and low for any target. "What am I aiming at?"

"Nothing yet. Just be ready. I'm not sure what that is or whether it cares about us."

Marella nodded and kept her arrow nocked.

Slowly, Lilit crept further down into the crevice, and Marella stayed close behind her. They descended until the light took on a hazy, almost-dusk quality and the pressure squeezed Marella's chest. Nothing moved toward them in the dimness, and whatever creature had been watching from above moved on. The absence of the creature meant a tiny increase in light, but not as much as Marella had expected.

"All right, let's see if we can find someplace to spend the night." Lilit sighed and glanced around. "I have no idea where we are. All the training excursions we did were at the north end, and we're somewhere in the south. I've never even seen a map of this area."

"Well, I've heard stories of ancient cities in the gorge, so maybe we can find the ruins. An ancient building would make a good shelter." Marella peered into a cavern taller than she was, hoping to see some hint of structure.

"That's not a bad idea. Do you have a lantern or orb with you? We'll need them soon." Lilit swung her pack off her back and pulled out a small iron lamp.

"I do. Should we both light them now, though? I thought we should take turns, that way they last twice as long."

Lilit nodded and swiped a finger up the orb, turning the

light up just enough to illuminate the growing darkness around them. "Good point. Save yours for later."

"Ready?" Lilit swung her pack onto her shoulders and led the way.

She kept them in the crevice they'd descended into but shone the light into each body-sized opening they passed. Eyes reflected back at them from most of the caves and holes. After half an hour of searching, Lilit found one that had no eyes shining in the darkness.

"In here," Lilit called. She swept a finger up the orb and the light intensified, revealing a pocked pumice cavern.

A clicking noise came from deep within the cave, and Marella rushed for the door. "This one's not empty! Hurry! This way!"

Lilit rushed out behind her, holding the lamp out to the side to avoid blinding either of them with the light. "Find somewhere small we can hide. We've woken it!"

A massive angler fish exited the cave behind them, clicking as it went. Marella ducked into a narrow crack in the wall and pulled Lilit in beside her. They waited together while the angler fish swam up to the crevice and swung its dangling bait ball into the crack toward them. When it realized they weren't taking the bait, it swam away.

Marella waited until the clicking had faded into the darkness before she emerged from the crack. "Do you think we can use that cave now? I've read that angler fish never return to the same place, and other predators should avoid it because of the angler's marks."

"That's a good idea. We'll see if we can find something better tomorrow, but this'll do for tonight." Lilit held the light up and they re-entered the cave side by side.

Together, they toured the inside of the pumice cavern

until Lilit spotted something and darted toward the back wall.

"There's another cave back here. This might be easier to defend if we're ever chased. We need something with a small opening the larger predators can't squeeze through."

Lilit held the light through the opening and peered inside. "I don't see anything. That angler fish must have kept everything else away. Let's go."

The hole was only big enough to fit through if they swam single file horizontally, but Lilit led the way and Marella eagerly followed.

The smaller cave didn't have the pocked look of the pumice cavern, and Marella took the light and held it up high. The room was at least as large as the main room in Marella's home in Kaulo, and carvings lined the ceiling and walls. The back wall held what had once been a stone door but had fallen from its rusted-out hinges and now blocked the exit.

"We've found it!" Marella said, trying to keep her voice down despite the excitement. "We've found one of the abandoned buildings of the ruined cities. Do you think it's Direpeak? Or Houndshelm?"

"I have no idea," Lilit set the light in the middle of the floor and reclined beside it. "And I don't really care. We'll use this as our base. Did you bring something to eat for tonight?"

Marella nodded and settled onto the floor beside her teammate. She dug out one of the pockets of kelp she'd purchased during her preparations. That shopping trip felt like forever ago, though it had only been a few days. They ate in silence and repacked their bags.

Lilit pulled out a wax stick and moved to an empty part of the wall. "We'll need a way to keep track of where we've searched, where we've found dragons, and which dragonets seem most receptive to bonding." She drew a grid on the wall and marked their cave with a circle. She drew the crevice over the top of the grid, so the gorge took up most of the space, but it was easy to see where they'd made their home.

"Tomorrow, we'll search this area," she marked a section of the right side of the grid, "and we'll make plans for each day the night before, while we rest and recover. I don't know about you, but my arm burns worse than fire coral stings." Lilit rubbed her arm and settled back onto the floor beside Marella.

"Mine does, too." She played with the idea of trying to use the crigoresi and runes to heal the sting but remembered what the admiral had said and discarded the thought. "You said you've been training for four years? Have any of your family members done the challenge before?"

Lilit sighed. "No. I'm the first. My father's a merchant. None of my grandparents were wealthy enough to qualify their children for the rite, so my parents never had a chance."

"Merchants? Have they ever been to Endael City?"

"No. My father organizes the caravans from here and keeps track of them with a system of messengers. I've heard it's lovely there, though."

Marella nodded. "It is. It's very warm and the water's so clear you can see for leagues. I like the mountains and rocks and crags around here, though. Everything at home's so flat, there's not much to look at besides the kidali fields."

"I've heard of that. It's supposed to be so full of nutrients that you don't have to eat anything else, ever."

Marella smiled. "That's true but eating one thing all the time would be really boring, so we eat all kinds of sea weeds.

Most everyone in Kaulo lives on plants, though. I'd never tried shrimp or eel or fish until the banquet in Pharlandzi."

"How could you live on only plants?" Lilit gaped at her. "I'd feel like I was being starved without meat at least once a day."

"I've heard people say that before, but you don't miss what you've never had." She decided to keep her views on killing to herself. She needed Lilit as an ally, after all.

Lilit shifted and smiled. "I guess that makes sense. Without the challenge to train for, what did you do with all your time?"

"I went to school and studied oceanography, biology, and sculpting. I've done a little drawing with wax pencils, but I'm not terribly good at it."

Lilit cocked her head and examined Marella. "What did you plan to do with your life, once you're grown, I mean?"

"I want to study whales in the southern oceans. After I finish my military time, anyway. In Kaulo, everyone serves a few years in the army. It's required."

"I grew up knowing I was going to try to get into the Dragonaxi Challenge, though I didn't fully understand what that meant until today. My mother died when I was little, and my father has never wanted anything more than a child who can ride dragons. I think he'd always wanted a son he could ship off to the military, but since that didn't happen, all those dreams fell to me."

"I'm so sorry." Marella tried to imagine growing up without her mother and failed. Her mother had been the rock that held her family together even when her brother had gotten into trouble for associating with a rebel faction outside Endael City and her father had had to ask her uncle for favors to get him released.

Silence fell, and Marella stared into the darkness beyond

the ruined building. "Do you think we can do it?" The question popped out unbidden and hung like a threat in the water.

"Of course we can. There's no sense thinking anything but positive. We'll stick together and find us some dragons, and we'll bring them back to the city and be famous forever. And of course we'll find that antidote while we're at it."

Marella smiled. "Of course. You're right. Sorry. I haven't had as much time to mentally prepare for this as you have. I wish I'd brought some of the scrolls along. They might have proved helpful."

"Nah. You don't need scrolls. You won't have time to look at them. Should we leave the light on to scare away animals? We need to sleep if we're going to find dragons tomorrow."

After a moment's hesitation, Marella nodded. "Yes. Let's leave it on low. We'll use mine tomorrow night."

TWELVE

Commotion

Two more days brought Errebeld and Keird to the rocky cliffs outside Talam. The current had shifted away from their course, and every mile since losing that assistance felt like ten.

"Stop for a bite?" Keird pointed to a cluster of shrimps beside a cave.

Errebeld winced but slowed his pace. He kept his back to Keird and pulled a handful of wilted kelp out of his pack. He nibbled slowly; the stale taste too bitter for him to eat quickly. At least it kept his mind off Keird's activities.

A piercing scream rent the afternoon quiet, and Errebeld spun toward Keird's position. Shrimp couldn't make that sound. His friend had gone pale and stared at something between the boulders where he'd hunted.

Errebeld crept closer, straining to see through the murky waters. "What is it?" he whispered.

"Three bultier. They got a dragon and babies. We go before they see us."

Keird swam back toward the traveling route, but Errebeld remained frozen. "I can't leave them."

He pulled out his bow and strung it without a sound.

"What you doing? Leave them be."

Another pain-filled scream pierced his ears, and Errebeld whispered, "I can't. I can't listen to that and not do something."

Keird grunted and pulled his spear off his back. "Fine, let's do it."

They swam hard toward the bultier attacking the babies, leaving the two who'd killed the mother with their meal. Another baby cried out and fell silent, and Errebeld took aim. As soon as he came into range, he released it, but a water flow he couldn't see blew it off course.

With a soft curse, he nocked another arrow and took aim. This time, the arrow went straight and true. It dug into the bultier's soft body, and the creature's skin flashed a brilliant blue, signaling its anger. Errebeld had been taught to flee from a flashing bultier, but he drew himself up to his full height.

The beast spun toward Errebeld's position, but he was ready. He released three arrows in quick succession, each one piercing the soft skin. Two went straight through, leaving the animal staggering.

A cloud of black surrounded the bultier, trailing from the wounds. It fell in a silent heap halfway between Errebeld and the dragonet it had attacked. Errebeld's stomach heaved, but he kept his meal down with effort.

Before he advanced toward the ransacked nest, Errebeld turned to check the location of the other two bultiers. Keird stood with his spear out in front of him. Black blood wafted from the tip, and one bultier lay still at his feet. The other paid them no attention as it feasted on the dead mother dragon.

"Is it dead?" Keird's voice startled Errebeld into motion.

He swam to the last dragon, which lay motionless in the remnants of the nest. The creature had tucked its head and legs in close to its pale gray body, but several small punctures on its neck showed the bultier's damage. Its chest moved gently with rapid, shallow breaths.

"It's alive, but barely. Bring me my pack."

Keird shook his head. "You get it. I watch that one." He gestured toward the mother dragon with the tip of his spear.

"Of course." Errebeld swam hard for the spot where he'd left his pack, grabbed it, and dashed back to the wounded dragonet. He dug through and found his only crig bead, popped it in his mouth, and waited, his hands poised over the dragonet.

When his heart rate sped and his stomach tied itself in knots, Errebeld used his pencil to draw a simple, four-lined rune on the dragon's back.

Blue light grew from the runes, and Errebeld pressed his hands to the creature's wounds, willing his strength into the dragonet. The punctures drew closed and healed into puckered, pink skin, and the baby's breathing evened out. When the crig ran out, Errebeld broke the link between himself and the injured animal.

"Well?" Keird whispered from much closer than Errebeld expected.

"He'll live, but —"

Keird sighed. "But not long. Mother's dead."

"Exactly. What do you know about dragons?"

"I am dragon trainer."

Errebeld smiled. "Of course. I knew that." His gaze

wandered to the scars on Keird's hands and arms. "So, what do we do to convince this one to come with us?"

"I, uh, I don't know. I never work with baby dragon before." Keird added a few soft swear words and ran a hand over his neck.

"We have to move it for now, so let's see if we can get it to swim to one of those caves."

Keird nodded. "I find empty one."

With his friend gone, Errebeld turned his attention back to the dragonet. They'd have to help it swim to the caves, and it wouldn't be strong enough to travel for several days, at least. Maybe even a week. He carefully kept his mind away from the beast he'd killed to save the dragonet. He'd have to deal with it eventually, but he wasn't ready yet. Soraya's disapproving face flashed in his memory, and he groaned.

"What?" Keird emerged from a cave less than ten lengths from Errebeld's position.

"I was just thinking of Soraya's letter. She's not known for her patience."

"She wait. New dragon for Society make her happy."

Errebeld smiled. "Of course it will. Is that one safe?" He gestured to the cave Keird had exited.

"It is. Let's go."

The two positioned themselves on either side of the dragonet and lifted. The creature was just barely larger than the eggshells strewn about the nest, so it had to be a newborn, certainly not more than a few days old, Errebeld realized. He grunted under the dragon's unexpected weight and gave thanks to Dalphein that he hadn't found a larger baby to save.

It took every bit of Errebeld's strength to settle the baby into the cave, and based on the redness in Keird's face, his friend wasn't in any better shape. They sat side by side against the cave wall, gasping for breath and staring at the sleeping dragonet.

"Now what?"

Errebeld chuckled. "Now we figure out how to feed it and keep it alive until it's strong enough to swim with us to Talam."

"Dragons eat fish."

Errebeld's smile vanished, and the memory of the lifeless bultier twisted a hot knife through his chest. "I know." He paused and added, "Maybe you can hunt, and I'll clean up after it and guard the cave?"

Keird nodded. "That maybe works." A huge yawn cut off whatever he'd been about to say next.

"You want to take a nap, and I'll keep watch for a bit?"

"You don't mind?" Keird yawned again.

"Nah. I'm too keyed up to sleep, and someone has to make sure that whatever scavengers come to that mess don't get curious about this cave."

Errebeld swam to the cave's mouth and surveyed the carnage. Five dragonets lay dead and partially eaten in the nest. Small fish and a few larger sharks picked at the mother's carcass. The red clouds hovering over mounds of twisted and torn flesh made Errebeld's head spin. Blackness threatened the edges of his vision. He lowered his gaze to the boulders littering the ground between the nest and his cave. He'd figure out how to atone for breaking his vow later. For now, he had to protect the baby sleeping off the rest of the bultier's venom.

The next day passed in a haze of worry and inactivity as Errebeld and Keird waited for the dragonet to wake. They'd spent hours discussing all the possible scenarios and still had no idea how to manage a wild newborn dragonet.

Errebeld paced in the cave's mouth, while Keird hovered over the infant. Its breathing hadn't changed. It hadn't moved or twitched a single muscle. It hadn't made the slightest sound.

What if the poison did something I couldn't fix? Errebeld worried. *What if it never wakes? It'll just starve to death in this cave.*

He considered trying to put a fish in its mouth but discarded the idea after a heartbeat. He didn't want to choke the youngling. Besides, that would be a horrible fate for the fish whether the dragonet woke up or not.

Several more hours passed before Keird swam up behind him. "I just remember something I hear once."

"Oh?" Errebeld spun, trying to cover how much his friend had startled him.

"Settle down. I not hurt you. Some baby dragon sleeps until mother brings food. Food wakes baby. Baby sleep to keep predators away. Other dragon kinds make big nest with many adults to protect babies. Those babies awake more." He took a breath and stared at the sleeping baby. "I not see many adult. I see one. This baby wake for food."

"Oh, Dalphein." Errebeld groaned. His stupid idea had been the right one. "Of course. I think I heard that once, too. You want to hunt?"

He held his breath until Keird nodded. Once his friend vanished beyond the cave's mouth, Errebeld leaned against the cave wall and pulled a wad of wilted kelp from his pack. Keird would eat something before he came back with fish, but Errebeld hadn't seen any decent seaweed in two days of traveling, so he'd have to make do. He gulped the bitter, slimy ball down without chewing and grabbed one of the daquiona beads out of Keird's pack to wash the flavor away. He chewed it slowly, enjoying the warmth of the liquid as it traveled down his throat. This time, he swallowed the casing. He'd need whatever he could get to keep his strength up.

Keird returned before the light began to fade and held a squirming, palm-sized perch in front of the dragon's nose. The creature's eyes popped open, and it charged at the food. Keird yanked his hand away a heartbeat before the dragonet snapped its jaws shut on the fish. Its luminescent blue eyes flicked over the cave for a long moment. When it realized they had no more food, it lay back down and resumed its unmoving slumber.

"I think it wanted more," Errebeld whispered.

Keird nodded. "It did. I bring more tomorrow."

The next day, Keird returned with two fish, each twice the size of the first one. Again, the baby scarfed them down and searched for more. Each day in the week following, the routine continued. Keird returned with more and larger fish. The dragonet ate them in a breath and searched for more. After the first few days, Errebeld found a small bed of seaweed where he could eat after he'd seen the baby fed.

After several days of this, Keird dumped his pack on the cave's stone floor and filled it with fish for the baby. He returned and freed the fish in the cave, with both Keird and Errebeld stationed at the cave's mouth to keep the fish or the baby from escaping.

This time, the dragonet chased the fish, one at a time, with all the glee you'd expect in a child playing tag with friends. Not a single drop of blood escaped to color the cave's water, though Errebeld's stomach churned at so much killing, so many fishes dead.

Keird flashed a wide grin. "You get used to hunting. I need help feeding youngling."

His shoulders slumped, but Errebeld nodded. He'd

suspected this day was close. One person just couldn't provide enough fish for the growing dragonet. And it was growing. The baby had added so much bulk they'd have to find a bigger cave soon.

When the first blue light filtered into the cave, Errebeld and Keird ventured out together. Errebeld carried his empty pack, though the weight of his chore bowed his back more than a full pack might have. He'd managed to justify killing a single bultier to save the dragonet, but how would he atone for killing dozens of fish?

"If we cannot feed it, the youngling dies. How is that better?" Keird eyed Errebeld's stooped posture.

Unable to find a suitable response, Errebeld shrugged. Perhaps his friend was right. What was the point in saving the infant just to let it starve? He'd have to find a priest in Talam to absolve him or give him penance.

Once this is over, I swear to Dalphein I will never again kill a living thing. Ever. For any reason. He repeated the vow again and again until they reached an open space above the cliffs, where schools of colorful fish danced in the morning light, throwing dazzling reflections all around.

"We not here to watch light show," Keird snapped. He made a show of swinging his pack off his back and opening it in one smooth movement.

Errebeld copied the motion, though his hands shook, and his legs felt as if they'd been made of kelp.

"You can do this. Youngling must eat."

Errebeld nodded and followed Keird in a slow ascent toward the shimmering masses.

A large fish dashed through and scattered the lowest school, but the one beside it simply shifted directions and moved straight toward Keird. Errebeld held his breath as his friend held open his pack and stayed completely motionless.

Without thinking, he did the same, and in seconds a dozen fish swam straight into his waiting bag. He tugged the strings tight and whispered an apology to the creatures struggling against the heavy waxed canvas.

"Let's go." Errebeld didn't wait for Keird but swam as fast as he could back to the sleeping dragonet.

This time, Keird released the fish in his pack first, and Errebeld held onto his until the baby had finished Keird's fish and started searching for more food. The infant's delighted grin was enough to take some of the weight off of Errebeld's shoulders. Feeding such an innocent animal couldn't be all bad, could it?

THIRTEEN

Dragons

A scraping sound woke Marella the next morning, and she blinked at the unfamiliar cave. She rose to find Lilit scratching a deeper mark around the area they planned to search that day.

"Oh, good. You're awake." She said when Marella rose. "The sun'll be up soon, so we should be ready to go."

Marella nodded and sat down to eat. She didn't know if she'd have time for any other meals that day, so she wasn't about to skip breakfast. Her arm throbbed, and the pain had spread up past her elbow and into her upper arm. She wiggled her fingers, relieved to find that they still obeyed her commands, though they felt swollen and clumsy.

"Mine hurts, too. Let's get this going, so we can find the antidote and cure ourselves."

"Good plan," Marella said through a mouthful of kelp.

They finished their meal and gathered their belongings. Marella tested her bow, changed the string, and swung both the bow and the pack onto her shoulders. She stuffed a bit of kelp and her knife into the pockets belted around her waist, buttoned them closed, and drifted toward the narrow opening.

"Ready?" Marella asked. Faint morning light shone through the hole, heralding the day's beginning.

"Ready. Let's do this." Lilit glanced back at the grid once more, extinguished her light, and followed Marella out into the morning.

They stuck Marella's light into every cavern they found and entered several larger caves to search for passages dragons might use to hide their nests. Marella searched her memory for any tidbit that might help her find a dragon nest but came up empty handed again and again. Frustration knotted her gut by midday, and Marella and Lilit snapped at each other repeatedly.

"Let me see that light," Lilit barked, grabbing the lamp from Marella and shoving it into yet another cave. Something snapped tooth-filled jaws toward her arm, and she pulled back and swam on before Marella could see what had been in the cave.

"We've been searching for hours." Marella said after three more failed cave checks. "Let's take a break and eat a bit, and we can regroup and go back to searching once we've settled ourselves."

Lilit wilted but nodded. "You're right. Let's take a little break. Sorry I snapped at you."

"I've been snappy, too. You're forgiven if I am. Truce?" Marella held out her hands, and Lilit grabbed them and gave a gentle squeeze.

"Truce. We'll get there. If the dragons were easy to find, this wouldn't be much of a challenge, would it?" Lilit chuckled, and Marella joined in.

When they'd finished their meal, Marella and Lilit continued their methodical search of the gorge.

After another hour of searching, Lilit found what looked like the entrance to a ruined building, similar to the one they'd chosen for their base.

"Let's check this one out." Lilit turned the light on and crept into the cavernous building.

Marella's hopes crashed into her flippers at the sight of the empty cave filled with small fish that darted away and out the door when Marella and Lilit entered. Surely those fish wouldn't be anywhere near dragons.

Still, she hoped she'd been wrong, and struggled against despair when her first instinct turned out to be correct.

"It's getting dark," Lilit said when they exited the cave. "Let's go back to our cave and mark off the areas we've searched."

Marella nodded, fighting the gnawing disappointment that chewed up her insides. "We'll have better luck tomorrow. I'm sure of it."

The next day was just as fruitless as the first, and they returned to their cave empty handed and frustrated.

The third day began much the same as the previous two. Marella and Lilit marked out their plan on the grid, packed their belongings, and headed out into the first light of the day.

"Today's the day, I can feel it," Lilit said, smiling at the brilliantly colored fish filling the gorge. "We're gonna find some dragons, and maybe get close enough to find the antidote to this cursed poison."

"I hope you're right." Marella tried to find a little optimism, but the past two days had beaten it all out of her. She'd begun to wonder if there even were any dragons in this part of the gorge. "If we don't find anything, I think we should head further north tomorrow. You said you found bunches of abandoned nests in that part of the gorge during your training excursions."

"If we don't find anything today, I'll probably agree with you, but let's finish today's search before we think that far ahead."

Marella didn't answer but tried to coax herself into thinking as Lilit did. Maybe her new friend was right. Maybe they would find dragons and cure the poison that made her entire arm hurt from her fingertips to her shoulder. Her fingers still moved on command, but every movement hurt, which made using the bow more painful with every passing hour. She still hadn't loosed a single arrow but had drawn the bow more times than she could count in the past few days. Each time had been more agonizing than the one before.

Lilit led Marella to an area they hadn't searched before, and together they began the methodical rhythm of checking every cave and cavern they happened upon.

Marella was about to ask to stop for a midday meal when Lilit froze. "They're here. We've found them."

Hope rose in Marella's chest, but she shoved it aside. What if they hadn't found them, but had found old, abandoned nests?

"Follow me, and be as quiet as you can," Lilit said, extinguishing the light and climbing into the cave.

The two swam slowly through the abandoned entry of an ancient building. Pillars rose on every side, each shimmering with inset mother of pearl designs and patterns. Broken crystal chandeliers littered the floor, light reflecting off them in a dazzling show of light. Marella saw nothing that marked this building as any different from the dozens of others they'd searched, but Lilit seemed sure, so Marella followed.

They crept along the wall toward the back of the cave, where a gaping hole where the wall should have been led into a deeper darkness.

Marella's stomach fluttered in anticipation.

I hope this is it. Please let her be right. She didn't know if she was praying to Dalphein or Ikeshalor some other Pharli god, but it didn't matter. Hopefully someone would hear and intervene.

They swam slowly, careful not to stir any dust from the floor and muddy the water. Lilit pressed her hands to the crumbling stone that made up what remained of the back wall and peered through the opening, and Marella positioned herself just above her friend to see what lay beyond the hole.

Massive piles of rock, wood, and debris had been arranged into perfect circles on the floor, and several piles had dragon heads peeking out the tops. Marella's breath caught in her throat, and she fought the urge to shout for joy.

Lilit clamped a hand around Marella's sore left arm, and she had to bite her cheek to keep from crying out. Instead, she used her good hand to pry Lilit's fingers free from the swollen skin.

Lilit looked down, and an expression of horror crossed her face. "Sorry," she mouthed, pulling her hand away. She motioned to the open water outside the cave and swam slowly away from the opening. Marella followed close behind.

They ducked into a nearby crevice and Marella felt her own grin mirror the ear-splitting smile on Lilit's face.

"What now?" Marella asked. "Do we just sneak in and find a bit of broken shell and cure ourselves first? Or try to make friends with a dragonet?"

Lilit shook her head. "First, we sit at the edge of the cave and let the dragonets get used to us. I didn't see any adults in there, but that doesn't mean they're not close enough to defend their babies if one sets up a cry."

"Right. Lead the way. I'll follow." Marella worked to still her shaking hands. Excitement and terror filled her chest. She'd never seen a dragon this close before, and judging by the size of the nests, the adults must be at least twice the size of the yearlings that had circled the ceiling at the banquet.

Lilit swam back into the abandoned building and clung to the wall as they'd done the first time. Instead of pausing at the hole, though, she continued through at the same slow pace. Inside the dragons' cave, she stayed near the wall and stopped to the right of the hole, halfway between the exit and the nearest nest. She settled onto the floor, and Marella lowered herself down beside her friend, careful not to stir the sediments up from the bottom.

They sat like that for what felt like hours. Marella enjoyed watching the baby dragons moving around in the nests. When they settled down, she tried searching the dimly lit cavern for signs of broken shells. No shells or bones or anything littered the ground between the nests, so she gave up quickly. Nothing changed for a long while, until something massive moved on the cave's far wall. The adult dragon rose and swam past the few occupied nests and the dozens of empty ones moving ever closer to the spot where Marella and Lilit sat.

Marella froze, her heart pounding in her chest, and kept her eyes down so the light wouldn't reflect off them and draw the dragon's attention. Beside her, Lilit sat still as a statue. The dragon swam past them, its tail undulating gently in the confined space, and moved through the hole and out into the open waters.

"She's gone. Let's find that antidote," Marella said, rising slowly. She moved toward the nearest nest, keeping her pace slow enough to not scare the dragonets inside.

"Marella!" Lilit's urgent whisper caught Marella's attention, but she didn't slow down. The poison burned her arm and radiated through her chest and down her left flank, and the pain was nearly crippling already. She couldn't see how she'd be able to swim at all if she waited another day.

On approaching the nest, Marella got her first look at the babies inside. Three dragons sat in the center of the ring of stones and debris, each roughly twice Marella's size. In the bottom of the nest, bits of shell crunched under the babies' feet. Small yellow fungus shaped in oddly-pretty ruffles grew on the shells, and Marella wondered how she was supposed to get the shells from under the dragonets.

"Marella!"

At Lilit's shout, Marella startled and turned. A massive dragon swam toward her, its jaws spread wide enough to easily bite her in half.

Marella darted for the opening as fast as she could and emerged into the open cavern a breath behind Lilit. Together, the two raced away from the cave. As they fled, Marella searched the gorge walls for any sign of a tunnel or cave small enough to hide them without letting the dragon in. The dragon grew closer, churning the water behind them and scaring off other creatures with its terrifying roar.

A hole just large enough for Marella to squeeze through opened on her right, and Marella shouted, "In here!" a heartbeat before she dragged herself into the cave. Lilit followed an instant later, and the two scrambled away from the opening.

Outside, the dragon roared and pressed one green eye to the cave's entrance. It swam away, and Marella drew a relieved breath. She turned to Lilit, ready to apologize for her stupid carelessness, when the dragon returned and slammed its clubbed tail into the wall of the gorge. Massive boulders fell from the ceiling of the cave, but none landed near Marella or Lilit. Marella gasped and pressed further back against the wall. The dragon beat its tail against the wall again, roared, and swam away.

Lilit glared at Marella. "How could you be so stupid?"

"I'm so sorry. I thought the adults were gone!" Marella tried to quell the trembling in her hands and quivering in her gut but couldn't shake the terror of the day's events.

"Do you even realize what you've done?" Lilit rose, towering over Marella's shaking form. "You've taught the babies that we're not supposed to be there. The whole point of sitting there and not moving is to let the dragonets get used to our presence so they approach us!"

"I said I'm sorry. We can still go back and start over. It might take an extra day, but we haven't lost everything." Marella found the spirit to defend herself and anger at Lilit's reaction chased the fear from her body.

"You think that adult's going to let us anywhere near that cave after your stupid stunt?" Lilit's shout scared the small creatures that had hidden in the cave with them, and dozens of fish and little scurrying things hurried away from her wrath.

Marella opened her mouth to respond, but Lilit cut her off with a wave of her hand. "Just forget it. We can't let the day end like this, though. Let's check a few more caves."

Lilit twisted around and squeezed between the boulders on the floor. When she reached the mouth of the cave, she darted through it without even checking to see if Marella had followed.

Marella had no idea how to make things right with her teammate, but she knew she had to try. She raced forward and swam beside Lilit, trying repeatedly to apologize. Lilit showed no signs that she'd even heard her, let alone accepted the apologies.

With a sigh, Marella fell back and followed Lilit at a close enough distance to keep pace, but far enough to give her room to recover from the afternoon's disappointment.

The worst part, Marella thought, *is that she's right. I ruined it. Dalphein! I'm an idiot.*

She hung her head and tried to muster a little optimism that the day could still be salvaged. They'd found one dragon den. They could find another.

They swam to the other end of the section of the gorge that they'd mapped on their grid and returned the methodical search of every cave and cavern that they'd refined over the past few days.

After an hour, they stopped to eat and rest, but Lilit still refused to speak to Marella. Dejected and angry at herself, Marella couldn't make herself eat much, and before much time had passed, both were ready to move on.

Lilit led the way to a section they hadn't explored before. Cheerful yellow and blue fish bobbed up and down among the coral. The little hairs at the back of her neck stood on end, and Marella struggled to put her finger on what about the area made her uneasy. No predators prowled overhead, no odd outcroppings of rock looked menacing, like the eels her mentor had warned her of. She peeked into another cave, found nothing, not even the small scurrying creatures that normally populated the caves, and pulled back, ready to abandon this section and move on to safer waters. She glanced up at Lilit, but she'd moved to the left and had her head in a different cave.

The lichen clinging to the rock wall swept downward, and before Marella could adjust, a current swept her away from the cave in a rapid descent. The force ripped her legs apart at the fingernail-like scales that normally kept them locked together, and her right foot snagged in a small cave. The bones in her lower leg snapped, searing pain through her leg and into her hip, and Marella couldn't hold back her scream.

Get away from the wall! Her grandmother's voice shouted in her mind. With her good leg and good arm, Marella shoved away from the wall and struggled to escape the crushing current. She'd gone too deep, too fast, and the pressure on her chest made it impossible to draw breath. Terror filled her mind, but she fought against it. She had to keep her head if she wanted to live. Her vision dimmed, and she didn't know if that was because the light had diminished or if she had reached the maximum depth and pressure she could take without fainting.

Drawing on every ounce of determination she had left, she kicked hard and pulled against the wall of water and broke free of the pounding current. Once free, she dragged a breath of ice-cold water into her chest, working hard against the crushing pressure, and hovered for a moment to regroup. She yearned to swim hard for the surface, to get away from the crushing pressure, but she held herself still.

Careful, now, she thought. *Don't climb too fast. You're deep, but not too deep. It's survivable. Climb too fast, and you'll die.* Her leg hung limp, her foot sticking out at an odd angle, but she used her good hand and foot to slowly propel herself into shallower water. The pressure on her chest eased, the light increased, and before long, Marella could see well enough to search for Lilit.

She checked all the caves near the down current without drifting close enough to risk getting caught in it again, but she saw no signs of Lilit. Alone, in pain, and fearful that her friend may not have survived, Marella searched for a cave large enough to hide in. She needed to fix her leg, and even if the crigoresi and runes couldn't cure the poison or the pain it caused, they could fix the bones in her leg and regrow the scales that had yanked free of her skin with the current's force, provided she could remember the runes and draw them perfectly. Her hands still shook with the terror of the current. She pressed them hard against her stomach and drew another deep breath. She'd have to wait until they were steady enough to draw the lines right.

She found a small cave that would serve her purpose, though it would be far too cramped to be comfortable. She winced with every movement. Moving slowly, she climbed inside and ducked far enough into the cave to be hidden from the outside.

There, with her back against the wall and her broken leg lying awkwardly against the hard stone floor, she paused. Should she leave some kind of mark outside the cave for Lilit in case she escaped the current and came looking for her?

Deciding that's exactly what she should do, Marella mustered the will to move her broken leg one more time. She found her wax stick and made a triangular mark similar to the ones she and Lilit had used to keep track of which caves they'd checked. However, instead of leaving it empty, Marella drew an arrow pointing to the cave's opening, so Lilit would know to look there.

A sense of accomplishment buoyed her, and Marella climbed back into the cave and settled carefully onto the stone. Even that movement shot searing pain through her leg and her left arm, and Marella leaned her head back against the wall and fought the urge to weep. Instead, she lay perfectly still and focused on breathing in and out slowly, feeling the water running over the gills lining her sinus cavity and throat, and reveling in the fact that she was alive. Everything else she could work with. She was alive.

She had no idea how much time passed, but eventually her hands stopped shaking and the stabbing pains in her leg eased to a more tolerable throbbing.

When she was sure she was steady enough, Marella pulled her wax pencil out of her pack and set it beside her. Next, she dug to the bottom of her belongings and found the little pouch Feena had given her to hold the two precious crigoresi beads. She pulled one out and popped it in her mouth, forced herself to swallow the slimy bead, and again cursed the waxy coating they used to protect the mineral from the sea. She waited until she felt the familiar tightening in her gut, the slight quickening of her pulse, and the anxiety that came from ingesting the crigoresi when she hadn't used any power.

Her cheeks flushed with the rush, though it was weaker this time than she'd ever felt before. That could be because she'd been under immense stress and had depleted her body's natural levels of the mineral, or it could be that she'd improved her overall fitness and could now withstand the crigoresi's effects without so much anxiety. Either way, she didn't mind the increased clarity and decided the reason didn't matter.

She picked up the wax pencil and positioned it above her leg but hesitated. She wasn't looking forward to the pain drawing runes on her leg would bring, but she had to do it if she was going to survive this challenge. Gathering her determination, she drew the rune as perfectly as she could on the uneven surface of her scales. A brilliant blue light rewarded her efforts, and heat filled the little cave. With a crunch and a snap, her leg popped back into position. Marella cried out at the sudden, intense pain, but settled back and let the power work. The light grew to a blinding intensity before it slowly faded away, leaving Marella healed but exhausted. As the admiral had promised, the power had done nothing to dull the pain in her arm and chest, and Marella had no doubt the poison would kill her if she didn't get the antidote.

More determined than ever, she gathered her belongings and headed back toward the cave she'd shared with Lilit. As she swam, she pointedly kept her mind away from all the general's warnings about lone challengers. She wouldn't think that way. Lilit had escaped somehow. She had to. Marella wouldn't even consider the possibility of facing this challenge alone. She couldn't. No matter how hard she tried to block it out, the soldier's voice echoed in her mind as she limped through the gorge.

"Stay together if you want to have a chance at survival."

How could she make it on her own? Hadn't she shown again and again how little she knew about this place and this challenge?

No. She wouldn't think that way. Lilit had survived. She'd be waiting at the cave when Marella arrived. She had to be. No other options were worth considering.

An eternity later, she found the cave she shared with her teammate. She shooed away a school of small fish hiding in the front cavern and dragged herself through to the place where they slept.

The cave showed no signs that Lilit had been there, and small fish and creatures had returned to claim it as their own. No new marks marred the grid, which was exactly as they'd left it that morning.

A powerful wave of grief and loneliness pressed Marella to the ground, and she lay there unmoving for an interminable moment.

No. No, no, no, no, no. She has to be alive. She just has to. Oh, Dauphine, what am I going to do? She can't be gone, can she?

The memory of that sudden downward pressure played through her mind again, but this time, she imagined all the horrible things that could have happened to her friend. What if the current had hit while Lilit had her head in a cave? Her neck would have snapped like Marella's leg had.

Nausea too strong to breathe through cut off that line of thought, and Marella remembered how helpful and gracious Lilit had been during all the times when Marella hadn't known what to do. Finally, the scene in the dragon cave played out before her closed eyes, and Marella wept. If she hadn't been so rash and foolish, her friend would still be alive.

Thick tears burned Marella's eyes, and she squeezed them shut against the pain. Memories of their brief friendship flashed through her mind. Pictures of Lilit drawing the grid on the wall and leading the way through the daily searches dominated her memories, and despair fought its way through. She wouldn't have had a chance without Lilit's help. How would she make it on her own now?

No. She wouldn't think that way. She was a survivor, and she would find a way to get through this. The poison burned through her arm and into her chest, throbbing in a rhythm that she decided would be her reason to live. She would live through this. She would find a dragonet — somehow.

Her stomach grumbled and reminded her that she still had to eat if she were to make the day's losses worthwhile by surviving the challenge. She hadn't eaten much at the noon meal — she wouldn't let herself think about why — and now her body demanded replenishment if it was to recover fully from the ordeal with the down current.

She pulled out her lamp and set it to a level just bright enough to see the edges of the cave. She set it in the center of the empty room and dug out a bit of kelp. It was past its prime and had started to get slimy. Back home in Kaulo, she probably would have refused to eat it, but her stomach rumbled, and she scarfed it down, ignoring the bitter taste.

Loneliness and grief weighed against her chest, but Marella grabbed her wax pencil and moved to the grid. She circled the spot where they'd found the dragons and marked the area with the down current with a big X. Beneath the grid, she made a note to herself that the X meant danger and sat back to study her handiwork.

This was the time when she and Lilit would have made a plan for the next day. Marella stared at the grid, trying to decide what her best course of action would be. Should she return to the dragon cave and attempt to undo the damage with the baby dragons? Or should she continue searching on her own? Which would give her the best chance to befriend a dragonet and get the antidote?

And win the challenge, a tiny voice in the back of her mind whispered.

She reclined against the back wall and pressed her pack behind her head as a pillow. From that vantage point, she could see the grid and continue to parse the options.

Her mind circled the problem endlessly without an answer until she faded into sleep.

Marella woke to a faint clicking sound well before dawn and groaned. Of course. It was just her luck that the angler fish would return now, with her alone and trapped in the cave behind its hiding spot. Unsure what else to do, and hoping the animal would go away and move deeper with daybreak, Marella ignored it and settled back down. She closed her eyes and focused on the lamp's faint light beyond her eyelids until she managed to fall back to sleep.

When the morning light filtered through the cave's opening, Marella stretched and rose, but her left arm hung limp at her side. She couldn't move her fingers or feel even the firmest pressure against her skin. The pain in her chest and down her side made every movement burn like the sting from a hundred urchins.

Loneliness, grief, and pain overwhelmed her, and Marella sank back to the cold stone floor and wept. She sat there in the dim light, imagining all the horrible ends that Lilit could have met, and struggled to find the will to continue the challenge. The circle she'd marked on the grid called to her, and she stared at the marking son the wall as if that map held all the answers.

FOURTEEN

Challenger

She struggled to rip her gaze away from the point on the grid that marked the dragons' cave as the previous day's events replayed in her mind's eye. During the process of reliving that horror, somehow, somewhere deep in the recesses of her mind, the tiniest inkling of a plan blossomed.

Her stomach grumbled, and Marella turned away from the grid in search of food. She dug in her pack for the dwindling supply of slimy kelp and choked down enough to give her the energy to face the day.

That finished, she swung her pack and her bow over her right shoulder and peeked out into the large open room that led back to her cave. The angler fish — if that's what had been there — had left at some point, and only a small cluster of tiny blue fish occupied the cavern. They darted away through the wide opening to the gorge when Marella emerged, their synchronized movements reminding Marella again of how alone she was.

She made her way to the dragons' cave, though she knew they might chase her away or kill her because of her rash behavior the day before.

Maybe that will be better, she thought. *At least then it won't hurt anymore.*

No fear fluttered in her chest or slowed her movements as Marella circled the stone wall toward the collapsed opening that led to the dragons' den. No creatures stirred when she entered the room with the enormous nests, and Marella swam to her left, away from the nest she'd disturbed before, and settled down against the wall.

Her scrolls and teachers had all said that dragons were curious creatures but could take a day or more to approach a supaerisi within their lair.

I'll have to be patient, then. Marella leaned her head back against the cold stone and closed her eyes.

Minutes turned to hours, and still she waited. Adult dragons shifted, left the cave, and returned, and still she sat.

The light had begun to fade when her stomach grumbled for food, but Marella decided to wait a bit longer before leaving. Instead, she pulled out another sad, faded, slimy bit of seaweed and forced it past her tongue.

After her meal, boredom set in, and Marella searched for ways to keep herself occupied. She used her long fingers to draw runes in the mud beside her spot, which occupied her for a while, but without the crigoresi to actually try them, the runes soon lost her interest, too. She yearned to watch the babies moving in the nests but feared scaring them off if they caught her watching.

Besides, I don't want to get my hopes up if I've already scared them off for good, she thought. Lilit's angry words echoed in her mind. *You've taught the babies that we're not supposed to be there!*

She sent up a prayer to Dalphein and Ikeshal and laid down to rest. Pain shot through her body with the movement, and Marella winced and bit her tongue to keep from crying out. The poison's movement was speeding up and had reached the middle of her body and started down her left leg. Marella pressed her legs together and flexed the muscles that unclasped the connecting scales, then moved each leg independently of the other. The movement shot pins and needles through her left thigh, but her right leg had healed completely while she'd slept. She pressed her legs together again and the scales caught, fastening her legs into one long flipper. She could use the stronger right leg to support the left for now, so she'd still be able to swim if she needed to.

The light faded to the purple hue that signaled the end of the day, and Marella rose to leave. The undulation of swimming upwards created more pain in her abdomen than she expected, and she cursed under her breath. The poison had definitely spread faster than she'd thought.

She made a last second decision not to return to the cave that night. Instead, she'd sleep with the dragons. No one had mentioned trying such a thing in any of her training, but she'd only had a week to prepare. She couldn't think of any reason not to stay with the creatures who were her only hope of survival.

The night passed in waves of rumbling and clicking sounds as the dragons moved and communicated with each other. Thumps and thuds woke Marella frequently, but she couldn't see in the pitch-black cave to tell what had made them. Twice, she woke to the sense of a large animal very close to her. She froze, prepared for the worst and stayed as still as she could. She barely allowed herself to even breathe. After a while, the dragon rumbled and chirped, the sound like something she'd expect from a whale, and moved away, leaving her trembling and on the verge of weeping.

By the time the dawn's first blush filtered into the

room, Marella had already been awake for at least an hour, lamenting her decision to share sleeping quarters with such large and noisy animals. When it was bright enough that she could see, Marella dug through her pack. This time, she bypassed the wilted and mostly rotten kelp in favor of something her mother had bought at the market. It didn't look like anything she'd eaten before, but the woman in the market had assured her that it was highly nutritious and was made up of seeds from a land plant. She poured the seeds the woman had called 'nuts' into her hand and stared at them, rolling them around in her palm and mustering the courage to try them.

She sighed, decided she was being foolish, and tossed the seeds into her mouth. They had a crunch she'd never experienced before, but it wasn't unpleasant. She finished the rest of the nuts in the pouch and spent a few minutes picking the remnants out of her teeth. They'd tasted good enough, she decided. She'd eat those until she ran out, then go in search of something else. Hopefully by then, she'd have made friends with a dragonet and cured the poison making every movement agony.

Settling back against the wall, Marella leaned her head back and prepared for another long day of waiting. Once more, she went through the most difficult runes, practicing the complicated lines in the mud and recalling what those runes were supposed to do and what color light they projected. When she'd gone through all the ones she knew, she whispered a list of whale facts she'd learned in school and wondered if she'd ever get to follow her dream of becoming a scientist.

A small-ish blue dragonet with wide splotches of green across its belly and back approached from her left, and Marella froze. She hadn't seen which nest the baby had come from, and she hoped it wasn't one who'd seen the adult chase her off before. Unwilling to risk scaring it off, she sat frozen and kept her eyes on her hands.

She held herself still while the creature scooted ever closer, approaching on her almost-completely-paralyzed left side. Marella had no idea what to do and wished she'd spent more time studying dragon behavior and bonding instead of focusing all her time on survival in the gorge.

She cursed quietly.

I thought I'd have a team, dammit.

Her heart pounded in her chest, and she waited, unwilling to move. She'd learned that lesson. She wouldn't risk ruining any chance of bonding with the dragonet.

The baby stopped less than an arm's length from her and settled onto the cave's floor, its back against the wall, in a perfect imitation of her posture. It hung its head down to stare at the dirt, its long neck arching into a green frill that sprouted around the back of its head. Its body was covered in tiny shimmery scales that formed patches of blue and green. Somehow, the animal sat up so its scrawny, clubbed tail fell along the wall, and it used its forelegs to wave towards her in an imitation of her writing movements.

Marella bit back a laugh and watched the dragonet out of the corner of her eye. Her cheek twitched with the effort of keeping her face smooth. She wanted to make eye contact, but that didn't seem like the wise thing to do. Instead, she returned to drawing runes in the mud, but she kept her eyes on her lap so she could see the dragon and the runes in her peripheral vision.

"What you do?"

The squeaky voice startled Marella, and she almost cried out. She waited until she was sure she had control of her voice before she answered.

"I'm practicing runes. You speak the common tongue?"

"Mmmm." The dragonet gave a high-pitched rumble. "Mother does. I learn."

"Well, you're doing very well. I'm Marella. Do you have a name?" Excitement bubbled up in Marella for the first time since she'd run from the adult dragon.

"Name? What is name?"

Marella frowned, searching for the simplest way to explain it. "Does your mother call you something to tell you apart from your brothers and sisters?"

Realization dawned on the dragonet's face in an almost comical expression. "Oh, yes. Mother call me," a series of chirps and clicks followed.

"Do you have another name? Something in this language? I'm afraid I can't make those sounds," Marella said, smiling. She'd turned her face toward the dragon without meaning to but hadn't made eye contact. She paused to control her reactions before her excitement got her into trouble.

The dragonet fluttered its undersized wings and situated itself closer to Marella.

"I think... Mother tell me once." The dragonet screwed up its face in an adorable look of concentration. "Ha—" the baby cleared its throat. "Hakkan. It mean 'little.' I littler than others."

"You don't look little to me." Marella dared a glance toward the dragonet's eyes, and it met her gaze with its coppery eyes. It had pupils that looked more like vertical slits than the round pupils Marella was used to seeing, but something about its features set her at ease.

"You littler than me. I—" the dragon trailed off, his eyes darting to the other side of the cave. "I be back later." He scampered across the muddy floor, taking little hops and trying to swim every few steps.

An adult dragon with similar coloring met the baby halfway to the nest. The adult eyed Marella for an uncomfortable breath but turned its back on her and focused on the dragonet.

The light streaming through the cave's mouth marked the time as near noon, so Marella pulled out another leather-wrapped packet of nuts and ate, watching the dragons move through the room as she did. The baby that had approached her had returned to its nest, one of the farthest from her location on the other end of the cave.

Good, Marella thought. *Maybe it doesn't know about my mistake.*

She turned her attention back to her lessons and wondered idly about the dragon's personality, whether it was male or female. She frowned. She had no idea if dragons even had male or female versions. Some of the animals she'd studied didn't. And others developed into whatever the local environment needed, so one animal could be both male and female at different points in its life.

That train of thought led to another, more curious line. Why hadn't her teachers ever included any information about dragons in her lessons? If they had, she'd be in a much better situation.

She massaged her numb left hand, which had become a habit she did almost constantly as she tried to feel something — anything — with that hand. She pinched the webbing between her fingers, willing some tiny signal to make it past the poison. Nothing happened.

The rest of the day passed in an endless parade of nothingness and boredom, much like the day before. Marella relived the conversation with Hakkan over and over in her mind, hoping and praying that she hadn't done anything to scare the little dragon away or insult it.

The new experience did make the afternoon pass faster, and before Marella realized the time had passed, the light faded to the dimness that warned of impending nightfall. She ate another packet of nuts and prepared herself for another long night of dragon noise. Fatigue made her dizzy, at least she hoped it was the fatigue, and she prayed to Dalphein she'd be able to sleep despite the noise and movement.

Night fell, and the palpable blackness returned. Marella longed to light her lamp but feared drawing the dragons' attention. She'd worked too hard to stay unobtrusive over the past two days to ruin it with a light now. She pressed her pack beneath her head and settled down to sleep. Exhaustion overcame pain and fear, and she fell into a deep, dreamless sleep almost before she touched the floor.

Daylight streaming across her face woke Marella the next day. It wasn't the pale light of dawn, but the full-bodied light of midmorning. She sat up, stretched, and bit back a groan. The pain had spread down her left leg to her foot and all the way across her chest.

Every breath hurt.

Her stomach rumbled, and Marella dug into her pack for more nuts. When she picked up the pack, dozens of tiny spider crabs skittered out of the flap and away into the cave, and Marella cursed.

Panic welled within her, and she pulled everything out of the pack, searching for the packet that contained her last crigoresi bead. She found it in the only pocket, untouched by the spider crabs. Her stomach growled again, and she turned her attention to her food supplies.

Frantic, she dug through her pack, searching for food

the spider crabs had missed, but every packet had been damaged and most were completely empty. Only one pack of completely rotten kelp remained.

Frustration, anger, and desperation fought for her attention, and desperation finally won. How was she supposed to find food with the poison paralyzing half her body? Her left leg was too weak to help her swim. Her left arm hung useless and limp at her side. If she left the cave, she'd probably sink to the depths of the gorge and die from the pressure.

What other options did she have?

Marella sighed and decided to wait to see if the dragonet returned that day. She could miss food for a day if she had to, but maybe Hakkan would be willing to bring her the shell fragments and the fungi they contained. The admiral had said only a dragonet could help her, so maybe this would be her day. At the very least, maybe the fungi could be a food source that would quiet her empty stomach. She sighed and winced at the pain that shot through her chest with the movement.

If a dragon doesn't help me soon, she realized, *I may die right here, against this wall.* She leaned her head back and raised her eyes to see what was happening in the cave. Nothing had changed. Clusters of dragonets bobbed and played in the enormous nests. Three adults lay against the far wall, watching the babies and keeping an eye on the cave's opening. Marella wondered how she hadn't seen them all that first day but realized her vision must have acclimated to the dim lighting in the cave.

She sat quietly and tried not to watch the dragons. Hakkan had approached her when she was busy with her lessons, so she resumed that activity. Instead of whales, she focused on cephalopods, especially squids. She listed facts about the family to herself but ran out of material after only an hour. At that point, she switched to octopus and listed all the facts she knew about those intelligent and flexible animals, though she kept her mind away from the deadly bultier and its venom.

Halfway through her recitation, Hakkan approached. The dragonet snuck up from the left side, as it had the day before, and settled onto the floor beside her.

"You not eat today," Hakkan said. "Why?"

Marella bit back a laugh at the creature's directness. "Spider crabs got into my pack and ate all my food."

"Why you no hunt?"

Marella sighed, unsure how much to reveal to the infant dragon. "I'm not feeling well," she said after a long pause.

"Oh. I help?"

Hope welled in her gut, but Marella punched it down. "Maybe?" Her voice was more hesitant than she'd intended. "Do you have any shell fragments or anything with a fungus or seaweed growing on it? That's what I eat most of the time."

The dragonet cocked its head and regarded her as if she'd said something very confusing. "Why you no eat fish?"

"I don't know. It's just how I was raised."

Hakkan stared at her for a long moment. "I help." It hopped away and disappeared over the edge of the tallest nest.

Marella leaned her head back and tried not to let hope get the better of her. She'd read stories from the great wars about prisoners dying from hope. The ones who kept it at bay and stayed practical were the ones who survived.

She closed her eyes and focused on those stories. She identified more now than she ever had before, though it wasn't an enemy army keeping her captive. The poison and her own lack of food kept her prisoner in the cave more effectively than guards ever could.

A soft thump brought Marella back to the present. She opened her eyes and nearly fainted with relief. Hakkan had brought not one, but four shell shards, each as long as her arm, and each completely encrusted in the yellow fungus.

Thick tears stung her eyes and Marella blinked them away. "Thank you." The words came out as a harsh whisper, and Marella cleared her throat to try again.

"I help?" The eager happiness in the dragon's voice almost brought Marella to tears again.

She smiled. "Yes, you've helped so much. I can't thank you enough."

Hakkan scooted the largest bit of shell closer to her, and Marella leaned forward to reach it. She pulled a chunk of fungus off the shell and swallowed it without even chewing. She didn't want to know what it tasted like. She didn't care. It was fresh and not slimy and would cure the poison paralyzing her body, and that was all that mattered.

After the first few bites, she started to chew and taste the fungus. Surely, the amount she'd already eaten would be enough to banish the dragonaxi's poison, she reasoned. The fungus had a pleasant flavor, similar to the nuts but with an underlying peppery taste that made her even more aware of her hunger.

She ate until her stomach swelled and ached from overeating, and only stopped when she couldn't force another bite down.

Marella couldn't say what she'd expected, but disappointment surged through her when she massaged her hand and felt nothing.

Don't be foolish, she scolded herself. *Of course it takes more than a few minutes to work. The poison took seven days to get to this point.*

Fatigue overwhelmed her, and the room spun.

"You no look good. I help?" The dragon's face loomed large in front of hers, and if she hadn't been backed against a literal stone wall, Marella would have moved back.

"You helped so much," Marella whispered. Her mind fogged, but she tried to reassure the worried dragonet. "I'm just very tired. I think I need to sleep a while, and hopefully I'll be all better when I wake up."

"I helped?"

Marella couldn't fight a sleepy smile. "Yes, you helped." She reached out and touched the baby's smooth, scaly front leg. "You saved me. Thank you."

The brilliant midmorning light had faded to the bleak violet of dusk when Marella finally woke. A cold blue nose poked in her face as soon as she opened her eyes.

"You all better now? You smell better."

Marella laughed, too relieved to fight the happiness. "Yes, I feel much better." The pain had left her chest and receded as far as her shoulder. Pins and needles shot through her hand with the tiniest contact, but she considered that an improvement after the complete paralysis of the previous few days.

"Eat more?" Hakkan nudged the fungus-coated shell closer to her, and Marella ate her fill once more. It didn't taste as good as she remembered, but perhaps the days' hunger and stress had made her enjoy it more than she normally would have. Regardless, she downed the fungus by the handful, and dropped back to sleep as soon as her stomach was full.

Faint light suffused the cave when Marella woke again. She couldn't tell if it was late evening or early morning, but for the moment, she didn't care. She could move her left hand again, and the pain had faded from an agonizing burn that occupied every thought to a dull ache she could easily ignore.

She stretched, relishing the ability to draw a deep breath and hold the water in her chest without pain.

Hunger pains rolled through her abdomen, stronger than any she'd felt in the week since the challenge began. Marella grabbed the closest shard of eggshell and broke off a chunk of the fungus. She stuck it in her mouth, ready to enjoy the fresh, peppery taste, but something tasted off and she spit it back out. It had taken on a rancid flavor that turned her stomach. She had no idea what the difference was, but the fungus didn't look any different than it had before. She grabbed handfuls of it and stuffed it into her pack, in case she needed it later. She'd have to go in search of food.

She gathered her belongings, checked the string on her bow and changed it when the one she had felt stretched and weak, and slung both her bow and pack over her shoulder.

"Where you go?" Hakkan asked. She hadn't seen the dragonet until that moment, though it was almost right beside her.

"I have to go find more food. I can't live on that." Marella gestured to the fungus. "I'm better now, so I'm well enough to hunt for what I need."

"You go at night?" Hakkan cocked its head and the ridges above its eyes drew closer together. "Dark is danger, Mother say."

"Is it night?" Marella peeked out the hole in the wall and tried to tell for sure what time it was. She wished she had Feena's time charm, but she didn't have enough crig to attempt it.

"Night coming." The dragonet flapped its growing wings and hopped from one side of Marella to the other, a distance of at least double her arm span. It was the farthest she'd seen it swim.

"Hey, you're getting better at that. Good job."

Hakkan preened and flapped and hopped closer. "I go far, yes? Like big dragon?"

Marella smiled. "Yes. You're doing very well, just like the big dragons. You'll be swimming everywhere in no time."

"When light comes, you go find food?"

"Yes," Marella said. "I'll have to. I'll come back before dark, though."

Marella unstrung her bow and tucked it into the loop on her pack. With everything set for the next day, she settled back against the wall, surprised to note that she actually felt like she could go back to sleep. She didn't think she'd ever slept so much in her life.

She stretched and lay back on the muddy floor, ready to sleep away the night.

Her body had other plans.

Like the first night she'd spent in the cave, Marella woke frequently to the sounds of dragons shifting, moving, and hopping. Heavy thumps punctuated the night, and more than once, the uncomfortable feeling of eyes watching her kept Marella awake.

The morning's first light came as a welcome relief, and Marella rose, dusted herself off, and gathered her belongings. She needed to get something to eat and return quickly so she could spend more time with Hakkan. The days had passed in a rush of illness and fatigue, and she had less than a week left of the challenge.

She strung her bow and headed out into the morning, feeling stronger than she had since the first day of the challenge when the admiral had stuck her with the dragonaxi's poisoned spines.

Unsure how to proceed, she swam close to the wall and considered how to best catch a fish. That had been Lilit's plan for surviving the gorge: she was going to eat what she brought until supplies ran low, then catch and eat fish from the surrounding area.

Perhaps she could use the bow?

That seemed unlikely, considering how slow the arrows moved in the water and how fast the smaller fish could swim. She couldn't eat a large fish by herself and didn't want anything to go to waste. The thought of killing a living creature turned her stomach, but she'd do whatever she could to stay alive and finish the challenge.

A school of small silver fish swam past her, and Marella reached out and plucked one away from the group. It squirmed and fought in her grasp, trying desperately to free itself. Marella watched the creature for a moment, then opened her hand and let it go. She couldn't kill something with such a strong will to live.

Dejected and hungry, she reconsidered her plan. If she couldn't kill a small fish, she wouldn't be able to make herself kill anything bigger. And the small, skittering creatures that ran away when she entered caves looked too disgusting to eat. It would take longer, but the only feasible plan she could come up with was to return to the sea floor above the gorge and find the seaweed beds she remembered passing on the way in.

FIFTEEN

Trust

For the next three days, Errebeld helped Keird with the hunting. Each day, the baby stayed awake longer and showed more interest in its surroundings. When it broke off its hunt to sniff at Errebeld, he struggled to stay calm and keep his breathing even. The baby cocked its head and examined him from head to fin, sniffed his face once more, and returned to its hunt.

Errebeld sagged against the wall for support as soon as the dragonet swam away. The infant had nearly doubled in length and girth and was roughly three times Errebeld's size. He worked to slow his racing heart and ignored Keird's chuckles from across the cave.

When the dragonet settled back down to sleep, Keird crossed the space. "It's time. He hunts with us tomorrow."

His stomach clenched, but Errebeld nodded. "I think you're right." He paused and imagined the dragonet in all the confusion of a hunt. "What do we do if he gets lost or confused or just takes off?"

"This is home. He will return." Keird waved a hand at the bare stone walls.

It didn't feel much like a home to Errebeld. "And if he doesn't?"

"He will. Go hunt your grass. I watch him sleep."

Errebeld wanted to argue, but his hunger made itself known. Keird laughed at the rumbling noises Errebeld's stomach made and waved him toward the cave's mouth.

~

"How do we wake him?" Errebeld stared at the sleeping dragon with no small amount of trepidation. "I mean, without him thinking we're food?"

"I don't know. Any ideas?"

"You're the dragon trainer, right? How do we train him to hunt if we can't wake him up?"

Keird raised his eyebrows. "How you know it's he?"

"I don't. I just have to call him something other than 'it.'" He sighed. "But we still have to wake him or her or it up to hunt."

"Don't shout. You wake sleeping dragon." Keird pointed to the dragonet, who had rolled over and opened its eyes. The baby stared at them for a long moment, glanced around the cave as if searching for food, and started to settle back down into its favorite sleeping position. Before it could curl up and lay its head on its forepaws, Keird shouted. "Come, baby. We hunt."

The dragonet raised its head and searched the cave again. Keird swam to the opening and waved the dragonet to him. "Come, Zakazely. Hunt." He waved with both hands, and the baby followed him.

Errebeld couldn't contain his nervous laugh but followed the other two out into the early morning light. "What did you call him? What is Zaká..."

"Zak-AH-zely." He said the word slowly, annunciating each syllable. "It means baby in Ashmoran."

Silver flashed overhead, and the baby took off into the morning's blue light. Errebeld kicked hard, working with all his strength to keep up with the young dragon. Other predators hunted those waters in the mornings, too, and many were larger than the dragonet.

Zakazely darted in and out of the undulating masses of fish, and each time he emerged with a mouthful.

After the first rush, Errebeld and Keird took up watch positions at each end of the wide field where they could keep the dragonet in view without having to maintain his frenetic pace. When the baby kept going until the midday light beat down through the water, Keird broke away to do his own hunting. Errebeld stayed behind and kept watch on the young dragon. He worried the baby would wear out and wouldn't be able to get back to the cave, but he had no idea how to interrupt the infant's hunt without becoming the second course.

Roughly five hours after they left the cave, Zakazely swam to Errebeld's perch and blinked. The exaggerated movement alerted Errebeld to the infant's fatigue, and he led the dragonet back to the cave. The baby settled into his spot near the back wall and his eyes closed in sleep before his head rested fully on his paws.

"How long he last?" Keird's voice woke Errebeld, who hadn't even realized he'd fallen asleep.

He blinked and ran a hand over his eyes. "Longer than I expected. I worried we'd have to carry him back here."

"Did you?"

"No, he made it. Just barely, though."

Keird smiled. "We hunt again tomorrow. Let him build strength. Leave soon."

"Can we take him to Talam? He's an untrained, wild, newborn dragon. Aren't there laws about that?"

"Ah, yes. We need to find trainer."

"I thought you said you were a trainer. Can't you teach him to obey?"

Keird shook his head. "I train big dragons. Dragons with mothers who know rules and obey."

"And this is different?"

"Yes, this different. Zakazely mother not teach rules." He pointed to his chest and to Errebeld. "We not teach rules."

"Right. No one's taught him. So, how do we start? He came back at the end of his hunt without being taught." Errebeld's mind whirled through the possibilities. He had to get the letter to Soraya's sister, but he couldn't abandon the baby, either. "Who do we know who can help?"

Silence fell, heavy and uncomfortable, and Errebeld leaned back against the wall.

After a long while, Keird said, "My sister. She know dragons. She want to pair with dragon. She find a way."

"Of course. That's perfect." The tension left Errebeld in a dizzying rush. "And she's just outside Talam, right?"

"No. She live in Belzon."

"Of course." Errebeld groaned. "When did she move? Never mind. It doesn't matter. I have to deliver Soraya's letter—"

"You take letter while Zakazely hunt tomorrow. We leave next day."

"Do you think he's ready?" Errebeld tried to hide his trepidation, but Keird laughed.

"If he hunt for hours, he swim for hours. He's ready."

The baby twitched in his sleep, his tail flicking back and forth in a sleepy imitation of swimming.

"We won't be able to travel far or fast, but—"

"Better than sitting another day."

"Agreed." Errebeld busied himself replacing all of his belongings in his pack. Since they'd been using their packs to hunt, he'd kept all his things in a neat stack at the back wall, beside the sleeping dragonet.

The next morning, Errebeld took his pack and rejoined the groups of people heading south on the current. He raced along the well-traveled route, using the current to propel him forward and saving as much strength as he could for the return trip.

He didn't slow when he passed the small inns and parlors along the outer edge of the town. Their distinct, angular windows and rounded walls spurred him faster. The cross streets came closer together, and Errebeld glanced at the direction Soraya had given him. He had to slow his pace to find the right street. He passed merchants calling out their wares and morning shoppers inspecting each cart. One merchant displayed a meager arrangement of land fruits, and Errebeld hoped the man didn't sell out before his return trip. He hoped for a little variety after weeks of eating the same bland seaweed.

Unbidden, his thoughts turned to the dragonet. He hoped the hunt had gone well again. The baby had grown large enough that most predators wouldn't bother him while he was strong and healthy, but if he got hurt, if he bled into the water, the sharks would still circle. And they'd win. The memory of the bandits flashed through his mind, and his pace faltered.

He shook his head to clear it of the disturbing images.

Focus. It took all his efforts to clear his mind and think only of the address he sought. Errebeld checked the numbers on the nearest house and cursed. He'd passed it.

He spun to go back the way he'd come and barely avoided colliding with a sea ox that had been about to pass him.

"Sorry, sorry," he mumbled to the driver as he passed the creature and its cart.

The driver, a stately woman dressed in fine, pale blue linen didn't even glance his way.

In moments, he found the right address and knocked on the triangular door. It swung open an instant later, and Errebeld swam into the dim interior. In the heartbeat before his eyes adjusted, he gained the impression of a crowded room and hoped he hadn't made a mistake.

"Who are you and why are you here?" A woman's voice called from the far end of the room.

Someone chuckled.

"I'm Errebeld. I carry a letter for Giselda Massot."

A slender woman with bronze scales and deep purple hair approached and held her hand out until Errebeld handed her the letter. "You're late. I expected you weeks ago."

"I, I'm sorry. I had—"

"I have already heard of your delays. Do you return to my sister now?" Her violet eyes flashed with irritation.

"No. I'm on my way to Belzon."

Giselda pursed her lips. "What business do you have in Belzon?"

"I beg your pardon, madam, but my business is my own."

Shouts of laughter echoed in the cramped room, reminding Errebeld of his audience. Supaerisi hovered or lounged on every available chair and along every wall, so closely packed that each stayed barely an inch from the next.

"I'm sorry to have interrupted your meeting. I'll be on my way."

"Please don't rush away. Let me get you a meal. You can rest while I finish this." She waved a slender arm toward the crowded room. "Come." Giselda eased her way through the room and opened a narrow door on the other side. She didn't wait for Errebeld but vanished through.

He rushed to catch up, his mind abuzz.

How did she hear? Is someone watching the cave? Has someone been following us, after all?

The doorway opened into a small dining nook, where a young girl settled a plate filled with kelp and three orange slices.

"I apologize. I normally have more to offer, but the food I had saved for you has spoiled while I waited."

"This is fine. I'm not picky."

Giselda raised an eyebrow and chuckled. "Aren't you?"

She laughed and exited through the door before Errebeld could think of a suitable reply.

His stomach chose that moment to remind him that he hadn't stopped to eat before he started out, so Errebeld helped himself to the food. The fresh taste of the kelp blended with the tartness of the orange, and Errebeld scarfed the food so fast he had to focus to avoid choking.

"I trust the food was to your liking?"

Errebeld startled, choked on the last bite of food, and spun to face Giselda. He hadn't heard her enter.

Instead of the woman he expected, he stood face to face with Soraya.

"I was quite surprised that my letter had not arrived before me. What kept you?"

"We were attacked by bandits, and —"

"I heard about that. You were injured? Two of the, er, bandits, were eaten by sharks."

Errebeld frowned. If only two were eaten, had one escaped? "Who were they?"

"Pharli flunkies looking for a chance to infiltrate our society. I'm pleased you kept my letter secure, even if—"

"They weren't dressed like the Pharli. They looked and sounded—"

"Wiktawan. I know. Our enemies are getting smarter. They want to protect the slavers that make them rich."

"I hope you're not spoiling our guest's meal, sister." Giselda swam in through the same door she'd used before and smiled at Soraya.

"Not at all. He's just about to tell me what happened after he and his friend were attacked." Soraya's voice held both a question and a warning.

"My shoulder," Errebeld wasn't prepared to answer questions about the dragon, so if they didn't bring it up, he wouldn't either. Instead, he moved his arm through a slow circle, wincing at the top of the movement. "I'm out of crig and had to wait for it to heal."

"And your friend? Was he injured also? Why is he not with you?" Soraya shot the questions at him rapid-fire, but Errebeld wouldn't be rushed. He'd dealt with high-born people and their attempts at intimidation since his birth, and these women wouldn't break him.

"He's still healing, yes."

"Why did you not bring him here? We could help him."

Errebeld shook his head and let out a heavy sigh. "He didn't want to be a burden. As soon as I was healed enough to swim, I brought the letter to you. I'll stay at my friend's place in the iron district tonight and head on to Belzon in the morning."

"You won't return to him?"

"No. He's settled at a family friend's inn for the duration of his convalescence. He'll be well cared for. I have other business to attend." Even as the lie left him, Errebeld wasn't sure why. He wouldn't be able to hide a dragon for long. Still, warning bells sounded in his mind, and he wove the lies he felt would best protect the dragonet.

"Odd," Soraya murmured.

Giselda swam to the door. "More of my afternoon guests are arriving. Is there anything else you need from him, sister?"

"No, I suppose not." Soraya sounded disappointed, but she followed Giselda to the door. "I trust you can see yourself out?"

Errebeld nodded and exited through a rear door. It led into a small receiving room lined with shelves holding all manner of bottles and boxes, but he didn't stop to investigate. Another door to his right stood open, and he exited out onto the busy market street.

Following a hunch, he darted around the edge of a building, where he could see both doors to the house. He'd barely had time to hide before two men left through the same back door he'd used. They scanned the street and swam off toward the iron district, where he'd said he was staying.

When they vanished around the corner, Errebeld joined the throng moving the opposite direction. He changed directions a dozen times and kept a careful watch for pursuit. Finding none, he left the city and swam back toward the cave.

While he traveled, he analyzed the conversation with the two women and his own reaction to them. Had he overreacted? Maybe. Why had he worked so hard to avoid telling them about the dragonet? He shook his head and checked behind him once again. It was probably best not to tell anyone until they knew if he could be trained.

The journey back to the cave took the rest of the day. Errebeld stopped often to make sure he wasn't followed, and between stops he stayed in with the steady flow of travelers so he wouldn't draw attention to himself. By the time he found the valley with its familiar boulders, the light had faded to deep twilight. Out of sight from the traveling route, he swam hard for the cave's opening, where it was hidden behind a scattering of rocks and boulders.

"Ah, you are back. I worried."

Errebeld dropped his pack beside the sleeping baby dragon and leaned against the wall.

"They asked more questions than I expected, then had me followed. It took me a while to make sure I wasn't noticed or tracked back here."

Keird cocked his head and examined Errebeld. "You not tell friends of Zakazely. Why?"

"I don't know. I guess I want to wait until we have him trained."

"You fear they take him."

"I—" Errebeld started to deny it, but thought better of it. His shoulders slumped and his breath left him in a rush. "Maybe. I just think we should wait to tell anyone about him until he can follow simple commands."

"Is good idea. We sleep now. Travel tomorrow."

Keird settled onto the cave floor beside the sleeping dragon, and Errebeld took his normal spot at the cave's mouth, leaned against the wall, and fell into a deep sleep in moments.

~

Morning dawned far too soon for Errebeld. He groaned and tried to hide his face from the light. Vibrations disturbed the water around him, and he sat up to see what had created so much movement. The dragonet swam laps around the cave, making excited chirps and grunts when his eyes met Errebeld's.

"Good morning, Zakazely. Are you ready to hunt?"

"Hunt." The baby said the word as perfectly as any person, and Errebeld struggled to contain his shock. He closed his mouth with a snap and grinned.

"That's right. Hunt. But only for a little while. Then we're going on a little adventure."

Keird slung his pack over his shoulder and waved to the baby. "Come, Zakazely. Hunt."

The dragonet darted out of the cave and dove straight for the brilliant schools of fish overhead. He played and screeched and ate, and Errebeld couldn't help but enjoy the baby's fun, even though it meant that fish were dying in scores. A tiny pang of guilt shot through him at the thought, but he brushed it aside.

Animals hunted other animals every day. That's the world Dalphein had made, and Errebeld would claim no responsibility for the dragon doing as he was made to.

Zakazely hunted and ate and played for well over an hour before Keird called him. Errebeld didn't expect the baby to react to the noise or his name and had to close his gaping mouth when the dragonet swam slowly away from the colorful clouds of fish.

"Hunt." The baby said as soon as he approached. He turned back to the fish.

"No." Errebeld waited for the baby to turn back to him. "We need to travel a bit. We'll hunt more when we get some distance behind us."

The dragonet cocked its head and regarded Errebeld with a soft brown eye. "What travel?"

"It's an adventure. Come let me show you."

Zakazely let out an excited coo and swam close to Errebeld, who took off at a leisurely pace toward the westerly route that would lead them to Belzon. Instead of joining the throngs of travelers, Errebeld swam parallel to the current, but far enough away that he couldn't see the other supaerisi.

The novelty of new places and views kept Zakazely close for the first hour. That ended when a cluster of blue fish nearly as large as Errebeld swam overhead. The dragonet dashed toward the fish, snagged one, and crunched it down in two bites.

"Dalphein save me from infants." Errebeld eyed the red cloud, the only sign of Zakazely's meal. "Let's get out of here before the sharks show up."

"This way." Keird waved a hand toward a narrow gap in the rocks, where they could shelter and let the baby rest — and avoid any predators drawn by the blood.

They settled down between the boulders, and the dragonet fell asleep in seconds.

"D'you think he's ready for this? How do we keep him from hunting whenever he sees a fish? Or worse, another supaerisi?"

"He is ready. He comes when called. We must call him faster." Keird nodded as if it were the most obvious statement he'd ever made, but Errebeld wasn't so sure.

"He's awfully quick. How will we call him faster? I didn't even see where he was going until he'd already caught it."

Neither spoke for a long moment, and Errebeld settled down to watch the movements overhead. As he'd expected, several sharks showed up and circled the area. Errebeld worried they'd follow the scent back to their hiding spot, but they swam off toward the north. When they'd gone, Errebeld relaxed and leaned back to wait out the baby's nap.

They resumed their trek an hour later, and Zakazely swam excited circles around Keird and Errebeld. A school of tiny yellow fish swam past, but the dragonet ignored them in favor of swimming upside down for a hundred lengths.

Errebeld's stomach stayed tied in knots until they passed a small group of supaerisi traveling with a heavily laden cart. The dragon swam up to the people and sniffed at them. A woman screamed.

"Zakazely, to me." Keird's call drew the baby's attention, and he left the travelers.

"They smell…" the dragonet cocked his head and a wrinkle appeared between his eyes.

"Different?" Errebeld offered.

"Ya. Diff'rnt. Like you. Not like you." He twisted his long neck around to examine the travelers again without turning his body.

"They're like us, but from a different place."

"Where?" The dragonet started toward them again, and Keird called him back.

"You stay with us. Not all are friendly to dragon."

The dragonet froze and stared at Keird. "Why?"

"Some are scared."

"Just stay with us, all right?" Errebeld smiled. "We're going to meet some people who love dragons and want to get to know you."

"Ooooh," Zakazely cooed. "We go now."

They traveled for the rest of the day without incident. Whenever the dragonet started to wander off, either Errebeld or Keird called him back and they continued on their way.

Long before nightfall, Zakazely slowed and fell behind. As soon as they found an empty cave to spend the night in, the baby tucked himself in a cocoon of wings and fell into a deep sleep.

Errebeld stayed with the dragonet while Keird hunted, then went out to find something for himself to eat. Once they'd both eaten, they settled in to play a game of stones until darkness fell.

SIXTEEN

Flats

Her decision made, Marella hurried toward the crevice she'd entered when she first arrived at the gorge. She shoved thoughts of Lilit aside. She didn't have time to grieve for her friend. She'd let herself feel that loss when she'd safely returned to Pharlandzi with Hakkan — or another dragonet, she corrected herself.

After spending so much time in the caves, Marella worried about ascension sickness. To avoid it, she moved slowly up the crevice toward the fields of seaweeds she remembered. She wanted to hurry. Her empty stomach reminded her of its urgency at least twice a minute, but she took her time and slowly climbed out of the gorge.

At the top of the gorge, she emerged onto the rocky ocean floor. She moved straight toward the boulders a hundred lengths ahead of her. If she remembered correctly, they protected a colorful array of seaweed that would easily keep her fed for the remainder of the challenge.

She ducked around the first boulder and found the field she'd remembered. Brown and red and yellow seaweeds grew in tight clusters, swaying in the gentle current. Small blue and silver fish darted between them. The fish helped Marella relax a bit. They wouldn't be staying there if predators were nearby.

She swam above the field, picking seaweeds and eating her fill. When her stomach no longer grumbled, she settled down in a dense patch of red seaweed and grabbed a handful to fill her pack.

Pain erupted in her right hand, burning its way up her arm far faster than the dragonaxi poison had. She raised her hand to examine it and saw the banded serpent hiding among the seaweed.

Oh no. No, Dalphein!

Her fingers swelled and went numb, and the redness spread over her hand and into her wrist. She gathered her pack and swam hard for the clear ocean floor on the other side of the boulder. She needed room to lie down after she used the crig. Without the mineral and sea's power, she'd die from the poison by the end of the day.

Her legs had already turned heavy and slow, but they still obeyed her commands. She pushed with everything she had for the safety of the empty ocean floor, that precious area where the ground sloped away from the boulders and the bare rock provided no place for any animals to hide.

Dizziness blurred her vision and made the rocks move in front of her, and Marella slowed. Nausea churned her stomach, and she turned right, toward the closest boulder. Her hands shook, but she reached out and grabbed the current-smoothed edge. She used every ounce of strength she had, but she pulled herself clear of the field and sank to the bare stone ground, her back to the boulder.

Her clumsy, thick fingers fumbled with the clasp, but she got the pack open and dumped all its contents onto the ground beside her. Her vision blurred and swam, but she blinked it clear and found the wax pencil and the precious, life-preserving, leather pouch.

She didn't trust her numb fingers not to drop the only bead she had left, so Marella opened the pouch and tipped it up over her open mouth and waited. The little bead slid into her mouth and down her throat, and she had to swallow several times to get it down. Her tongue felt as thick and numb as her fingers, and swallowing took more effort than she'd expected.

While she waited for the mineral to take effect, Marella worked at putting her belongings back into her pack. Between her blurred vision and her weak, clumsy hand, that task was next to impossible.

She had no idea how much time had passed. Time meant little to her poison-slowed mind. She dropped the packets and pouches into the bag one at a time, though several times she dropped one and had to try again. The last item she replaced in the pack was the little knife her father had bought for her. At last, her heart rate sped up and the faint anxiety in her stomach alerted her that her body had absorbed the mineral.

The numb, swollen fingers on her left hand dropped the wax pencil twice before she managed to get it in a proper grip, and Marella blinked several times to clear her vision. She'd never tried to draw runes with her left hand before, but this one needed to be on her right hand, so she'd have to do her best.

She closed her eyes and tried to steady her nerves, opened them again, and pressed the pencil to her hand. She moved the pencil in tiny increments, working hard to make the lines as straight and perfect as she could. Straighter lines meant stronger runes, which meant more complete healing. If she'd had more crigoresi, she wouldn't have worried as much, since she could have done a quick, sloppy rune first and healed herself enough to be able to concentrate, then she would have done a second, better one to rid herself of the poison completely.

Four lines, each perpendicular to the others. Two lines bisecting the four, each at an opposite diagonal. Brilliant red light erupted from her hand. The two puncture wounds burned hotter, turned pink, and closed. The angry redness retreated down her arm. Her vision cleared, and the swelling left her fingers. Little by little, the light faded.

Relief flooded through her, and Marella leaned her head back against the boulder. She needed to get back to the cave. She worried if she stayed gone too long Hakkan might think she wasn't coming back.

She slung her pack and bow over her shoulder and tried to ignore the bone-deep exhaustion that made every movement an effort.

She started toward the gorge but thought better of it and turned back to the field. She could still gather some food to get her through the rest of the challenge.

This time, instead of recklessly sticking her hand into the dense patches of growth, she brushed her pack over it, first. If nothing emerged, she then moved the leaves aside to check for dangerous creatures, and when she was sure it was safe, she pulled the leaves off the stalk and shoved them into her bag.

She repeated that process until her pack bulged with food. When she was satisfied she had enough, she headed slowly back toward the gorge.

The day's events had left Marella disoriented, and she swam much farther than she expected before she realized she was moving in the wrong direction. She took stock of her surroundings and spotted the black scar of the gorge in the distance on her left.

She heaved a sigh and switched directions, hoping she could find the same crevice again so she wouldn't have to wander around in the gorge, searching for familiar landmarks. She wanted to be back in the dragons' cave before night fell, which would be difficult if she got lost. She wondered if the little dragon had looked for her while she'd been gone.

Fatigue made the swim more challenging than it would have been if she hadn't had to use the crigoresi, but she swam hard enough to keep the current from sweeping her off course.

Behind a small hill almost halfway to the gorge, something moved that didn't fit the environment, and Marella slowed. She squinted to get a better look, then kicked hard to approach. Beneath her, one of the dragonaxi challengers lay writhing in the mud. Faint lines of blood wafted away from him, and she winced. That, especially when added to his squirming, would draw every predator for miles around.

She swam down to him, unable to leave an injured person to suffer and die alone. He had the green skin she'd come to associate with natives to Pharlandzi, with brilliant orange hair and violet eyes.

"What happened?" His right arm twisted at an uncomfortable angle, and his left arm lay limp at his side, swollen and covered with the familiar red blotches the dragonaxi poison caused. The scales that held his legs together had been torn loose, and the blood trailed from the open sores where they should have been.

He shook his head. "Tried to swim with porpoises for protection. They decided I didn't belong."

Marella nodded. She'd heard stories of supaerisi traveling with pods of dolphins and other porpoises but hadn't read anything in her lessons that would lend credibility to the legends. She didn't think she'd ever be brave enough to try it on her own. Another, more horrifying thought occurred to her.

"Did you find the fungus? The cure?"

He shook his head weakly.

"I can help with that, at least, but it's not instant." Marella dug through all the plants she'd shoved in her pack until she found the palm-sized chunk of the eggshell fungus.

She started to put it in the man's hand, but realized he'd never be able to get it to his mouth. Instead, she supported his head with her left hand and fed him the fungus with her right. He ate it as ravenously as she had that first day and asked for more when he'd finished it.

"I didn't bring more, but if we can get you back to the cave, I'm sure Hakkan will bring you all you want."

"Who's Hakkan?" The man asked. He frowned. "Who are you? I'm Dyfan."

"I'm Marella, and Hakkan is the dragonet I've been trying to bond with. He brought me the eggshells."

"You found dragons? Can I stay with you? Where's your team?" Dyfan let his head fall back against the stone ground.

"Gone," Marella said, her voice clipped. She assessed the young man's injuries again. "Can you swim at all?"

"I don't know. I can try."

"No." Marella pressed a hand to his chest and held him on the ocean floor. "You'll just hurt yourself more. Do you have any crig? I know the runes, but I'm out of beads."

Dyfan's eyes opened wide, and he turned his head, scanning the horizon for something.

After a long moment, he shook his head. "I do. I, I mean, I did. It's in my pack, but I don't know where my pack is."

Marella wasn't sure what she hoped to hear but had to ask. "Where's your team?"

"Dead." Dyfan's eyes glazed over. "I think so, anyway."

Marella nodded. "Well, let's team up, then. If we can get you swimming, anyway."

She assessed each individual injury, running her hands over the bones to find the fractures and estimating how much power it would take to heal him. Could she risk it without the mineral?

"I can see what you're thinking. It's too risky. It's too much." Dyfan shook his head again.

"Can you move your feet? You're bleeding. We have to do something, or we'll have sharks circling in no time."

Dyfan paled and flinched. "If you're sure you can do it without risking yourself." He turned his face away from her. "You should probably just go back to your dragon and leave me to my fate. I deserve this. I—"

"No!" Outrage filled Marella at the idea of leaving him to die alone. "Of course I won't leave you. Let me find my wax stick." She didn't have to search long, since she'd had it out so recently. "Look, I had to heal myself from a snakebite a couple hours ago. I might still have enough crig in my system to heal you, at least enough to get you moving. If we can just get you back to the cave, you can rest and heal there."

Dyfan looked uncertain but didn't object when she pressed the pencil to his hand and drew the healing rune. She pressed both hands to his chest, willing her energy into him. Faint blue light emanated from the rune, and Dyfan cried out. The wounds on his legs puckered and turned pink, but Marella didn't lift her hands. He had to draw the healing energy from her, or he'd never survive it.

Adrenaline surged in her, giving her strength she didn't know she had, and the snap of bones realigning filled the space between them. Dyfan grunted.

A familiar weakness ran through her arms and made her head feel heavier than the boulder to their backs, and she pulled her hands away. The blue light died, and Marella lay down beside Dyfan, her chest heaving with exertion.

"I can't do more. Can you swim?" She asked between gasping breaths.

Dyfan sat up and moved his right arm and both legs. "I, I think so."

A shadow passed over them, blocking the light for a heartbeat.

Dread lodged in her gut, and she raised her eyes to the waters above them. Six sharks circled nearby, drawn by the scent of Dyfan's blood.

"Good, let's go. We have to get out of here, now." Marella swung her pack onto her back and grabbed Dyfan's paralyzed left arm.

The power and the day's exhaustion had drained much of her strength, and she couldn't move as quickly as she wanted.

Dyfan swam beside her, but his scales hadn't reformed, so swimming with his flipper separated made the movement awkward and slow. Together, they fled toward the gorge, away from the threat of the sharks circling above. With neither of them bleeding, the sharks weren't likely to chase them, but she couldn't help checking every dozen lengths. The ominous shadows still circled above but hadn't moved with Marella and Dyfan.

They swam along the edge of the gorge until they found

the crevice Marella had used as her landmark for the entirety of her challenge up to that point. The light had started to fade when they finally found the dragon cave and slumped against the wall in the dim inner cavern.

Weak purple light filtered into the cave, illuminating the dragonet who swooped and hopped over to where Marella lay.

"You bring brother?" Hakkan cocked his head and examined Dyfan. "Brother broken?"

Marella laughed. "He's my friend. This is Dyfan, and yes, he's hurt. He just needs a little time, and some of your eggshells, if you're willing to share."

"I help?" Hakkan swung his head around to look behind him, then back to Marella. "I help. No leave." He gave her a severe look that made her bite her tongue to keep from laughing again.

When he'd left to gather the eggshells, Dyfan grabbed at Marella's hand. "I have to apologize." His voice cracked, and he cleared his throat. "I didn't believe you. I really didn't. I didn't think you had a chance, not when all of us who trained for so long failed. I'm sorry I underestimated you."

"Let's not celebrate yet. We've still got a huge part of the challenge left to go."

"How so?" Dyfan leaned closer. "You've already bonded a dragonet. You've basically already won. All you have to do is get back to Pharlandzi."

Marella shook her head. "Watch him. He can't swim yet. He's too little to leave the nest."

Dyfan laughed, and anger welled behind Marella's eyes. "No really, he's smaller than any of the other dragonets."

"Size has nothing to do with it, especially at this age." Dyfan laughed again. "I thought you were studying to be an oceanographer or something. Didn't you study dragon development?"

"No," Marella snapped. "My studies focused on whales and arctic life. I didn't sign up for this challenge, but here I am. I had eight days to prepare, and I used those days to learn how not to die in the gorge. I thought I'd have a team to help me with the dragon parts."

Dyfan nodded and leaned back against the wall. "So, what now?"

Before Marella could answer, Hakkan swooped back, carrying several dinner plate-sized shards of eggshell, each coated in the yellow ruffled fungus.

Dyfan grabbed one and shoved handfuls of the fungus in his mouth, barely chewing before swallowing and inhaling another mouthful.

"My brother to meet your brother," Hakkan said, his voice more hesitant than Marella had ever heard it. "This good?"

"That would be wonderful," Marella said. "Dyfan would love to meet your brother."

Beside her Dyfan gulped, choked, coughed, and cleared his throat. "Absolutely. I couldn't be happier to meet anyone."

Hakkan nodded and hopped away, and Dyfan met Marella's gaze in the fading light. "Did that make sense?"

"No, but Hakkan didn't seem to mind," Marella said, laughing. She frowned, an idea striking her. "How do you tell if they're male or female? I haven't been able to figure that out."

"He's a male. You have to look beneath the tail. Females have a pouch there, where they grow and hold their eggs before they lay them. Males have a couple large scales there, where... erm..."

It was Marella's turn to laugh. "I get it. I've studied reptilian biology, remember?"

"I thought you said whales. Whales aren't reptiles."

"I didn't just study whales. I studied all kinds of animals that live in the arctic and the tropics." She frowned. "Just not enough that live in between the two."

They both laughed and fell silent when two dragonets landed in front of them.

Hakkan bowed to Dyfan in an adorable attempt at formality. "Almost time for sleep, but this Deinnu."

"It's lovely to meet you, Deinnu," Dyfan answered with as much of a bow as he could manage without raising up from the floor.

The shadows had lengthened and deepened while they talked, and Marella stifled a yawn. "You still sick?" Hakkan said, shoving his nose right up against hers. "Egg goo not make you better?"

Marella couldn't fight the laugh that bubbled out that time. "It made me perfect. I'm just tired now. It's been a busy day."

"I sleepy, too. Deinnu, we go sleep. You meet more when light comes." Hakkan hopped away toward his nest, and Deinnu followed close behind.

"Thank you," Dyfan whispered. "I thought I was gonna die alone, and now I have a chance to finish the challenge. You're amazing."

"I did what anyone would have done. Let's get some rest. You need sleep to let your body get rid of the poison and finish healing."

"Um, I think you need to finish healing, too, right? Didn't you say you got bit by a serpent today?"

The last of the light faded from the cave, leaving only a

darkness thick as pitch. "Yes. Let's rest. We'll work everything else out later."

Fatigue and dizziness pressed Marella to the floor, and she sank into unconsciousness before she even had a chance to adjust her pack beneath her head.

A series of soft thumps and a low growl woke Marella before the sunrise. She sighed, rolled over, and went back to sleep.

SEVENTEEN

Time

Dawn brought a dizzy nausea Marella hadn't felt since her earliest days of using crig. She'd overdone it, and she'd depleted her reserves of the critical mineral. She groaned and moved to her side. Inch by inch, she pushed herself to sitting.

"'Rella sick?" Hakkan's blue nose swam into her vision, almost close enough to touch her forehead. "'Rella smell sick. Stay here. I get shells."

Marella tried to object but didn't know how to explain her current ailment to the young dragon. She'd choke down more of the fungus if it meant keeping Hakkan happy.

The dragonet reappeared a moment later, his brother in tow, with a dozen shards of eggshells and a happy expression that made her smile despite the weary dizziness.

"Thank you." Marella bowed and accepted the gift. She broke off a small bit of the fungus and ate it, trying not to notice the muddy taste and unpleasant texture. Grit crunched between her teeth, but she forced down another bite.

Dyfan sat up and stared at the bounty. "I'll take some of

that." His left arm twitched as he sat up, but he didn't use it to stabilize the eggshell when he broke off a fist-sized chunk of fungus. He devoured it as if he'd never had anything more delicious, and Marella realized he'd only had a small taste from her pack, and a little more when they'd reached the cavern the evening before. She'd eaten handfuls of the stuff and slept for a full day before the poison had left her system.

She nibbled at the bit of fungus in her hand and remembered how delicious it had tasted with the poison coursing through her.

When Dyfan had had his fill, he leaned back against the wall, his eyes drooping. Moments later, soft snores emanated from him, and Marella turned her attention back to the little dragon.

"Brother sick, too?" Hakkan asked. "All better with shells?"

Marella smiled. "Yes. He's still sick, and the eggshells will make him better. I just need a little time and rest. I think I overdid it yesterday."

"What is 'overdid?' You know stories?" Hakkan settled down in front of her. "Tell me story? Where you come from?"

Marella leaned her head back and struggled to think of a suitable tale. "Oh, of course. I can tell you all about Dalphein. He's the god of the sea, and he protects my people and all the creatures in the sea." She chuckled. "He's sort of a trickster, though.

"A long, long time ago, when gods roamed the land, Dalphein was born to Fuagi, the god of fire, and Amphitrite, the goddess of water. As an infant, Dalphein was afraid of many things, but above all, he feared the dark. His mother despaired of ever getting him to sleep on his own, so she took to lighting lamps in every room of the castle she shared with Fuagi."

"Lights in cave would be nice, but hard to sleep," Hakkan said. He cocked his head. "How sleep with light all night?"

Marella smiled. "I don't know, but his father was the god of fire, so darkness probably felt uncomfortable to him."

Hakkan cocked his head, first to one side, then to the other, as if concentrating on a faraway sound.

"I guess. I understand. Finish story."

"All right." Marella bit back a chuckle and tried to hide the wave of dizziness and nausea her nod triggered. "Amphitrite was tired because he kept her up all night, and she didn't think she'd ever get him to rest when the sun slept. She got so desperate, she tied a lamp to his head. The light helped him sleep, but it caused all kinds of problems, too. He constantly bumped it into things, and accidentally set her temple on fire with it."

The dragonet hopped about in front of Marella. "What is lamp? What is fire?"

Marella pulled her lamp from her pack and demonstrated how to turn it on and off. "This is a lamp. I've never seen fire, but my Nannu told me fire is like being stung by a thousand jellyfish all over, and it can ruin buildings and take down cities. I've never seen fire before. It can't live in the sea."

Hakkan frowned and fluttered his growing wings, but didn't say anything else, and Marella continued.

"When Dalphein grew into adolescence, his lamp caused even more trouble. He used it to illuminate the sleeping rooms of beautiful women, and the light blinded them to his intentions, and he fathered many children with the women of the seaside towns. His mother was outraged at the number of grandchildren he provided, and struck him down, saying, 'You must not behave in such a way. We are gods and must behave with dignity and grace among our people.'

"But Dalphein didn't listen. Instead of settling into a life of helping the mortals in the ocean and on land, he tried his hand in politics. He whispered secrets to kings in back rooms, and soon every nation within his reach was at war with every other. Again, his mother despaired. This time, she cast him into the sea and ordered him to look after all the creatures there.

He found a community of supaerisi there, near the Zegellen islands, and found their beauty to be beyond his ability to resist. He coupled with many of the women and created another race, with his bronze skin and colorful hair. He spent the rest of his days watching over his descendants and helping the youths get into as much mischief as they could manage."

Marella drew a breath and swallowed the bile rising in her throat. "I'm afraid I'm not a very good storyteller," she whispered.

"That wonderful. Tell another?" Hakkan scooted closer, his head almost in her lap.

"Let me take a break first." Marella scrubbed a hand over her mouth. "I'm not feeling very well."

"Mmmmmm," the dragonet rumbled and dragged himself closer, his haunches stirring up the mud and clouding the water. "We rest together. I sleepy, too."

He lay down beside her, and Marella set her head on his smooth foreleg.

The feel of eyes boring into her woke Marella sometime in midmorning, based on the light streaming through the cave's mouth. She searched the room for the source of her discomfort and found an adult sitting in the nest Hakkan usually slept in. The dragon had its head cocked to one side and stared at Marella with an intensity that made a shiver run up her spine.

The tremor woke Hakkan, who rumbled and stretched. He looked around, following Marella's gaze, and gave a startled little hop.

"Mother!" He scurried across the cavern, rushing in close to his mother's side. She stretched wide green wings around him and glared at Marella.

A quiver of fear ran through her, and Marella pushed herself to sitting. She leaned her back against the wall and hoped the mother dragon wouldn't act on the rage burning in her eyes. With the weakness and dizziness from overusing her crig, Marella wouldn't have any chance at outrunning a full-grown dragon.

Her head spun, and she closed her eyes. She resisted the urge to immediately open them again, reasoning that seeing the dragon coming for her wouldn't lend her the strength to escape.

Beside her, Dyfan stirred. "What's going on?" he mumbled.

"Nothing." Marella didn't open her eyes, but felt the tiny currents created by motion beside her.

"Why's that dragon staring at us like that?" A tremor in his voice gave away his unease, and Marella forced her eyes open.

"I think she's Hakkan and Deinnu's mother. I fell asleep with Hakkan earlier and woke to her watching me. I think she's angry the dragonets are spending so much time with us. You've spent years getting ready for this, right?

What do you know about how to not get ripped in half by an angry mother?"

Dyfan massaged his left hand, wiggled his fingers, and fidgeted with the webbing between his long fingers. "Not much. None of the flight like to talk about their time in the gorge."

Marella made a face. "Gee, I wonder why." Her voice dripped acid, and she lowered her head. "Sorry. It's not your fault."

"Don't worry about it. We'll figure something out before it's time to go back to Pharlandzi." He stopped and stared at his hands. "How many days have passed, anyway? I have no idea how much time we have left."

Marella used her finger to mark the mud. Day one was when she and Lilit had descended into the gorge together. They'd been chased by the angler fish and found a cave to sleep in. They'd spent two full days searching and working the grid Lilit had drawn on the cave wall. On day four, they'd found the dragons and Marella had recklessly rushed in, searching for the fungus.

She pushed her memory past that day's disastrous end. She'd spent day five alone, healing from her injuries and recovering from using the crig. The next day, she'd returned to the dragons' cave and met Hakkan. That was the day she'd gotten the fungus and cured the poison. Day seven the spider crabs had eaten her food, but she'd been too weak to find more. She slept through most of day eight as her body purged the poison. The next day, day nine, she'd left the cave and gone to the flats, where she'd encountered the serpent and found Dyfan.

Yesterday. That was only yesterday. Marella marveled at how the time had passed. It felt like she'd just entered the gorge a few days ago and that she'd been there forever at the same time.

"Today's day ten if I've counted right." She shook her head, letting her mind roam over the insane events of the previous nine days.

"Well, we have six days left, then. That should be enough time to convince the babies to come back with us. We'll need to plan a day to hide out from the adults, though. I've never heard of a rider getting out with a baby without the mother chasing them."

Marella couldn't hide the fear that coursed through her at the thought.

"Don't worry. You just have to get in a small cave and wait it out. The mothers never hang around more than half a day."

"With as slow as the babies swim, should we give ourselves extra time to get to the city?" Marella tried to remember how far the swim had been but found her memory of that day muddled and blurred.

"That's not a bad idea." Dyfan's stomach growled, and they both laughed. "What've you got for food? I'm not sure I can eat more of that." He gestured to the eggshells coated in fungus laying between their spot and the dragons' nests.

"Yeah, once the poison's gone, that stuff doesn't taste very good." Marella gave a weak smile and pulled her pack out from under her. Her stomach clenched at the memory of the spider crabs and she sent up a silent prayer to Dalphein and Ikeshal that their food was safe.

She pressed a hand into the pack and pulled out a bunch of red and yellow seaweed. Relief coursed through her and she handed the first handful over to Dyfan.

"Is this all? You don't have any fish or anything?"

Marella shook her head and stuffed the seaweed into her

mouth. When she'd swallowed, she said, "No one where I grew up eats fish. I'd heard of it, of course, but I'd never tried it until the night of the banquet." She made a face. "I think I like seaweeds better."

Dyfan shook his head. "How do you go more than a few days without fish or eel or some kind of meat? Don't you stay hungry and cold all the time?"

"I've never been cold until we came north. The waters where I lived stay warm all year, so it's never been an issue. I guess it wouldn't make sense for your people, though. There's not enough places to grow seaweed around here. Especially not kidali like my people grow. It needs a lot of flat space."

"I guess so," Dyfan said. "I'll probably try to catch some fish today, if that's all right with you."

"Are you strong enough?" Marella eyed the puckered pink scars on his legs — proof that he hadn't finished healing yet. "I know the crig didn't fix everything. You should probably spend a day or so healing before you head out there." She hitched a thumb toward the cave's mouth.

Dyfan gave her a sour look and ate a handful of seaweed. "You know, that's not half bad. I guess I can live on it for a day. We'll fish tomorrow."

They ate in silence until they'd both eaten their fill. Marella closed up her pack and leaned it back against the wall. She hadn't forgotten the mother dragon, but had deliberately kept her gaze away, as Lilit had instructed. Now, she couldn't resist the urge to check, and found the mother had curled up in her nest with her babies. It looked to Marella as if she was sleeping, but she wasn't about to get close enough to check.

She kept her chin down and watched the animal through her eyelashes while she pulled her hair out of its braids, combed all the debris and dirt out of it, and tied it back up.

"Why tie it like that?" Dyfan asked. "I've heard the women where you come from keep it long and loose, right?"

Marella nodded. "I was warned to keep it up, so it doesn't get tangled around dragons' tails or gear. Besides, it's probably safer this way here, anyway." She gestured toward the gorge.

Dyfan said nothing and turned his attention back to the dragons. "It's a shame none of the others found this cave," he said quietly. "There's probably three dozen dragonets in here."

"I know. I tried to find others but had no idea where you'd gone into the gorge. I think they kept us all pretty far apart."

Dyfan heaved a heavy sigh. "What happened to your team, Marella? I have to know. Did they abandon you?"

Thick tears stung her eyes, but Marella blinked them away. "No." She told him how Takvor had left before the dragonaxi sting and gave a brief account of the events at the down current. "I kept hoping she made it out, but she never went back to our cave, at least not that first day. I haven't been back there since I came here."

She dropped her chin to her chest and fiddled with her fingers. "I want to believe she's still alive, but that would mean she abandoned me and went out on her own. Honestly I wouldn't blame her if she did after I made such a mess of that first day. What about you? You said you got beat up trying to escape with porpoises but what about your team?"

"I..." Dyfan stopped and swiped a hand over his face. "We got in a big fight. They had a good plan, like the grid you said Lilit drew, but I was impatient. I wanted to find the dragons and cure the poison. We came to blows, and they threw me out of the cave." He sighed again and leaned back against the wall. "I've heard the same things everyone has — that there's no chance at winning this thing alone, that the team either stays together or dies separately.

"I decided to make a break for it, thinking maybe someone in the village knows another cure for the drago-naxi poison, but I was too weak to swim that far alone. My left arm wouldn't work at all.

"I heard the porpoises and remembered stories my mother told me when I was little, and you found me a few hours later."

A soft thump alerted them to a dragon's movement, and a heartbeat later, the mother swam past them and out the mouth of the cave. She didn't turn her head toward them, but Marella shivered. The mother held herself stiffly, like a woman who's angry at her lover. Except that this time, the dragon was angry with her.

Fear sent a shiver up her back, but Hakkan hopped over, and all her worries evaporated.

The rest of the day passed in a flurry of stories and laughter. Before long, Hakkan laid his head on her lap, and Deinnu sidled up close to Dyfan. Visions of returning to Pharlandzi with the dragonets swam through Marella's mind, but she pushed them aside. She was running out of time to convince the dragonets to return to the city with them, and then the mad dash to get the babies away from their mother. She needed to focus on surviving those events before she could daydream about the celebration back in the city.

The next day rushed by in a repeat of the one before.

EIGHTEEN

Training

The trip to Belzon took twice as long as it would have without the dragonet, but after eight days, Errebeld called a stop. The buildings had come closer together, and more and more travelers had eyed Zakazely with suspicion and fear.

"We'll have to find a cave we can stay in for a while." Errebeld eyed the lighting overhead. "There's plenty of daylight left."

"We find cave, and I find Faize." Keird grinned. "Is better than solstice gift for her."

He swam away toward some promising rocks to their left, and Errebeld called Zakazely to follow. The baby hunted a school of midsized fish while they waited for Keird to find a suitable cave.

"This way. Zakazely, to me." Keird waved his arms over his head to get the dragonet's attention. The baby tucked his wings and dove toward Errebeld, who laughed and ducked left to avoid being crushed by the enthusiastic dragon.

They swam into a wide cave occupied only by a few

small crustaceans. The dragonet crunched them down, settled onto the sandy floor, and went to sleep.

"Is good I ate first." Keird laughed and dropped his pack beside the dragon. "I go find Faize."

He didn't wait for a response but vanished into the light beyond the cave's mouth.

Errebeld leaned back against the wall and daydreamed of loungers, chaises, and other comfortable furniture. He'd even be happy to have a cot to keep him off the ground. It had been more than a month since he'd slept on anything but cave floors and open ground beside the traveling route. He sighed and shook the thoughts from his head. It would be months longer before he slept on a lounger since someone had to stay with the dragonet.

Maybe we can take turns sleeping here and with Faize. Surely, she has a spare lounger.

"You sleeping?"

Errebeld jumped up and tried to act like his friend hadn't startled him. "Nah. I was just daydreaming. You found her already?"

"This is the baby? He's huge!" A plump young woman with shimmering green skin and purple hair swam into the cave. "I thought you said he's a newborn!"

"He is baby." Keird placed himself beside the sleeping dragonet, and Errebeld sat back and stared.

Errebeld had to admit it: Faize was right. The dragon had tripled in size since they'd rescued him. At least. His tan and brown hide had thickened into neat rows of shining scales, and the beginnings of a ruff had sprouted around his head.

"And you keep saying 'he'? I'm no expert, but I'm pretty sure this is female." Faize swam close to the dragon and lifted a wing to peer underneath. "Definitely a female.

See these markings? Males don't have them." She pointed to silvery stripes on the leathery wing.

The dragonet grumbled and pulled her wing free, and Errebeld sighed. "We didn't know if it was a boy or girl, we just couldn't keep calling her an 'it.'"

"What does she answer to?" Faize put her hands on her hips and glared. "Tell me you gave her a decent name."

"I, we've just been calling her Zakazely."

"You named a dragon 'Baby'?" She screeched.

The dragonet chirped and shifted his — no *her* — position. Errebeld stumbled mentally over the sudden change, but realized he'd have to get used to it.

All three supaerisi stayed silent until the dragon settled back to sleep.

"We didn't really name her." Errebeld waved a hand toward the baby. "We just had to call her something besides 'it,' and we didn't know if she was a boy or a girl." He shook his head. "I sound like an echo."

"Well, now that you've been calling her that, we'll have to pick something that sounds similar or she'll never answer to it."

"Like what?" Keird ran a hand over his face and stared at the dragon.

No one spoke for a long while, until Errebeld leapt up. "What is 'Zaká' in Pharli? Isn't it something feminine?"

Keird shook his head, a blank look on his face, while Faize furrowed her brow in concentration.

"Is it beauty? I think is beauty."

"I think you're right. Will that do? She is beautiful." A wave of triumph out of proportion to the tiny victory swelled Errebeld's chest.

"Yes, that will do." Faize beamed at him, and Errebeld

fought the urge to puff out his chest. "Does she wear a harness?"

All the joy evaporated and Errebeld's face fell. "We haven't tried." At her disapproving glare, he added, "In all fairness, we didn't exactly plan to find a dead mother dragon and wounded baby. And we haven't passed any villages that would have dragon harnesses for sale, not that they'd let us anywhere near a settlement with an untrained wild dragon in tow."

Keird said something Errebeld didn't understand in rapid Ashmoran, and Faize snapped something back. They argued in the unfamiliar tongue for several minutes before Faize spun away from her brother.

"He is right." She glared at her brother and turned to Errebeld. "You did all you could. We start from beginning." Faize blinked and shook her head. "*The* beginning. I apologize. It is not easy to switch sometimes."

Errebeld waved a hand as if to drive her apology away. "You do just fine. Do you know how to start? The dragon training, I mean."

All three turned to stare at the dragon, and Errebeld's stomach sank. He'd heard dozens of trainers say a dragonet that wasn't harnessed inside a week never would be. Zaká was at least three weeks old.

"I'm not sure."

"We find a way."

Faize and Keird spoke at the same time.

"Let me find a harness. I will return tonight." Faize spun and swam out into the daylight before Errebeld could react.

"Did you eat?"

Errebeld kept his gaze on the dragonet. "I haven't. I'm

not hungry yet, if you want to hunt first. I'll stay with him — I mean her."

If Keird detected the lie, he said nothing. Instead, he followed his sister out into the light. A rumble from his empty stomach would have given him away, if Keird had stayed another moment in the cave.

Worry gnawed at Errebeld's insides until Faize returned less than an hour later. Instead of a harness, she brought a stooped old man who wore a leather belt with dozens of tools and attachments over his silvery scales. His blue skin and silver hair created a striking contrast, and Errebeld wondered where the man had come from. He'd never seen such a color on a supaerisi before.

"This is Hamalin Brinon, the finest dragon outfitter in Belzon." Faize rushed over to the sleeping dragon but hesitated and turned to the old man. "How do we begin? I don't want to startle her."

"Quite right." Pale blue eyes reflected the cave's low light back to Errebeld. "Can you call her? Wake her up so we can see what size harness she needs?"

"If I wake her, I'll have to feed her." Errebeld judged the light outside the cave. "Do you think we have time for both?"

"Of course." Hamalin gave a wide smile. It took Errebeld a moment to decipher the thick, exotic accent. "I'll just take half a moment, then she's free to eat until dusk if she'd like."

Keird called the dragon, and the baby stirred and raised her head. As soon as her eyes blinked open, the old man rushed in with tapes flailing behind. While he worked, he murmured to the dragonet, but Errebeld couldn't make out what he said.

True to his word, Hamalin had the dragon measured

faster than Errebeld could believe and led the small group out into the waning light.

Keird and Faize supervised the dragon's meal, and Errebeld went off in search of his own. He hadn't eaten since morning, and his empty stomach wouldn't be put off any longer. He feasted on a bed of colorful seaweed fifty lengths south of the dragonet's hunting grounds.

~

The next morning, Errebeld woke to a strange clanging noise. He leapt to the ready, his knife in hand.

"Calm yourselves." Faize let out a nervous laugh. "I should have woken you. I apologize. When Hamalin said he had it finished, I thought we should get started right away."

"Quite right." The old man eyed Errebeld's blade and shifted his gaze further into the cave. "May we?"

"Of course. I'm so sorry. It's just—"

"No matter. If you'll wake the dragon, we'll get started." Hamalin shifted the weight of the heavy chain harness draped over his shoulder.

"Of course." Errebeld winced. He sounded like a fool repeating himself like that. He sheathed his knife and turned to the dragon, but Keird had beat him there.

"Zaká, up."

The dragon shifted, grumbled, and made a great show of taking a long moment to open her eyes. "Hunt now?"

"Not yet." Keird laid a hand on her side and smiled at the dragon. "Try something new first."

Without waiting for an introduction, Hamalin swam to the dragon, murmuring in a language Errebeld couldn't identify. The old man flung the harness over Zaká's head, and in a flash, the dragon flung him away and hooked a back claw through the chain. The heavy iron shattered as if it had been made of glass, and Errebeld called out to soothe the baby.

"It's all right. Just give it—"

Before he could say more, Zaká had Hamalin in a foreclaw.

"NO!"

Errebeld's scream echoed in the depths of the cave, but it had no effect on the angry dragonet. She closed her claw, piercing the old man's chest. He opened his mouth, but no sound came out.

Zaká crunched Hamalin down in two bites, releasing a cloud of red into the cave.

Errebeld's empty stomach heaved, and he retched, the sound mingling with Faize's terrified scream.

Keird's shouts of "NO! No, no, no, no, no!" Echoed over the top of the other voices.

Unable to support himself, Errebeld slumped against the cold stone wall. Thick tears stung his eyes, but he blinked them away. He couldn't move. He couldn't think. What was he supposed to do?

Keird approached the dragonet with his arms out straight in front of himself. "Easy baby. Easy Zakazely. You all right."

The dragon stuck out her tongue. "Mean fish taste bad."

"Oh baby, he not mean. He try to help you."

"Help?" Zaká cocked her head, a confused wrinkle showing between her eyes.

"That's right. Help. You need harness to go with us." Keird waved a hand to the ruined chains.

"I go with you now." The baby shook her head. "We hunt?"

Errebeld forced a smile and swam to Keird's side. "Yes. Let's hunt." His stomach churned, but he forced himself to turn and swim out into the early morning light.

The dragonet swam through the schools of colorful fish as if nothing had happened. Errebeld couldn't fight off the fear of sharks and other predators descending on their cave, drawn by the scent of blood in the water.

He shook his head to rid himself of the images. "Do you think I can go see a priest later today? I—"

"Go now." Keird waved him off with kindness shining in his eyes. "You not used to killing. Go to priest. Ease your mind."

Errebeld didn't give him a chance to change his mind. Tears blurred his vision as he swam away from the dragon and his friend. He tried to blink them away, but nothing he tried worked. The tallest spires in town beckoned him, and he swam blindly toward them, toward Dalphein's temple and the priests and priestesses who could absolve him.

An eternity passed before the doors loomed in front of him, but Errebeld finally reached the simple wooden doors. The wood shone blue and clean in the morning light.

Those look new. They must have replaced them recently. The thought passed unbidden through Errebeld's mind, and he shook it away. He had bigger things to worry about than doors.

His knees trembled as he pulled the door open and swam into the cavernous temple. In the center of the entryway, a gleaming silver statue of Dalphein caught the morning light. Shining gold and bronze fish glittered in his crown and flashed against the polished silver trident he held over his head. His other hand held a small lamp, which gave off a cheerful yellow glow, even though daylight lit the chamber. Marble columns surrounded the statue, holding the ceiling high above the gleaming monument.

Errebeld fell to his face before the figure of his god and wept.

"I'm sorry, I'm sorry, I'm so sorry. I didn't mean to," he cried the words over and over, unable to think clearly enough for a more articulate prayer.

Time passed, though he couldn't say if it had been minutes or hours.

"Rise, my child."

A gasping sob escaped, and Errebeld pressed a hand to his mouth. A middle-aged man floated beside him, his purple skin and green scales telling of his Pharlandzi heritage, and his soft middle revealing the lack of physical effort required of a man of Dalphein's priesthood. The man smiled down at Errebeld and held a hand out to help him off the floor.

"I'm sorry, your, your h-h-holiness. I'm, I'm not f-f-fit to be in your p-p-p-presence." Errebeld took the offered hand but sobbed even harder.

"Rise, child. Tell me why you weep."

Several long minutes passed while Errebeld struggled to bring himself under control. Finally, he wailed, "I have taken a life, your h-h-h-holiness."

"In what manner did you take this life? Tell me the tale." The young priest rested an arm across Errebeld's shoulders and pulled him close. "Dalphein does not judge in haste."

The words tumbled from Errebeld's lips in a waterfall of emotion. He told of the bandits who'd attacked them and how the sharks had killed them. He told of finding the bultiers and saving the baby and lingered on how he'd shot the attacking bultier until it stopped moving toward him.

When he reached the part about helping Keird hunt for the baby, Errebeld dissolved in helpless tears again and several long minutes passed before he could continue.

When he could speak again, Errebeld told the priest of the journey to Belzon. In between gasping breaths, he told the story of how Zaká had killed the old man.

Finished, spent, and sure the priest would toss him out on his ear, Errebeld waited with his forehead resting on the polished marble floor.

"Rise, my child."

Errebeld didn't move. He couldn't bring himself to face the priest's judgement.

"Rise, child. You are clean. You have only killed to save, not for the sake of killing alone. You have saved a valuable life, and in her life, you will find your forgiveness. Rise, my child."

The words washed over Errebeld like a healing balm. "Are...are you sure?"

"Of course, child. Dalphein does not judge those who protect and care for his beloved creatures as you have done. Rise and dine with me as one of his exalted."

Errebeld struggled to hide the pained sniffling as he rose and wiped the thick tears from his eyes with the back of his sleeve.

"Now, you will need to make penance for the two supaerisi you have not saved." The priest kept his eyes on his hands as he tore colorful seaweed leaves into manageable pieces. "A life for a life will be sufficient. You must save two lives to atone for the two you failed to rescue."

Panic washed over him, but Errebeld swallowed it down. "Of course, your holiness. That sounds fair."

How? How do I save anyone? I've never saved a single soul, and now I have to save two? How? His mind reeled, touching on a dozen made-up scenarios where he might save people from Zaká.

The priest set the platter on the low marble table between them. "Eat, my child." He set his words in action and stuffed a bright yellow leaf in his mouth.

Errebeld followed suit, though he couldn't bring himself to do more than nibble at the colorful food. His stomach churned with grief and guilt, unrelieved by the holy one's words.

"Let your mind be still. Dalphein will present you with opportunities to make your penance. Until he does, think no more of it. You are young, and you have your whole life to equalize the balance."

"Thank you, your holiness." Errebeld gulped down enough of the meal to be polite and rose to leave.

The priest bowed low and left the room. Errebeld returned the gesture, though he bowed toward the statue rather than toward the priest's retreating back. He sank to the floor and sat in the statue's shadow for a long while, meditating on the priest's words and searching for the peace he should feel in the temple. After more than an hour, he finally found a measure of calm and rose to leave. The priest waved from the doorway, and Errebeld bowed to show his thanks.

With a final glance up at the smiling face of his god, Errebeld shoved his way out of the temple and into the bright light of midday. The door swung shut behind him and closed with a final clang. The forlorn sound echoed through his chest, and Errebeld drifted back to the cave he shared with Keird and the dragonet, his mind blank and his chest aching.

NINETEEN

Fishing

Somewhere around midday on the third day in the cave, Marella mustered her courage. She leaned back and set a hand on Hakkan's neck but resisted the urge to make eye contact. "Do you think you'd ever want to come back to the city with us?" she asked. "You'd have a good life where you're worshiped and fed and treated like a god."

Hakkan cocked his head and stared at her, but she kept her eyes on his chest. "What a god? What worship? Where city?"

"A god is someone that's more important and more powerful than people, even supaerisi, like me and Dyfan. Worship is when we," she gestured between herself and Dyfan, "make sure you have everything you want and need."

"And the city isn't far away," Dyfan said. "It's close enough you can come back here whenever you want."

"I ask Mother?" Deinnu swung his head around on his long neck and stared toward the empty nest near the far wall. "When she done hunting?"

Marella shook her head. "I don't think that's a good idea. She doesn't like us very much, does she?"

"No." Hakkan swiveled his head between the nest and Marella. "I like you. Mother say you steal me away. Now you want go city? Maybe Mother right?"

"No, of course we don't want to steal you." Marella ran a hand down the baby's neck, trying to soothe his worry. "We want to be a part of your family, but you'd still have your mother and your brother."

Dyfan drew the dragon flight's emblem in the mud. "Does your mother have a mark like this on her tail?"

Deinnu and Hakkan stared hard at the mark. "How you know that?" Hakkan asked after a long moment. "She hide it from everyone."

"That's the mark of the Pharlandzi dragon flight, so if you come with us to the city, your mother will be there in a week or so." Dyfan smiled. "So if you come with us, you'll get to spend every day with her."

"I spend every day with her here." An obstinate expression Marella had never seen before crossed Hakkan's face.

"That's perfectly all right." Marella swallowed hard and worked to hide her disappointment at Hakkan's reaction. "You don't have to come with us, but we can't stay here much longer, either." Marella ran a hand down the dragon's front leg. He'd grown larger even in the few days she'd spent in the cave. "We have to go back to our people in a few more days, but I'd love to spend that time with you, if that's all right."

A grin transformed Hakkan's face, washing away the worry and fear and replacing them with a delighted expression that made Marella smile back.

"Right. You stay. I friend. Story?"

Marella searched her mind for a story she could tell the

little dragon that might pique his curiosity about the city and its inhabitants but came up blank.

"I know a good one," Dyfan said. "It's about Pharlandzi, the city where we live."

Hakkan and Deinnu settled their heads down onto the cave's floor, their eyes glued to Dyfan in rapt attention.

"Long, long ago, before the city in the trench had been built, a man named Pharli came to the gorge on a fishing expedition. He'd entered a contest to see who could catch the largest fish in three days' time, and his rival had an unbeatable lead.

"Pharli wouldn't give up, though. He continued fishing the area, searching for something large enough to win him the prize and feed his family for the next week.

"He found a swordfish longer than he was and chased it toward the mountain. It was fast, but he was faster. He chased the creature out over the gorge, but didn't see the warning signs and got caught in a wicked down current. The cold water pushed him down, down, down, so deep that noon looked like midnight and the pressure squeezed all the water from his chest.

"Pharli struggled to escape the current, but couldn't get free, and it pushed him even deeper. His vision went black, but he didn't know if that was from the pressure or the darkness from the depths, but what he did know was that he was going to die. He couldn't get free. He couldn't survive the pressure that deep.

"Just when Pharli was ready to give up, something brushed against him. He couldn't see what it was, but an enormous creature pressed against him and pushed him free of the current. His body smashed into the rock wall, breaking both of his legs and one of his arms, but the animal slowly, gently pushed him toward the surface.

"Pharli had no idea what was going on, or whether the creature saving him from the current would eat him as soon as he was free, but he didn't have the strength to fight it. He let the animal push him toward a cave and maneuver him inside, though with the fading daylight he couldn't see much. He slept through the night in the foreign cave, without a care for what manner of creature had saved him and stowed him in the cave.

"When morning came, Pharli woke in terror. Three dragons hovered over him, staring at him and nudging his injured legs and arm.

"His ribs hurt too much to scream, but he gasped and immediately whimpered from the pain. The noise alerted the dragons that he was awake, and the smaller one settled onto the ground beside him. It rumbled and chirped and made a clicking sound he couldn't interpret, but he guessed that it was trying to communicate with him.

"He pressed a hand to his chest and tried to talk to them. 'I'm Pharli. You saved me. Thank you.'

"The small yellow dragon repeated his words, and the two spent the next three weeks learning to communicate with each other while Pharli healed from his wounds. The dragons brought him fish to eat and kept scavengers away from him. By the time he'd healed, he and the yellow dragon, who called himself Lanidzi, had become fast friends."

Hakkan lifted his head. "Oh, Mother tell us story of Lanidzi! She say he very brave and wise, and saved mer king and loved by all. Pharli is king, yes?"

"That's right, Pharli became the king when he returned from the gorge with his new dragon friend. Together, they designed and built the Pharlandzi palace, which is large enough inside for many dragons to swim together."

"Oooh, that is big." Deinnu's eyes had grown wider with each word Dyfan spoke. "I see it someday?"

"Of course you can. Marella and I will take you there any time you want." Dyfan grinned and met Marella's eyes. Triumph shone in his gaze, and Marella smiled back.

Dyfan and Marella took turns telling the dragonets stories of the city's grand streets and historical battles. When the babies retreated to their nest for the night, Marella leaned close to Dyfan.

"I have an idea. You've been wanting to go fishing, anyway, right?" Dyfan nodded. "So why don't we catch some salmon or something big enough to tempt the dragonets? If they see that we'll feed them, too, then we may just win them over and convince them to go with us."

"That's not a bad idea. Let's get some sleep. We'll see how the morning goes and try to get out and go fishing early."

Late the next morning, after telling several stories, Dyfan urged the dragonets to get some rest with their siblings while he and Marella went in search of food. They had depleted the seaweed supply already, since Marella had only picked enough for herself, so she needed to leave the cave, anyway.

Dyfan moved slowly, but the scales that held his legs together had grown back enough that a few could latch and hold while he swam. Neither had enough strength or stamina to chase the bigger fish, so Marella pulled her bow off her shoulder and checked the string.

"Watch this," she whispered, taking aim at a large salmon feeding on a school of little blue fish. She took a deep breath and reassured herself she could do this. She wasn't killing it for herself. She had to do this for Hakkan.

Without him, she'd be exiled from Pharlandzi, and her father would lose his position.

She waited until the fish turned sideways, checked her aim once more, and released the arrow. Thread unwound from a spool at her waist, making a soft whirring sound that took Marella back to the hours she'd spent at the practice range. The arrow pierced the water with deadly accuracy and struck the fish in the flank, and Marella pulled back on the thread, keeping the wounded fish from dropping into the depths of the gorge.

"Well done! Can you do that one more time?" Dyfan danced side to side behind her.

"Of course." Marella reeled in the fish and re-wound the spool. Once she'd handed the fish to Dyfan, she cut the thread with her belt knife and tied it onto the next arrow.

When she'd nocked the arrow, she raised the bow to search for her next target. The little blue fish had reformed into their dizzying school, but two more salmon circled the bunch. Marella waited until one salmon circled back to her side of the milling fish, took aim, and loosed another arrow. Again, it struck true, and Dyfan whooped.

"One more time and we can both eat for a week!"

Marella gave a sickly smile. Her mind wandered back to the banquet and the slimy concoctions she'd choked down. That felt like forever ago. She'd been cold since she'd entered the gorge. Perhaps a little fish, especially fatty fish like salmon, would help her stay warm. She'd read about creatures that used fat from their food to keep from freezing in arctic waters, so the same principle should help her. The thought of eating those vibrant, living creatures made her shudder, but she focused on the fish.

She drew a deep breath and took aim once more. She pushed all thoughts out of her mind, as Coline had taught her, focused on a single scale on the salmon's side, and released the arrow.

Again, it drove through the water with all the accuracy and speed her years of practice could produce and struck the salmon in the side. Marella pulled it back and stuffed it in her pack, not looking up at Dyfan while she worked.

"Where did you learn to do that?" Dyfan asked after a long silence. "I thought you said you don't eat fish."

Marella sighed and swung her pack and bow over her shoulder. "I don't, but everyone in Kaulo's required to spend three years in the military. Those of us who train ahead of time have a better chance at getting the best assignments. I want to serve with my friends in the watch towers, not get stuck patrolling the slums."

"I guess I can see that. Great shooting, though. I didn't even know you could shoot arrows in the sea and have them work. I've heard stories of people doing it on land, but never in the water."

"I hear that a lot from travelers." Marella pulled out an arrow to demonstrate. "The arrows are different, heavier, than the ones on land, or well, that's what my mother said anyway." She handed it to Dyfan, who examined it from one end to the other. "And instead of feathers to keep it going straight in the air, it has these wooden fins."

"I see. How did you learn to shoot it? And what's the bow made of? And the string? How do you keep it from fraying?"

Marella laughed. "One question at a time." She explained all the details of undersea archery while they swam back to the dragons' cave.

"Everyone thought you'd be dead in a day," Dyfan said before they re-entered the cave. "I can't believe how wrong we all were. You're pretty amazing."

"Um, thanks, I think." Marella frowned, trying to decide if he'd complimented her or admitted to thinking she'd be an abject failure — or both. "Let's find the babies and give them these fish."

"You don't think the other dragons'll smell the blood and come looking for a share, do you?" Marella asked, eying the packed cave and searching for Hakkan in the dim light.

Dyfan shrugged. "I don't think so. How would the mothers feed their babies if they had to worry about their neighbors stealing their food?"

Still irritated at Dyfan's admission that he'd expected her to fail, Marella returned his shrug. She didn't want to admit he was right.

They settled down against the wall together to wait for the babies to return, and she turned to face her companion. "What happens after this? We go back with dragons and 'win' the challenge. Then what?"

"No one explained that to you?" Dyfan frowned. "Well, everyone—"

"No one explained anything to me! I spent the few days between being nominated and the start of the challenge learning how to hopefully not die down here." Marella struggled to keep from shouting out her frustration.

"That's fair, I guess. Everyone that comes back with a dragon is automatically a part of the dragon flight. For the first few years, you're grouped according to your dragon's age and ability level, and you train together as a team." He shrugged. "For most of us, it's a big step up in status because you're almost royalty if you have a dragon. I don't know that it'll be that much of a change for you, though, because you already have a king for an uncle."

"Is that why you did it? For the status and glory?"

Dyfan chuckled. "No. I guess it's sort of expected of

me. All my cousins have won the challenge, so now it's my turn. I'm the oldest in my family, so I set the example."

"Oh." Marella turned back to the cave's activities, confused by the massive number of dragons there. "What's happening? Why are there so many?"

"I think they're taking the babies out to swim for the first time. It's a big deal. We can't take them to Pharlandzi until they can swim in the gorge, and their parents can't leave them to return to the city until they can swim and hunt, so they do this every day from now until the parents leave."

"Does it matter which parents are in the dragon flights? What happens to the ones that aren't going back to the city?" Marella tried to wrap her mind around the natural process and what, if anything, the Pharli people had done to change it.

"They're getting ready to get back to their solo lives in the deeper ocean." Dyfan gestured to the mass of dragons. "They only come here to breed and raise their young, but most of the time they're alone or in groups of two or three."

"Oh." Marella mulled that information over in her mind and squeezed back against the wall when the dragons filed past her. Hakkan nodded to her but didn't stop or otherwise greet her when he passed. She sent up a prayer to Dalphein for his success and safety and added one to Ikeshal just to be safe.

While they waited for the dragons to return, Marella and Dyfan pulled out the salmon she'd caught for them to share. She fought the urge to gag when Dyfan cleaned the scales off the fish and sliced a bit of meat off. He handed the first cut to her and waited, watching her face.

She bit off a small piece and swallowed it down without

chewing. It had an unpleasant fishy taste that triggered her gag reflex, and she fought to keep it down.

"You really don't eat meat, do you?" Dyfan's voice held a note of wonder and surprise, and Marella met his eyes.

"No, I really don't. That's the only reason I found you. I couldn't make myself kill the little fish I trapped, so I went to the flats to gather seaweed."

"I didn't think it was possible to never eat fish and not die of starvation." He stared at her as if she were some bizarre species, and embarrassment heated her cheeks.

"It's not that uncommon, at least where I'm from."

A clatter of dragons returning cut off his reply, and Marella sagged with relief. She wouldn't have to explain her diet any more that day.

As soon as Hakkan entered the cave, he headed straight for her spot.

"I did it, 'Rella! I swimmed across the deep all by myself. Well, Mother was beside me, but she didn't touch me. I swimmed it myself." He puffed out his chest and Marella smiled.

"Very well done. I've brought you a salmon as a reward." She held up the first fish she'd caught, and he grabbed it from her.

"Thanks! I hungry. Mother not hunt because she help us. She go hunt now." He devoured the salmon in two bites and was licking the remnants off his chops and paws when Deinnu swam over.

"What you eat?" He asked his brother.

"'Rella gived me fish."

Deinnu raised his head and stared at Dyfan, eyes wide with hunger and hope. "Fish?"

"Yes, we have one for you, too." Dyfan pulled the last

salmon out and handed it to Deinnu, who inhaled it as quickly as his brother had.

"I take it you swam the gorge, too?" Dyfan asked when the dragonet had finished his fish.

"I did. I swimmed it fast. I the fastest."

"'Rella?" Hakkan sat beside her, his face nearly touching hers. "Mother says she and other big dragons go to city soon. Is same city you go to?"

"Yes, it's the same city. Do you want to go back with us? You'll be able to see her every day." She hoped her impulsive promise wouldn't turn out to be a lie.

"I go to city." He laid his head on his shoulder and Marella swallowed against a sudden lump in her throat. She'd done it. She'd convinced him to return with her, and she'd made a friend in the process.

"I go, too," Deinnu squawked. "We all go together."

Dyfan grinned at Marella and the two had a quiet moment of celebration in the darkening cave. Soon, the adult dragons returned with claws full of fish, and the dragonets returned to their nest to eat and sleep, and Marella laid back, her mostly-empty pack wadded up to cushion her head.

TWENTY

Rumor

Errebeld scrubbed his hands over his face to blot out the unpleasant memories. "Well, does anyone have any other thoughts? We can't try another harness for a while."

Keird shook his head, and Faize knotted and unknotted her hands in her lap, the action stretching and relaxing the fine webbing between her long fingers.

"We have to try something, right?" Errebeld reached for the only option he could think of. "Isn't there an archive or something in Belzon where we can find a scroll or two on dragon training?"

"There is." Keird met Errebeld's gaze with the first spark of hope Errebeld had seen since the failed attempt to harness the dragon.

Faize dropped her hands and rose. "It's close to my home. Can we go now?"

"I stay with Zaká." Keird drifted closer to the sleeping dragonet. "You go."

"Are you sure?" Errebeld would have pressed harder, but Keird had already settled in to rest beside Zaká.

Faize turned and swam out of the cave without another word. With one more glance at the dragon, Errebeld hurried after her.

Instead of following the main roads he'd taken to the temple, Faize turned down the first narrow alleyway they came to. Stone buildings taller than anything he'd seen in his hometown loomed high on either side, but Faize swam on as if nothing were out of the ordinary.

Of course, she lives here. She's used to it. He struggled to keep from gawking at the women, clad only in narrow swaths of pale fabric draped over their torsos, reclining against the bottom of one building.

Faize swam on without any sign she'd noticed the women. She vanished around a corner twenty lengths ahead of him, and he kicked hard to catch up.

Errebeld chased her around several more twists and turns as the buildings blurred into a massive, unbroken wall on each side.

Without warning, Faize stopped short, and Errebeld had to back-kick as hard as he could to keep from running into her back.

Beyond her, something glittered in the darkness, and Errebeld couldn't tear his eyes from the shining building. Six columns, each taller than four of his uncle's palaces stacked atop each other framed double doors large enough for ten supaerisi to swim abreast through them. A wide marble ramp rose from the sandy ocean floor to the shining doors. Dalphein's temple, the beautiful place he'd visited just that morning, would have fit inside this building at least three times over.

Faize waited until he'd paused beside her before proceeding toward the imposing building. She moved slower, and after the breakneck race through the streets,

Errebeld struggled to match her pace without running ahead.

When they approached the entrance, a small opening set into the right door swung open. Errebeld hadn't noticed the smaller doors before that moment, and the sudden opening startled him to a complete stop. Once he recovered, he had to hurry to catch up to Faize again.

Inside, Faize paused by a wide table bolted to the marble floor beside the door. She murmured something to the young woman seated there, but she kept her voice low enough that he couldn't hear what she said no matter how hard he strained.

Rows upon rows of shelves held more scrolls and tomes than he'd ever seen in one place. Small signs at the end of each row announced what manner of information readers could hope to find on that set of shelves.

The woman behind the table pointed to a stack behind her and made several motions with her hands. Faize nodded and turned back to Errebeld.

"This way." She swam in the direction the woman had indicated without pausing to see if he followed.

Errebeld hurried to keep up, taking in all the scrolls and tomes surrounding him. Most of the spines were written in languages he didn't understand, but here and there he found something labeled in the common tongue.

Dragon Breeds and Characteristics

Dragon Temperaments and Testing

How to Avoid Offending Your Dragon – now that one might be helpful. He eased it off the shelf and carried it with him.

All the titles he could understand had something to do with dragons.

He smiled. *Well, at least I know we're on the right path.*

"It should be somewhere in here, if it's here at all." Faize stopped and searched the shelves to her right.

They spent the next hour searching every title on every shelf in that section. Several titles came close, and they gathered those into a basket Faize had picked up somewhere along the way.

When they had a heavy stack, they proceeded to one of the tables set in the center of the cavernous room and set the books out on top of it.

Errebeld grabbed Wild Dragons and How to Live with Them and flipped through the heavy, oiled vellum pages. At first, he read every page with interest and enthusiasm. After the first chapter, he skimmed the pages for another hour.

"I give up." He slammed the book shut and reached for another. "Let's try this one."

Faize closed her book and set it atop the one he'd discarded. "This one's useless."

They spent the next few hours skimming and setting aside book after book and scroll after scroll.

When the daylight dimmed and the attendant lit the orb light on their table, Faize rose.

"We should go. It's too dark to go to the cave. Are you all right with staying at my place tonight?" She hesitated, and Errebeld smiled.

"I'd love to. It'll be nice to sleep someplace other than a cave floor, even if it's only for a night."

He followed her through the building and up to the double doors, which had been propped open. A name murmured in quiet conversation beside the door caught his attention, and he froze halfway through.

"...Marella del Kapat... into the gorge. Yes, really... part of the Dragonaxi Challenge... Have you ever heard of such a thing? ...No, I don't think there's much chance she'll come out alive."

He only caught pieces of the conversation, but it chilled him to his bones. Surely it couldn't be. His sister wouldn't be foolish enough to join that death challenge. Would she?

Doubt crept in, and he hovered by the door, hoping for another whispered word, but the woman had moved too far away for him to hear anything else.

Disappointed and worried, he followed Faize out into the twilight.

~

"Just let me send a letter to my parents. They can tell me whether the rumor is true."

"You overheard strangers whispering in a library. There's probably nothing to it, but I see no harm in verifying. That gives us more time to search the library, too."

The next morning, Errebeld paused at the desk in the library and purchased a bit of reinforced canvas and a new wax pencil. He wrote a short letter, found a messenger to deliver it, and hoped his parents would reply quickly. While he waited, he'd occupy his mind and time with the search for information about dragon training.

A week passed in a blur of books and scrolls and searching fruitlessly for answers. Errebeld strained his ears to hear what the other patrons in the library had to say, but no one else mentioned his sister.

The waiting set his nerves on edge, so when Faize arrived at the cave with Soraya in tow, it took all his self-control not to scream that he'd worked too hard to keep the dragon a secret for her to ruin it. Instead, he plastered a serene expression on his face and bowed low.

"Soraya. I didn't expect you here."

"I was in Pharlandzi and someone needed a messenger to deliver an important letter. Imagine my surprise when it was addressed to you." She pulled a folded letter out of the pouch at her waist and presented it with a flourish.

Errebeld took the letter and broke the wax seal but couldn't hide the trembling in his hands. He scanned the text, then read it again, more slowly.

"Well? What's it say?" Faize ducked her head in front of his face, but he turned his head away and handed her the letter.

"Just read it aloud so we can all hear it," Soraya ordered.

Faize nodded and began with a tremulous voice, "To Errebeld del Kapat, I won't waste your time on pleasantries. Your sister has gone into the gorge as part of the Dragonaxi Challenge, which as far as I can tell is a Pharli tradition going back hundreds of years.

I have heard nothing from her or any other participant since they left two weeks ago, and I fear for her safety as she has had none of the training the other challengers have benefitted from. I had hoped to tell you in person, but this is the next best thing, I suppose.

Please make haste and come to the city. Within the week, we shall either have a celebration or reason to grieve. I'm holding onto hope for the first, while the royal court is preparing for the second. Your Loving Father, Vazken del Kapat."

"Well, I guess that settles that. We should leave immediately." Errebeld lifted his pack and made a show of checking his belongings."

"I need to grab a few things, but I'll be back before Zaká finishes her hunt." Faize and Soraya turned and left.

Without a word, Keird woke the dragon and led her out into the morning.

Less than an hour later, Faize and Soraya returned and the four struck out for Pharlandzi. Errebeld couldn't shake the feeling he should have gone there to begin with like Gallien had said.

TWENTY-ONE

Searching

Hops and whispers and the flutter of leathery wings against the cave walls kept Marella from sleeping well, and she tossed and turned through the night, until the cave fell quiet just before dawn.

An angry rumble and roar brought her awake not long after, and she bolted up off the floor in search of the threat. Two angry dragons towered over the rest, searching every nest in the cave. Marella moved to nudge Dyfan awake and realized with a start that the spot where he normally slept lay cold and empty. Her pack was missing, too.

Frantic, she scanned the cave for Hakkan's cheerful face, and instead met his mother's furious glare.

Cold realization blossomed in her stomach, followed by a rush of rage and terror. Dyfan had left in the night, and he'd taken both the dragonets with him.

Many pairs of eyes turned to face her, and Marella darted out the cave's mouth, certain they weren't going to ask for her side of the story.

Dawn barely lit the gorge, and Marella searched every hole and crevice in the wall for a place to hide. She'd barely made it ten lengths when the first dragon burst from the cave behind her, and she chose the closest cave she could reach. It wasn't empty but was only occupied by a few small turtles chasing a handful of jellyfish. Marella steered clear of the long tentacles and pressed herself against the wall on her right.

Her arms trembled with fear, but she worked to keep her breathing even. She didn't want to draw any more attention than she had to. She'd just started to hope that the mother dragon hadn't seen her dash into the cave, when those hopes dissolved like a thin strip of metal rusting over the summer. A wide nose pressed to the cave and churned the water. Marella flattened herself against the wall and wished she could disappear into the stone. A deafening rumble filled the cave, and the turtles and jellyfish swam in frantic circles, their escape route cut off by the very creature they were trying to flee.

A tremor shook the cave, and several stones the size of her head or larger fell from the cave's roof. It took every ounce of self-control Marella had to keep herself still. She couldn't flee. Dyfan had said she could wait out the mother, so that's what she'd do.

Her stomach rumbled, and she mourned the last shreds of seaweed in her pack.

How could he? The question repeated over and over in her mind. *How could he steal my food and supplies? How could he take off with the dragons I introduced him to?*

Shock and fear and anger blanked her mind and kept her from finding any answers or thinking of anything else. The dragon rammed the cave wall again, and more stones shook loose, falling in a deadly cascade. One struck a turtle's shell and rolled off, and Marella winced. She hoped the animal wasn't hurt because of her.

And it is my fault, she reasoned. *I brought Dyfan to the dragons. I introduced him to the dragonets. I healed him at the cost of my own strength. I should have left him where I found him.*

She shook her head at that last one. No. She couldn't have lived with herself if she'd left him to die. Besides, the old woman had warned her that kindness was her only chance to win.

And where did kindness get me?

The dragon rammed the cave again, and this time a crack climbed along the wall at her back. Marella longed to run but had no way to escape the cave.

Another impact shattered the back wall and left a gaping hole large enough for her to swim through. Faint light filtered through the new opening, revealing an open structure supported by carved columns.

Without hesitating, Marella darted through the opening. The light came through a tiny opening on her right. She could probably fit her arm through it, but not more than that. To her left, another opening beckoned, this one large enough she could fit through easily. This cavern had less light than the first, but cool, fresh currents of water told her it wasn't sealed off. She waited for her eyes to adjust and saw a gaping hole in the ceiling. This time, she went more cautiously. She stopped to peek through the hole before swimming into the cave.

Marella froze. Four dragonaxi undulated toward her, and her stomach clenched in terror. She retreated back the way she'd come and tore at the narrow hole she'd scoffed at only a few minutes before. Her fingers scraped along the rock, but slowly she pulled away enough chunks of the crumbling stone that she could squeeze through. She paused on the other side, listening for any sign of the dragons. The pounding blows had stopped, but that didn't mean they'd left. An eerie silence filled the space, and she checked to make sure the dragonaxi weren't sneaking up on her.

Undefined shapes moved in the dimness, and Marella's chest tightened. The admiral had said the animals hid in dark caves, so she needed to get to the light to escape them. She drew a breath, listened again for any signal that the dragons were still outside, and poked her head out into the open water of the gorge.

Her head swam with relief. The dragons had abandoned their pursuit of her and had faded to tiny undulating blobs at the edge of visibility. Marella moved further out into the gorge, putting as much space between herself and the dragonaxi as she could.

She hovered there for a long moment, oblivious to the schools of fish that swam around her, enveloped her, and left her behind.

She longed to chase after Dyfan, to find the babies and bring them back to Pharlandzi with her. She stared off into the distance, stretching her mind and searching her memory for any hint of information Dyfan might have given her in the days they spent together. He'd said his team had entered the gorge well south of their position in the cave, but how far south could they have gone? Lilit's grid had only gone to the outcropping of rock where they'd encountered the down current.

Marella shuddered at the memory and sent up another prayer that Lilit had survived. Unbidden, the sound of Dyfan's voice when he admitted he hadn't thought she had a chance filled her mind, and she narrowed her eyes. She couldn't let him win. Not this way. Somewhere deep down, she knew he'd taken the dragons back to the cave he'd shared with his teammates. She knew with equal confidence that she had to find them. Somehow.

She took off toward the south, staying well away from the walls until she was sure she'd passed the sheer cliffs that rested against the tall mountains. Those areas were most prone to down currents, if she remembered right from that lesson she'd half ignored. She wasn't willing to take that kind of risk again. She swam until the light reached its brightest and started peeking her head into the larger caves. She moved slowly, careful not to disturb predators that might be waiting in those dark confines but found nothing more threatening than jellyfish.

Her empty stomach rumbled to remind her of the breakfast she'd missed, but she had no food, and now, no bow or arrows, so she'd have to survive the day with the reserves she'd built up. She cursed Dyfan again under her breath and pressed a hand to her belly. She thought the salmon should have lasted her a few days. A wave of guilt hit her with the force of a wall at the memory of the salmon. She'd never killed a living creature before, and she didn't think she'd be able to do it again without the babies to feed. She worked the area with the same thorough pattern she'd used to look for dragons with Lilit, but this time her quarry was more cunning than the dragons alone, and Marella wondered if they'd see or hear her coming and move away before she could see them.

She let her mind replay the days she'd spent with Hakkan. She'd grown to like the little dragon, even though he complained about being the smallest and having to work harder to do the things his brothers and sisters did. He'd been a perfect match for her.

No. She wouldn't think of him in the past tense. She wouldn't allow it. She'd find them and bring Hakkan back to Pharlandzi with her. No other option was worth considering.

Even as the thought occurred to her, her mind was busy developing and discarding contingency plans. The gorge was hundreds of leagues long and contained millions of caves and caverns. Dyfan and his crew could be in any one of them.

If she didn't find them that day, which was looking more and more likely as the daylight faded, Marella would return to the dragons' cave and try to befriend another dragonet, though the thought made her chest ache. She only had three days. She hoped it would be enough.

With that plan solidifying in her mind, Marella made her way back to the cave where she'd spent the first half of the challenge. She hadn't been there in over a week but couldn't think of anywhere better to go. It was easy to defend and would provide a safe place to spend the night.

Hunger left her weak and tired when she finally made it back to the cave.

The smeared wax grid on the wall intensified the aching grief in her chest, but she ignored it and settled down against the wall to sleep. Images of Hakkan swirled in her mind. She pictured the concern on his face when she'd been ill, his eager happiness at being able to help, his excitement when he'd swum the gorge, all the thought he put into agreeing to go with her to the city. The day's events flashed above those memories, a crushing weight she couldn't hold back any longer. Tears flowed from her eyes until she finally cried herself out and fell to sleep in the blackness of the cave.

TWENTY-TWO
Merchants

"Zaká, this way." Keird waved the dragon back to them for the third time in an hour.

The dragonet made a soft chirping sound and glanced between Keird and the kelp bed she'd been swimming toward.

"I know it looks fun, but we're going this way for now." Errebeld made his voice as soothing as he could and mimicked Keird's wave toward the group. Zaká chirped again and swam back to Keird. She flipped end over end as she came, and Soraya laughed. "Is she always like this?"

"Usually, yes," Faize said. "Unless she's sleeping or eating."

"What else is there for a young dragon to do?" Errebeld couldn't hide his own smile. Zaká spun and flipped around them as they moved ever closer to Pharlandzi.

They'd been traveling for six days, and Errebeld thought they must be getting close, though they'd moved slower than his normal pace and avoided all the villages and towns along the way, so he wasn't certain. They'd argued the first day over the speed, but there was no way to hurry with a young wild dragon in tow.

Lost in his thoughts and worries for his sister, Errebeld didn't notice the merchant wagon until the travelers surrounded his group.

"Ho there! Is that a young haingana? I've never seen anyone train one of those before. Always thought they were just too wild. Look at her come when you call, though. Well done."

The man who spoke swam toward Errebeld. He had bright silver scales over his tail and bronze skin, so Errebeld assumed he must have been from the narrow sea, southeast of Kaulo.

"I'm so sorry for letting her get so close to your group." Errebeld tried to wave Keird toward Zaká in the hopes that they could get the baby away from the group. "She's a bit of a handful still."

"I believe that. Is she friendly? I've always wanted to meet a dragon." The man laughed and swam toward Keird and Zaká.

Errebeld struggled to keep the panic out of his voice. "I–I don't really know, sir. I'd stay back if I were you. She's friendly to us, but she hasn't been tested around strangers." The scene with the harness-maker replayed in his mind, and Errebeld struggled for breath.

After what felt like an hour, the man stopped and turned back. "Not tested, you say? Well, I probably shouldn't be the first, then, should I?" He laughed again, though it sounded forced. He glanced back at Keird and Zaká once more and returned to his wagons.

A petite woman swam out of the nearest wagon and started swatting at the man as soon as she could reach him.

She kept her voice down, but Errebeld caught a few louder words here and there.

"Stupid... were thinking... died. What would you..."

It didn't take much imagination to fill in the gaps, so he swam toward the dragon and clear of the woman's wrath. That thought made him laugh out loud. His father had always said he'd do anything to avoid a woman, and here he'd just proved it. That brought Gallien to mind, and Errebeld wished they'd traveled together. Gallien would have adored Zaká and probably would have had some idea where to begin training her.

"Ho there! Don't let her scare you off! Come join us for some chow!" The man's voice echoed off the tall cliffs beside the path, and Errebeld paused.

"You go. See what they know of your sister. Merchants carry news. I stay with Zaká." Keird waved him away and shooed the women after him with promises of a demonstration of the merchants' wares. "I join you when Zaká sleeps."

Half an hour later, Errebeld laughed at a joke one of the merchant men had told. None of them had heard any news of Marella, but they had plenty of jokes and stories to keep the whole group entertained. Keird swam into the circle and settled himself onto the ocean floor.

"Well, where ya headed with that baby?" A pale blue woman asked. "She'll need someone what knows how to manage such a wild thing."

"Pharlandzi," Keird muttered. "Lots of trainers there."

"Of course! And it's such a beautiful city." The man who'd tried to greet Zaká smiled and bobbed his head. "I don't guess you'll take that one into the city proper, though, not for a while at least."

"Of course not. I've heard there's trainers in all the villages around the city." Errebeld smiled and waited for someone else to speak. When they didn't, he added, "We should be able to find someone to help without angering the guard. I understand they're strict about which dragons they allow in the city, and with good reason."

"Yes, of course. As they should be. And I'm sure there's trainers all over the country, as you say. You'll just have to find one what knows something about haingana." The man laughed as if he'd told the funniest joke he'd ever heard, and Errebeld gave a weak smile.

"I think I'll check on Zaká. She doesn't take such long daytime naps anymore." He swam toward the outcropping of stone where the dragon had laid down, but when he turned the corner, the space lay empty. "Hey! She's gone!" He made sure to project his voice so the others would hear.

He didn't wait for his friends but searched the area until he found scrapes along the narrow rocks that showed where Zaká might have gone. He followed a scrape here and a tail mark in the sand there for half a mile. After that, she must have swam upward, because no marks showed on the ground or the rocks around the area.

Desperate panic swelled Errebeld's gut, and he swam upward after her.

She couldn't have gone far, could she? They hadn't left her alone for more than twenty minutes.

He spun in the water, straining his eyes for any sign of her, though her brown and tan markings would hide her completely in the murky waters and rocky terrain.

"Zaká!" He shouted as loud as he could, and his voice echoed back to him from a dozen directions.

The echoes faded, replaced by a deafening silence.

Before he could shout again, Keird and Faize swam up beside him.

"Any idea which way she might have gone?" Faize asked.

"With the current, probably. Based on the way your hair is moving, I'd say that way." Errebeld pointed to his left. "We should spread out a bit but stay close enough to see each other."

Keird nodded and swam off in the direction Errebeld had indicated. Faize followed, keeping half a dozen lengths to her brother's right. Errebeld took the other side, keeping Keird in the center of their slow procession. A movement beyond Faize caught his eye, and hope flared bright in his mind, only to be dashed when he recognized Soraya's slender form.

They crept forward, calling for Zaká every few lengths. A school of shiny blue fish swam overhead. They scattered, reformed their ball, and darted off into the murk when Keird shouted.

The sight tightened a band around Errebeld's chest. His dragon would have loved darting into that ball of fish.

My dragon. I have to find my dragon. I have to.

He screamed her name into the growing darkness and waited for any sound to puncture the endless silence.

Soraya appeared out of the dim water ahead of him, and he stopped to avoid running into her. "We're not going to find her. She could be anywhere out here, and she's big enough to take care of herself—"

"No—"

Soraya pushed on as if he hadn't spoken. "You did your job. You fed her and taught her to hunt and now she's back in the wild where she belongs."

"No. I'm not—"

She held up a hand. "I know it's hard, but it's for the best."

"I'm not leaving her. You—"

"She's right." Faize set a hand on his arm. "There's no way—"

Errebeld shook his head and opened his mouth to speak, but she continued.

"—we're going to find her out here. We don't even know where the road is now."

"You go back, then. I'm not quitting." Errebeld refused to acknowledge the tiny voice in the back of his mind that said they were right. Keird's silence spoke the loudest of all.

His shoulders slumped as he quietly gave in. A steel band squeezed against his chest, making it difficult to draw a breath. He fought the urge to sob outright like a child who's lost his favorite pet but somehow managed to keep it in.

Numb, but aching, he allowed Faize to pull him in the direction they'd come from. Keird's face looked exactly the way Errebeld expected his own to look — eyes downcast, lips tight, a picture of grief and disappointment.

A scream of pain and terror pierced the silence, and Errebeld spun to face it before the echoes through off his sense of direction. He darted toward the sound, dread replacing the grief if only for a moment.

He reached for his belt knives and wished he'd brought his bow. He didn't know what kind of threat lay ahead.

Beside him, Soraya drew a sword and Keird readied his spear. At least they'd come ready. He couldn't see Faize and guessed she must be behind him somewhere.

Another scream brought him up short before he lunged forward with all his might. That was Zaká. He'd know her voice anywhere. And she was in trouble.

He darted past an outcropping of rock and nearly fainted on the spot. Zaká faced off against a fully-grown orca. Behind him, a marlin darted about mindlessly, its skull showing through the gashes in its torn flesh.

"Dalphein help us," he murmured. His fingers loosened around his knives. They wouldn't be terribly useful against an orca.

An arrow flashed past him and buried itself in the whale's thick hide. It spun away from Zaká, leaving her bleeding and sinking rapidly to the bottom. Errebeld let the others take on the whale and kicked hard toward the wounded dragon.

He pulled his last crig bead out of the pouch on his belt and swallowed it down while still chasing Zaká. She didn't try to swim, but twitching movements of her legs let him know she was still alive. A red cloud grew in the water behind her, but he didn't let himself dwell on that. He couldn't. He had to focus.

The dragonet settled in a heap on the ocean floor, and Errebeld reached her a heartbeat later. He didn't pause to examine her wounds before he grabbed a stick and used her own blood to draw the healing rune on her chest.

The blue light blinded him, but when it faded, deep gashes remained on her legs, neck, and torso. At least she'd stopped bleeding. He set his head on her chest and listened for her heart. It beat out a steady, though rapid, rhythm, and he breathed a sigh of relief. She'd survived. Somehow, he'd get her to someone who could heal the rest of her wounds.

Keird settled into the sand beside him, the unasked question written on his face as if in script.

"She's alive." Errebeld's voice came out in a raspy whisper as raw as he felt from the day's events. "Barely, though. D'you have any crig?"

Keird shook his head and set a hand on Zaká's still foreleg.

"We have to move her." Faize swam down and surveyed the scene. "It won't take long for sharks to follow all that blood."

"I don't know if we can. Do you have any crig? I can try to heal her a little more?"

Faize dug a single bead out of a pouch inside a pouch on her belt and handed the tiny white pearl to him. Beside her, Soraya did the same.

"Please let it be enough. Dalphein help her." He prayed out loud, not caring what his friends thought of his ancient religion. They could — and probably would — tease him for it later, if Zaká lived.

TWENTY-THREE

Night

A plaintive cry woke Marella in the night, a wailing as if a great creature had lost something dear. The painful sound brought a pang of tears to her eyes, and Marella hoped it wasn't what she thought. Unable to help herself, she crept toward the cave's opening. Faint light streamed into the outer cave, and she used that light to make sure nothing dangerous lurked in the dark before she exited her haven.

Outside, something large swam past, blocking out the light for a long moment. Marella waited until the shadow had left the cave's mouth before she approached. She stuck only her head out, peering into the dimly lit gorge. The mother dragon swam away to her right, and Marella swallowed an unexpected lump in her throat.

The sad cry echoed off the walls of the gorge, answered by smaller voices far away. Marella's chest hurt from the pain in the mother's cry, but she could do nothing to ease it. Dyfan's assertion that mothers didn't miss their young for more than a few hours rang in her ears, and she marveled that he'd been so wrong.

Maybe, she thought, *that means he underestimated other things just as badly. Like how willing the babies would be to return to the city without me.*

Hope blossomed in her mind, but she shoved it aside. She had no reason to believe Hakkan wouldn't go with him. The dragonet had been willing to leave her asleep in the cave the night before, so why wouldn't he follow through and go all the way to the city?

Loneliness and defeat replaced the hope, leaving a hollow soreness deep inside her that she doubted would ever heal.

With nothing better to do, she retreated back into the cave and tried to sleep. Memories of the early days with Lilit, the down current, and the days she'd spent with the dragonets tormented her, and she slept in pained bursts darkened by nightmares.

Dawn found her no more rested than she'd been the night before, and her hunger refused to be ignored any longer.

Marella crept out of the cave, wary of any night predators that might still be lingering in the gorge's shallower waters. Seeing none large enough to pose a threat to her, she left the cave behind and swam toward the crevice she'd used as her entry and exit point since the challenge began.

Again, she paused at the top, careful not to disturb any creatures who might be lurking and waiting to capture unwary prey leaving the crevice. Without her pack to throw ahead of her, she broke a fist-sized chunk off the crumbling wall beside her and tossed it up. Hoping that anything stalking her position would chase the stone and wouldn't see her come up after it, she peeked up over the side.

A few small sharks swam in circles, but they weren't large enough to trouble her, and she continued out of the crevice and toward the boulders that marked the edge of the flats.

She moved as quickly as she could, though hunger made her movements weaker than they would have been otherwise. She slipped through the water, leaving the tiny sponges and creatures waving gently in her wake.

The boulders felt farther away than before, but she pushed onward, envisioning the colorful array of food that lay on the other side. When she reached them, she paused. The purplish light of early morning filtered down onto the boulder. Small creatures were very likely still feeding in the flats, and larger predators may be nearby stalking them.

Cautious, she peeked around the nearest boulder just in time to see a serpent like the one that had bitten her snatch a hand-sized fish out of the water above the rippling seaweed.

Great. She searched the ground for something she could throw to make sure she didn't get bitten again but came up empty handed.

Hungry, weak, and dizzy, she leaned back against the boulder. Self-pity lingered at the edges of her awareness, but she refused to give in to it.

She closed her eyes and focused on her breathing, in and out, in and out, until calm returned and she could think clearly.

When she opened her eyes again, she moved to her left and slowly circled the boulders, searching for anything she could use to make sure the seaweed clusters weren't harboring deadly predators before she stuck her hand in them.

She circled each boulder, looking high and low for any stick or rock or bit of debris that would help her, but found nothing. Finally, something shiny gleamed in the silt to her right. Marella moved toward it, hopeful but cautious. Some predators used shiny scales to lure unsuspecting prey close enough for them to strike, and she wasn't about to fall victim to such a simple scheme. She stayed well above the shiny bit and used the trailing frill on her fin to move the water and sweep away the dirt. Each swipe of her fin revealed more of the object, which wasn't a predator or anything alive, but looked like some sort of metal strip.

Again, she used the frill on her fin to sweep everything away from it and reached down to flip the thing over. It was as wide as three of her fingers together and as long as her arm. She lifted it gently, pleased to discover that nothing but little scurrying things hid beneath it.

Its weight surprised her, but she slung it over her shoulder and carried it to the flats, where she used it to beat at the seaweed at the edge of the field. Leaves fluttered outward, revealing the paths the creatures hiding beneath them took to escape the metal strip.

When the fluttering stopped and she was sure the serpents and other creatures had fled, Marella hovered above the field and used the metal strip to isolate a bit of seaweed, which she plucked and devoured as soon as she'd ascertained that nothing still lurked beneath it.

She ate until her hunger abated but didn't stuff herself. She needed to be able to move quickly if she found Hakkan and the others. When she was ready to move on, she stuffed as much seaweed as she could in the small leather pockets she wore around her waist. It wouldn't last more than a day, but hopefully she wouldn't need more than that.

With her pockets and her belly full, Marella raced back to the crevice. She had three days until the challenge ended. She'd make the most of every single one.

She picked up her search where she'd left off the day

before, checking each cave, but also calling constantly for Hakkan. She didn't know if he'd come to her calls, but she'd heard that dragons had better hearing than supaerisi. Maybe all he needed was to know she missed him and was looking for him.

Marella refused to consider the possibility that he might have bonded to another challenger already. Somehow, she was reasonably sure that had been Dyfan's intent when he'd stolen away in the middle of the night.

I hope he shoots himself in the fin with an arrow. The bitter thought surprised her, and she laughed. It was an amusing image, and she spent the next few hours picturing Dyfan wounding himself with her supplies in one way or another.

The imaginings lightened her mood, and soon they morphed into images of the dragonets discovering how uncouth Dyfan had been and turning on him. As satisfying as those imaginings were, though, they led only to worry. The babies weren't big enough to manage without someone to help them. She hoped they didn't try to venture off on their own.

When the light reached its midday peak, Marella paused and decided to return to the flats for a bit more food. She didn't want to have to rely on her pocketed supplies alone. Instead of returning to the crevice and finding the boulders as she'd done so many times before, Marella swam up to the top of the gorge where she was and peeked over the edge.

Rolling hills led away from the enormous scar on the ocean floor. Off to her right, a distant shadow indicated the boulders that protected the food.

Nothing but a small school of tiny silver fish moving in undulating waves broke the shimmering light between her and the distant hills, and Marella braved the open waters and swam up out of the gorge.

The hills rose and fell beneath her. She stayed just high enough that her fins sent plumes of silt into the water as she swam by the higher hills.

She hummed a soft tune and planned for the coming week.

Since I haven't found Dyfan and the babies, she decided, *I'll eat and return to the dragons' cave. Surely, I can meet another dragonet and find someone to bring back to Pharlandzi.*

While she ate, her mind replayed the conversations she'd had with Hakkan, the stories she'd told, the myths Dyfan had relayed, and the bonding time she'd spent with the little dragon. A pang of guilt shot through her at the thought of befriending a new dragonet, but she shoved it aside. She had no other choice. If she returned empty handed, she'd be turned away and exiled, and her father's position as emissary would be revoked. If she failed to return at all, she'd be assumed dead. Either way, all the people in the city who'd bet against her would win.

She squared her shoulders. She wouldn't let that happen. She couldn't. Her family counted on her. Her uncle, king of Kaulo, counted on her, whether he knew it or not. She remembered the promise she'd made and hoped his feelings weren't hurt from the lack of correspondence. She hadn't dreamed she'd end up in such a nightmare challenge when she'd left.

Lost in thought, Marella drifted toward the gorge, back to the dragons' cave. Back to square one. She refused to indulge the sadness and loneliness, instead focusing on what she had to accomplish. She could do it. She'd done it once already. And this time, she wasn't weak from poison

— either from the dragonaxi or the serpent — and she hadn't used the crig and worn herself down. She may not have had her pack and supplies, but she was stronger and healthier than she'd been at any point since the challenge began, and she'd accept nothing but success.

She raced back to the crevice and slowed only when she approached the dragons' cave. She stopped inside the first cave, the one she'd come to think of as the foyer and listened. Whispers of movement and soft thumps reverberated from inside, and Marella wondered how she'd missed those sounds the first time she'd found the cave.

Nerves fluttered in her stomach, but she pressed onward and slid into the dimly lit cavern that housed the dragons. Instead of returning to the same spot she'd spent so much time in — where she'd gotten to know Hakkan and Dyfan — she moved to the left and clung to the wall until she'd made it halfway to the back. There, she settled down to watch the babies in the nearest nest and hoped one would give her a chance. She had precious little time but approaching them the first time had been disastrous. She wasn't willing to repeat that mistake.

She sat quietly and waited through most of the morning, until a rumble against the far wall drew her attention. The rumble turned to an angry scream, and Hakkan's mother charged toward her.

Marella ducked behind the nearest nest and kept her head down. She raced between nests and swam as hard as she could for the exit. The dragon's claw snagged her fin fringe, but Marella pulled and let the fringe tear. It ached at the place where it attached to her ankle, but not enough to slow her down.

She grabbed the side of the wall and used her arms to pull herself through the opening and out into the smaller cave but didn't slow. She pushed herself faster and swam out into the open gorge. The dragon's bellows told Marella the mother was right behind her, but she didn't look back. She passed the tiny cave where she'd met the dragonaxi without hesitating. She'd rather face the angry mother than a swarm of those awful beasts. Instead, she squeezed herself into a narrow crevice in the wall and swam upward, searching for something to hide behind or a part of the crag that would offer more protection.

The mother dragon bashed her tail against the wall below Marella's position, and a shower of stones fell from the impact. She pressed herself further into the tight space and prayed to Dalphein for deliverance. When the mother slammed her tail into the wall again, she sent a prayer to Ikeshal, too, just to be safe.

Another blow from the dragon's tail rocked the wall and sent a shower of stones tumbling into the gorge's depths. Marella moved further up, hoping against hope that there would be an escape somewhere along the way.

The dragon's pained cries spoke to Marella's own broken heart, but she had no way to comfort the animal. She missed Hakkan, too. And nothing she said would convince the mother that Hakkan's disappearance wasn't her fault, especially since Marella already blamed herself for the dragonet's theft — and he had been stolen, she was certain of that.

The stone wall around her shuddered under another blow, and Marella cringed. She pressed her back into the crevice, where little cracks and rocks dug into her back. She eased the pressure just enough to make sure the stones didn't break the skin. She couldn't afford to attract more foes with the scent of blood. In the distance, another dragon let out a cry, and the mother dragon raised her head.

The call repeated, and Marella went limp with relief when the mother turned and raced toward the sound, leaving her trembling and alone in the crevice.

She braced her arms against the wall across from her and wept in frustration and relief. How would she ever befriend another dragonet if the adults wouldn't let her near the babies? She couldn't risk returning to the dragons' cave again. She wasn't sure she'd be able to outrun that mother again, even if she had a head start.

It wasn't worth the risk, but what else could she do? She hadn't found a second dragon cave in any of her searches.

She recounted the days on her fingers. *This is day fourteen. I only have two and a half days to return to the city. That's not enough time.*

She stayed hidden in the crevice for what felt like hours, dragging her mind over any option she could think of. There weren't many.

Finally, she gave up. She'd return to the city and beg them to waive the exile requirement since she'd been unprepared for the challenge. They had to give her credit for surviving, didn't they? She'd found the antidote and reversed the dragonaxi's poison. She'd survived alone, or mostly alone, for two whole weeks in the gorge, even after most had written her off as dead.

That has to count for something, she told herself. Dyfan's words replayed in her memory, telling her none of the other challengers had expected her to last even a day in the gorge. A pang of sadness struck her hard, knocking the breath out of her. When he'd said that, she'd mentally finished it with, "but I'll prove them all wrong." Now, she wasn't so sure.

Was there any chance they'd let her back in the city without a dragon? She had no idea. But she had to try.

TWENTY-FOUR

Help

Blue light flared around him, and Errebeld concentrated on giving as much of his strength to Zaká as he could. Slowly, the worst of her wounds pulled closed and scabbed over. Something in her neck snapped back into place, and Zaká whimpered. The tiny sound sent a jolt of triumph through Errebeld. She might still make it. The light faded too soon, and the dragonet curled into a ball on the sandy ocean floor.

A gentle hand settled on his shoulder. "We have to move her."

Errebeld sighed. The healing had left him drained and exhausted, and all he wanted was to lay down beside Zaká and sleep, but Faize was right. They couldn't stay here.

Slowly, he eased himself off the ground and swam over to the others. "She can't swim yet."

Keird took up a position beside her right foreleg, and Faize took the other. Errebeld supported her left wing and left Soraya to get the right one. Together, they lifted the sleeping baby into the water and swam toward the rocky cliffs to their right. Errebeld hoped they could find a safe place for Zaká to recover without worrying about predators.

They moved slowly, searching every indent in the rock for a shelter. After nearly an hour, they found a suitable spot.

As soon as they settled Zaká into the tight little nook, Soraya brushed herself off and straightened. "I'm going back for our things. I'll give our apologies to the merchants." Without waiting for a response, she swam off into the hazy water.

Errebeld barely noticed. He ran his hands over the dragonet, searching for any serious injuries he hadn't healed. She still had broken bones in both her forelegs, scrapes and scratches all over her body, and a worrisome mark across her belly that Errebeld hoped wasn't as deep as it looked.

"She needs food," Faize whispered. "I'll see what I can find."

Without looking up from his examination, Errebeld nodded. He hoped she'd be strong enough to eat whatever Faize brought back.

"Can I help?" Keird hesitated beside Errebeld, one hand outstretched, but not quite touching Zaká.

"Talk to her. Let her know she's not alone." He hoped that would be enough to quell the aggression injured wild animals typically displayed. The few times he'd healed animals in the past, he'd made sure he was far away before they woke.

"Ah, Zakazely, why you pick fight with whale?" Keird kept his voice soft and soothing, but his words jangled Errebeld's already-frayed nerves.

He fought the urge to jump to Zaká's defense, reminding himself that Keird wasn't blaming the baby, he was just looking for anything to say to soothe her. Keird gave up on the common tongue and said something Ashmoran that Errebeld didn't understand.

Through his bilingual monologue, Zaká made no sound and didn't twitch a single muscle.

After a while, Faize returned with a silver fish as big as her torso and dragged it over to Zaká. A wave of relief washed over Errebeld when the baby lifted her head and gulped the fish down in two bites, then fell back to sleep before her head was even on the ground.

Errebeld leaned back against her, careful to avoid her injuries, and let his eyes drift closed. Between the shock of finding her gone, the strain of the search, and the work involved in healing and moving her, he had nothing left. He let his head fall to her chest and slept.

"Should we wake him?"

"What do we do now?"

"I don't know. How long? It'll take weeks for all that to heal."

"We can't stay here for weeks."

Soft conversation woke Errebeld in the dim light of early morning. He stretched and took a moment to get his bearings. The memory of the previous day's events flooded him, and he spun to check on Zaká. She lay with her eyes closed, her head resting on her red-striped arms, twitching in her sleep from time to time. Her chest rose and fell in a gentle, even rhythm.

Reassured, he turned back to his friends.

"What do we do now?" Soraya repeated. "We can't stay here long enough for her to heal."

"Does anyone have any crig left?" Errebeld asked the

question without much hope and didn't respond when the others all responded in the negative.

"How far to Pharlandzi?" Keird eyed the dragonet with a calculating eye.

"Another day, day and a half maybe," Soraya said. "Why? What are you thinking?"

"If we give her a day to eat and get some strength, I think we should be able to get her to Pharlandzi." At Soraya's disbelieving stare, Errebeld added, "We got her this far, didn't we?"

Keird gave a little smile. "It might work."

"And if it doesn't?" Soraya gestured to the sleeping dragon. "What do we do if we get her to the flats and can't go on? There's nowhere to hide her there and plenty of hostile dragons who'll defend their territory."

"I have to try." Errebeld caressed the dragon's forepaw and met Soraya's eyes. "I know you didn't sign up for this. You don't have to wait for us. But I won't leave her here to die. I have to do what I can."

"Yes, this. We will try." Keird shifted closer and set a hand on the dragon's tail. "We save her again."

Faize grinned. "It's settled then. We move on tomorrow."

They spent the rest of the day taking turns catching fish and eels to feed Zaká. Each time, she ate without fully waking, but Errebeld thought she attacked the fish with more energy as the evening waned.

Errebeld stayed with Zaká while the others hunted. He wouldn't break his vows again if he could help it. Zaká slept peacefully, shifting without a sound every now and then. Errebeld hoped she'd have the strength to go on by morning, though he didn't think she'd make it to the border villages unaided. They'd have to support her, but he wouldn't give up on her.

~

When morning dawned, the friends fed themselves and caught more fish for Zaká. This time, she woke up to eat and eyed the group.

She made a sad cooing noise and held up her broken leg for Errebeld's inspection.

"I know, love. We're going to make that better, but we have to swim a little first. Can you swim?"

She repeated the sad little noise and lifted herself off the ground. The effort pained him to watch, and after a moment, Errebeld placed himself under her left wing. Keird took a position under her right wing, and together, they lifted the baby and began the journey to Pharlandzi.

After an hour, the strain had Errebeld breathing hard, and after two, he had to stop. He rested for half an hour and resumed his position under Zaká's wing. They repeated the process six times, but the last time, he only made it half an hour before he had to stop. His legs shook from the effort of supporting the dragonet.

"You still think you can do this for two days?" Soraya's sharp tone brought Errebeld's hackles up, but he didn't have the energy to spar with her.

"You're free to go on. You don't have to wait for us."

Faize placed herself between Errebeld and Soraya and crossed her arms beneath her breasts. "Why have you stayed with us? I thought you had some important business to rush back to Pharlandzi for?"

"I just want to see how far you'll carry this idiocy. You don't even know if she's trainable, but you're willing to risk your own lives to carry her into another nation?" Soraya's harsh laugh echoed off a series of sunken ships in the near distance.

Errebeld let his gaze wander the broken line of ships and worked to ignore the woman. He'd come this far. He wouldn't abandon Zaká now. He did the calculations in his mind and smiled.

"I think we're making good time. This is the Horoz field, isn't it?"

Keird whooped and laughed. "It is! We made it to Pharlandzi."

"Well, we made it to the border." Faize said. "It'll be harder from here. Past those ships there's nowhere to hide a dragon. We'll have to find a village and get help before dark."

The light had the soft, gray quality that meant clouds obscured the sun on the surface, which made it impossible to judge how long they had until nightfall. Errebeld cursed softly and shook his head. "Should we stop here for tonight and carry on in the morning?"

They found a place to hide, a little nook hidden on three sides by smooth boulders and half covered overhead by a sheet of metal that looked to Errebeld like a rusted-out door. As soon as they had the dragon settled, Keird and Soraya took off to hunt and Errebeld foraged in a nearby bed of pale yellow seaweed. It had no flavor, but it filled his belly, so he ate by the fistful. Faize stayed close to Zaká, saying the dragon needed to know they were close. Errebeld winced. She wouldn't be hurt if they hadn't left her alone while they gossiped with those merchants. He wouldn't repeat that mistake. He'd make sure she was never alone again.

TWENTY-FIVE

Pharlandzi

Determined to return to the city and daydreaming of her parents welcoming her back, Marella swam to the top of the crevice and peeked out over the side. When nothing moved toward her, she kicked hard away from the gorge and hoped she'd left it behind forever this time.

Frustration, relief, fear, elation, and anticipation warred for supremacy within her, with each winning out over the others for only brief moments before being swallowed by the melee once more. Marella eyed the light above and tried to ignore her rumbling stomach. The brilliant light told her she'd lost the morning already, and it had taken roughly half a day to swim from the city to the gorge, so she needed to get moving if she was going to make it back before nightfall.

Her shoulders slumped in defeat, Marella swam slowly toward the boulders that had been her point of reference throughout the challenge. Hopefully, she'd be able to find her way back to the city from there. Visions of city guards turning her away threatened to steal away the last shreds of her courage, but she pushed them aside and swam on. She couldn't think like that.

The priestess had said she would win if she was kind, and Marella had been as kind as it was possible for her to be.

She reached the boulders and couldn't ignore her empty stomach any longer. Marella reached into her pockets but found the seaweed she'd stashed away had been crushed into a slimy pulp in her mad escape from the angry mother dragon.

Disgusted, she dumped her pockets and used her hand to swirl water into her pockets and remove the last of the mess. Since she was already at the boulders — and the flats they protected — Marella decided to stop and gather food. She'd need something to eat later if the guards wouldn't let her back in the city, anyway.

She searched the area around the boulders until she found the strip of metal she'd used and abandoned there the day before. Only a thin layer of silt covered it, and it shone up at her beside the second boulder she checked.

Using the metal strip to move the leaves and check beneath, Marella picked and ate seaweed and stuffed her pockets with more for later. Small creatures scurried away beneath the metal strip, but Marella ignored them and continued her work until all four pockets were full and hunger no longer gnawed at her gut.

Disappointment sat like a stone in her gut, leaving her without as much of an appetite as she'd expected. With a final glance back at the gorge and a whispered goodbye to Hakkan, Marella swung the metal strip over her shoulder and swam in the direction she thought would lead to the city.

She'd only made it a few lengths when a menacing shadow loomed on the horizon. It stayed just far enough away that she couldn't quite see what it was, but the creature was larger than her, and its gaze made the hairs on the back of her neck and down her arms prickle in alarm.

The shadowy creature circled around behind her, toward the flats she'd just left behind, and Marella made an impulsive decision to follow it there. Every sense she had screamed at her to turn around and leave whatever it was in peace, but something deep in her mind thought it looked familiar enough to approach.

Thankful she'd thought to save the metal strip, Marella moved slowly around the boulders. She peered between the hulking rocks at every junction, keeping the creature in view between and around the boulders.

She lost the animal when it ducked behind the boulders but didn't let that slow her. Her heart slammed against her ribs in an endless beat of alarm and anticipation. She knew that shape. She couldn't place it, but she knew it, and it was dangerous.

Slowly, careful not to disturb even the tiniest bit of sand or the smallest creature, Marella moved toward the flats. She ducked behind the first boulder she reached and strained her ears for the faintest sound. Only the faint rustling of leaves and scurrying of tiny legs met her ears, and Marella wondered if she'd misread the creature's destination.

A frantic struggle broke out on the other side of the boulder, and Marella ducked closer to the ground to escape whatever threat may lie in the field of seaweed. The thrashing sounds lasted less than a minute, though that minute felt like an hour, and silence fell once more.

Marella waited for some sign that whatever creature had survived the struggle might not be a threat to her, but after a long minute of waiting with no sound beyond the gentle flapping of leaves in the current, she braved a peek around the boulder.

Shock froze her in place. Marella opened her mouth to call out but couldn't force any sounds from her throat.

"You!" Dyfan's voice echoed off the boulders and broke the spell. "What are *you* doing here?"

Marella swung the metal strip off her shoulder, prepared to defend herself as Dyfan swam toward her.

"I should ask you the same question. How dare you use me to meet the dragonets, then sneak off in the night like a burglar?"

"A burglar? Is that what you think? No, I saved Hakkan from a miserable life spent with a nothing like you. You don't know the first thing about dragons. You think you could take care of him? Really?"

Dyfan's words struck at Marella's deepest insecurities, but she bristled against the attack.

"He chose me, not the other way around," Marella spat. "And I certainly wouldn't be alone in caring for him, would I? I ignored my own faith and killed salmon for him to eat. Yes, I think I could do just fine in caring for him, especially with help from the admiral and the Dragoni back in Pharlandzi."

"You'd put your dragon in someone else's care? You just proved my point."

Rage boiled in Marella, and this time she didn't try to contain it. "I never said I'd give him away. I said I'd accept help from experts on how to care for him."

"Like that's any better. You just admitted you don't know what you're doing."

Marella shook her head. "Are you being deliberately obtuse or are you always this stupid?"

"How dare you? I'm anything but stupid, unlike you, who think you can just show up and win a challenge that hundreds of well-trained people have died in."

"You're not worth my time. Where's my dragon?" Marella glared and lowered the metal strip to her side.

"What do you think you're going to do with that?" Dyfan chuckled. "I hope you're not looking for a fight. I'm more than twice your size. You don't stand a chance."

Marella raised an eyebrow but said nothing.

"What, you think you can defeat me?" Dyfan smacked his chest, and Marella rolled her eyes. "You don't have your precious bow this time. What do you think you're going to do, beat me with that?" He pointed to the metal strip she held loosely at her side.

Again, Marella held her tongue. Her eyebrows drew together when his face turned scarlet with anger. With a furious shout, he dove toward her, but Marella stepped aside, and he crashed into the boulder behind her.

She backed away toward the center of the flats without taking her eyes off him.

Dyfan straightened and faced her, his face livid. The side of his face swelled, but he hadn't knocked himself out as she'd hoped. Marella prepared to dodge another attack, but instead he shouted, "What's wrong with you, Marella? What makes you think you're so special?"

"'Rella?" An eager little voice sounded from somewhere nearby, and Marella turned to search for Hakkan.

Dyfan took advantage of the distraction and rushed toward her. She heard him coming, but didn't react fast enough, and this time his punch landed square in her gut. Marella gagged and bent at the waist.

"'Rella!" This time, Hakkan was closer, his voice filled with shock and worry. "Why you hurt 'Rella?"

"Stay out of the way. This isn't about you." Dyfan's voice had a deep, guttural sound, and Marella straightened. Between the rage on his face, his savage punch, and the growling voice, Marella knew with certainty that he'd kill her given half a chance. She wouldn't allow it. She'd come too far and survived too much to let him win now.

She raised the metal strip in front of her like a sword but kept her grip loose and her movements fluid.

"I missed you," she whispered to Hakkan.

"Really?" The surprised hope in his voice hit her harder than Dyfan's punch. "He say you no want to go back to city with us. He say you want stay in gorge alone instead."

"No, he tricked you. I'll explain it all later, but right now—" Marella cut off as Dyfan charged at her again. This time, she was ready, and she brought the metal down hard on his right shoulder.

Dyfan cried out but kept charging. He twisted and hit her in the chest with his left shoulder, knocking her backward and toward the bed of seaweed below.

Creatures rustled the seaweed, moving toward Marella's location. She saw the danger and kicked hard to stay afloat. Serpents wouldn't behave that way, so something worse hid beneath the leaves. She wasn't about to find out what it was.

Marella lifted herself further away from the ocean floor, swimming up and over the top of the boulder behind her.

"'Rella, I help?" Hakkan swam up beside her and pressed his nose against hers. "You hurt. I help?"

Unsure what he meant or what he could do, Marella nodded. "All right. You can help."

Instead of doing something to heal her injuries, minor though they were, Hakkan spun and charged toward Dyfan. The little dragon — who had grown to almost triple Marella's size — let out a frightening roar and swiped at a stunned Dyfan with razor-sharp claws. Clouds of blood blossomed into the water around him, and his face and neck disappeared in a horrifying array of bone-deep cuts. He let out a gurgling cry and tumbled into the churning seaweed below. Half a dozen arm-length dragonaxi shredded the seaweed and attacked the injured man with a voracious appetite.

Unable to watch, Marella turned and swam away, but she hadn't gone far before she heard Hakkan beside her.

"I do good? He no hurt you 'gain."

Marella sighed and gave him a little smile. "Yes, you did good. I didn't know you could do that."

The dragonet flexed his foreclaws and eyed them with wide-eyed wonder. "Me either."

"Where's Deinnu? We should get him." Marella didn't relish the thought of telling Dyfan's dragon that he wasn't coming back, but someone had to. She couldn't leave him waiting.

"Oh, he with others. I show you."

Others. The word hurt more than she'd expected. Even though she'd guessed he'd returned to his team, she'd somehow hoped he'd been more loyal than that — even after he'd stolen her dragon and left her to face the adults alone.

Marella took a moment to compose herself before she spoke again. "How many others?"

"Many?" Hakkan cocked his head to the side and the expression of confused concentration on his face made Marella burst into laughter. Of course the little dragon didn't know how to count.

"I'm sorry. That was a silly question. Do you know their names?"

The dragon swam in a circle around her, repeating her question in a singsong voice. "Names, names, I know their names."

Marella laughed again.

"Names are Lilit—"

Marella froze, her arms and legs turned to stone, and Hakkan spun to face her. She couldn't hide her shock.

Lilit had survived? Why would she join the other team instead of going back to their cave? Cold realization dawned. *Of course, she didn't think I'd survive the night by myself, and after I messed things up with the dragons, she was awfully mad.*

"That the one Dyfan want me to join with. And Hasmig and Kasbar. That all the names."

The other two meant nothing to Marella. She couldn't even pair them with faces in her memory. They must have been Dyfan's teammates.

"Will you show me where they are?"

"They over here." Hakkan bobbed up and down in the water, apparently unaware of Marella's shock and dismay.

He led her to a small opening in the side of a nearby hill and down into a much wider cavern than she'd expected. While they swam, Marella explained that Dyfan had lied, and that she really did want to stay with Hakkan forever.

"Well, well, well, look what the dragon dragged in." The cold sarcastic voice stopped Marella in her tracks. "I didn't believe Dyfan when he said you'd survived the current. Now, here you are. How many times do I have to kill you?"

Marella shook her head. "I wouldn't try, if I were you."

"Yes, Dyfan told me all about your skill with the bow, but you don't have that now, do you? And you're alone, and I'm not. No, I'm not worried."

Two men swam in and took up positions on either side of Lilit. "Where's Dyfan?" The one on the right asked.

"He hurt 'Rella. I stop him. See?" Hakkan held out his

claws, two of which still had chunks of flesh clinging to them.

The man on the left retched, but the other two showed no reaction.

"You hurt Dyfen?" Deinnu entered from a back entrance, but Marella didn't take her eyes off Lilit.

"He hurt 'Rella. He lie to me. 'Rella not want to stay alone in gorge, he not want me to bond her." He gestured to Lilit. "He lie and lie and lie. He not lie 'gain. 'Rella nice. 'Rella not lie."

"That's right," Marella said, her voice as soothing as she could make it. "I've never lied to you."

"What do now?" Deinnu asked. He turned his attention to Marella, ignoring the other three.

"I think we should leave. We need to get back to the city. It'll be dark soon."

Lilit laughed. "Oh no you don't. You're staying here, and we're going to the city. You can't beat me."

Hakkan flexed his claws again. "You leave 'Rella 'lone!"

"Now, now." Lilit glared at Marella and transformed her face to a mask of patience for Hakkan. "I haven't lied to you, have I? Have I been anything but kind to you?"

"You say you kill 'Rella. That not true." Hakkan nudged Marella back toward the cave's mouth and put himself between her and Lilit. "You not hurt her now."

"Hakkan," Marella interrupted. "Do you know where my things are? Dyfan took my pack and my bow when you left the cave. I need those back."

"I get it," Deinnu chirped. "It here."

No one in Lilit's group moved to stop the dragonet from leaving through the back exit and returning a heartbeat later with Marella's pack and bow dangling from his front claws.

"Just leave those here with me, Deinnu," Lilit commanded, her voice firm, but gentle. "She won't need them."

"I need them, Deinnu. They belong to me. She doesn't know how to use them." Marella mirrored Lilit's tone, and the little dragon swam to her and dropped her belongings onto the cave's sandy floor.

"Let's go," Marella said in the same voice. "It's a long trip back to Pharlandzi, and we need to get there before dark." She turned to leave the cave, and Lilit screamed and lunged for her.

"No!" Hakkan called, in a tone that sounded more like a mother scolding a child than a baby trying to stop a lethal attack.

"I will not lose," Lilit ground out between clenched teeth.

"You lost the moment you tried to kill me in the down current," Marella said. "Even someone as dumb as me can see that." Her voice dripped sarcasm for the last part.

"That's where you're wrong." Lilit pulled a dagger from her belt and advanced toward Marella.

"No!" This time, Hakkan sounded angry. "You not hurt 'Rella. We go now." He lowered his head to Marella's eye level. "You hold on me? I go fast. Deinnu come too?"

Marella nodded and searched for someplace to grab. Hakkan held out his front paw, his claws closed to create a steely circle. Marella grabbed a claw and held on, and the dragon took off in a burst of speed that shot burning pain through her shoulder and into her chest. Her fingers went numb, but she somehow managed to keep hold of the claw.

He swam hard, his tail driving them forward at break-neck speed. Marella tried to focus on the landscape around her, but it all blurred into one confusing green mass of water and hills. She couldn't tell how long they traveled, but it felt like hours had passed before she heard a man's shout. The voice screamed for them to stop, and Hakkan slowed to a more normal pace before stopping in front of the city's wall.

Guards rushed out to meet them, shouting commands to each other and at Marella, who stared at them dumbly and tried to shake some feeling back into her arm.

"Are you injured?" someone asked. Gentle hands massaged her shoulder. "I think it's dislocated."

Around them, more voices joined the fray, and Hakkan stayed close by her side. "'Rella? That lot of people. They nice? They like you? Or like others?"

Marella sighed. "They're nice, Hakkan. We've left the not nice ones behind." She wished she could be as certain as she sounded, but for now at least, she needed the dragon to allow the men close to him.

"Care to introduce your dragons, miss?"

That voice sounded familiar, and Marella raised her head.

"Admiral," she began. "I—"

He shook his head. "No one thought you had a chance, girl, and now here you are with not one, but two dragonets. I'll have to look, but I don't think that's ever happened before. How did you manage it? Never mind. Let's get you to the infirmary to fix that shoulder."

Marella shook her head and pulled away from the admiral's strong grasp. "I beg your pardon, sir," Marella kept her eyes down but straightened her back. "But I need to stay with Hakkan and Deinnu for now. They've had a tough day and I won't leave them to strangers."

"I can respect that." Surprise tinged his voice, and Marella glanced up. The grudging respect on his face warmed her. "Come along, then. We'll get them settled and bring the healer to you. Will that do?"

Marella nodded and let herself be towed through the massive city gates. Crowds lined both sides of the boulevard, and this time, all of them watched her progress toward the palace between the two baby dragons.

Heads bowed and people murmured and exclaimed, but no one approached her. Marella wondered what she looked like. She hadn't bothered with her hair in nearly a week, and she had to be covered in bruises from her run-in with Dyfan and the breakneck dash for the city.

She decided it didn't matter, set her uninjured left hand on Hakkan's paw, and held her head high until they passed through the wall and into the brightly lit interior of the palace.

TWENTY-SIX

Waiting

I nstead of leading her back to the room she'd used before the challenge, the admiral took a winding path to the peak of the left-most tower.

"I'm afraid we don't have any suites that will fit two grown dragons, so we'll have to figure something out before they grow much more."

Marella didn't know what to say, so she simply nodded and hovered over the lounger until both Hakkan and Deinnu settled down into the large nest set up at the far end of the room. Within seconds, soft rumbles told her they'd fallen asleep, and Marella smiled.

"Let me find someone to heal that shoulder," Admiral Ferroa said. "And someone will be in shortly with food. I expect you'll want to see your parents, too?"

Before he'd finished the last sentence, Marella's mother burst through the door and raced over to the lounger.

"Gently, madam, she's injured," the admiral murmured as he backed out of the room. He swept down the hall and out of sight an instant later.

Marella's mother stopped a hair's breadth from gathering Marella in one of her warmest hugs, a look of fear and worry on her face. "Injured? What's wrong? What happened out there? Everyone said you didn't have a chance."

"So I keep hearing. Thankfully, no one told me that until after I'd already found and befriended a dragon." She glanced over to the nest. "Or two."

"But you're hurt? Where? How? What happened?"

"Now, Yeva, let her have a bit of space. She's been through quite an ordeal. I'm sure she'll tell us everything as soon as you let her get a word in."

Marella smiled at the warmth in her father's voice. She'd missed them both so much.

She leaned her head back against the lounger and propped her right arm up on the armrest. The movement was awkward and painful, and she had to use her left arm to accomplish it.

"You *are* hurt! How can we help?" Yeva positioned herself on Marella's uninjured left side and hovered. "Are you hungry? Look at your hair! Where's that maid? How about a pillow? There's a few over here. We need to get you some clean clothes. Is that blood on your shirt?"

"Yeva!" Her father kept his voice below a shout, but only barely.

"Sorry. Go on, Marella. You were going to tell me what's hurt." Yeva gave a sheepish smile and squeezed Marella's uninjured hand.

"I'll be all right. It's just a dislocated shoulder." Marella shifted and winced. "And maybe a few broken ribs."

"Oh, that sounds dreadful. How did it happen?"

Marella glanced at the sleeping dragonets and lowered her voice. She worried they might overhear the conversation. "Some other challengers didn't find dragons, so they tried to steal mine. They were tricky, and almost won. I'm only here by sheer luck, really." She thought back to the day's events and marveled that she wasn't dead, though she carefully avoided picturing the fight with Dyfan. "Well, a little luck and a lot of help from Hakkan." She gestured to the sleeping dragons.

She relayed the more mundane details of the weeks she'd spent in the gorge but avoided telling her parents about the dragonaxi and down current and the multiple times she'd fled from the adult dragons. She told of the trips to the flats for seaweed but left out the bit about the serpent. By the time she'd finished, it sounded like a grand adventure in one of the resorts near the shore. A little pang of guilt pierced Marella's chest, but she ignored it and turned back to the babies.

"I hope they bring food soon. I'm starving, and I'm sure they'll wake up hungry." She smiled at the memory of Hakkan inhaling the salmon and wondered what she'd feed him now.

"Marella, I know you've left out some details, dear." Her father hovered just far enough away from her right side to avoid accidentally brushing her injured shoulder. "And I'm guessing you don't want to talk about it much, but how did you manage to bring back two dragonets when everyone says it's all but impossible to find one?"

"I..." Marella paused, searching for the right words. "I bonded Hakkan, and another challenger bonded Deinnu. The other challenger stole both babies in the middle of the night, thinking he'd give Hakkan to his friend, but I found him, and we fought, which is how I got hurt. I won, and Deinnu stayed with me. He and Hakkan are brothers."

"That sounds much more dangerous than you've let on," her mother said, frowning and fussing with a blanket she'd found. She set the blanket over Marella's legs but avoided touching her anywhere above the waist.

"Thank you, Mama," Marella said, thankful for her mother's care more than the blanket. Her stomach growled, and Yeva shot up off the lounger like an arrow.

"I'm going to see what's taking them so long with your food. They were supposed to be here by now."

Before she reached the door, it swung outward and three servants entered. Each struggled under heavy-looking trays that had them panting and red-faced by the time they set the trays on the tables between Marella and the sleeping dragonets. The last servant in the room bowed as soon as she emptied her arms of the tray.

"I'm sorry it took so long, Miss Marella, but they didn't have enough food ready for two babies. We had to scramble a bit to find something for them. I remembered you said you don't much like fish, so we brought you seaweed, fruits, and some shrimp and eels. I hope that's all right."

Marella sifted through her memory in search of the green-skinned servant's name. "That's all right, Feena, I know my arrival was unexpected." She hoped she'd gotten the name right.

The girl bowed low. "Most unexpected, miss. I've never heard of someone coming back with *two* dragons, and neither has anyone else in the kitchens."

Marella smiled and bowed back to the girl but refused to answer the question in the servant's eyes.

When she realized Marella wasn't going to explain, Feena led the other servants out of the room and closed the door. Marella turned to her parents, unsure how much to say or how to explain her worry.

"Look, it's probably best if we don't mention the other challengers or that fight to anyone," she finally said. "All the other challengers trained for years for this thing, and I won by dumb luck. I almost got myself killed more times than I care to think about just because I didn't know what dangers to watch out for." She sighed. "Besides, I don't want to make trouble with other families over this. All the other participants were from powerful families with a lot of money. That's how they got chosen."

"I understand your concern," her father said. His brows knit together like they did when he was working out a particularly difficult problem. "And I've heard from others that the challenge is very elite and difficult to get into. Have you figured out how you managed to get in?"

Marella shook her head. "I honestly haven't had much time to think about it. Someone had to put my name in, but I have no idea who or why." She eyed the platters of food and her stomach rumbled again.

"Oh, dear me. Let's get you fed." Yeva sprinted to the table and lifted the lids off the platters.

Two contained piles of fish, octopus, eels, and other meats that Marella assumed were meant for the dragons. Her mother replaced those lids almost as soon as she'd opened them. The third platter held heaps of yellow and red seaweed, alongside carefully arranged dead sea creatures. Marella said a short prayer to Dalphein for their lives lost on her behalf and moved them to the platters meant for the babies.

Marella barely tasted the seaweed as she inhaled it. She swallowed some bites almost whole and didn't slow until she was full to bursting.

"Before the day gets away from me, I have to say you were right." Her father sighed and motioned for her to keep eating when she would have answered. "If you had taken the carriage back to Kaulo, your mother and Coline and I would have been exiled right behind you. I went out to see you on your way, and when I got back to our rooms, the maids were already packing our things. So thank you. You saved our position here."

Marella gulped down the bite she had in her mouth. "I had no idea. That's horrible, but somehow I'm not surprised by much anymore."

Silence fell in the room while Marella finished off the platter of food.

While she ate, a soft knock at the door announced another visitor. The door swung open before anyone could move to open it, and an older woman with brilliant yellow hair and lime-green skin swept into the room.

"Admiral Ferroa says you're injured and in need of healing. Yes, I think I see the problem already." The woman set a small black bag beside the lounger and pulled out a handful of crig beads. She swallowed two and gave two to Marella. "Go ahead. You'll need that to heal properly."

She paused and stared at Marella, who held the beads in her hand and stared blankly.

Marella had never considered swallowing more than one bead at a time. It took her half a year or more to save up enough for one. Two was an extravagance reserved for kings.

"What's the problem? Swallow them. Let's get this done. I've got others to see, you know." The woman paused, cocked her head, and frowned. "Oh, me. I haven't introduced myself, have I? I'm Bengisu Emek, healer to the dragon flights. I take care of all the dragons and all the riders, so I've got a lot of work this time of year, so let's get on with it. Swallow those."

Marella did as she was told. As soon as she swallowed, Bengisu produced a wax pencil and drew a complicated rune on Marella's injured shoulder. Blue light filled the room, but Bengisu didn't stop there. She moved to Marella's chest and drew a different rune. Purple light joined the blue, and a burning ache seeped into every bone in Marella's body. Bones snapped in her shoulder, and Marella bit her lip to keep from crying out.

Soon after Bengisu left, Marella lay back on the chaise and reveled in her victory. She'd survived. She'd won the challenge. Nothing could harm her now. Moments later, she drifted into a deep sleep. Now that she was safe, she slept harder and deeper than she had since she'd heard her name at that banquet. No dreams troubled her, and she slept until the midday light streamed through the window and landed on her face the next day.

"Oh, you're awake," a high-pitched voice cooed. "Let's get you cleaned up. I've already fed your babies. Are you hungry?"

Marella blinked and took a minute to orient herself. She'd done it, she remembered. She'd won the challenge and returned to the palace with Hakkan and Deinnu.

Alarm shot through her, and Marella bolted upright, searching for the dragons.

"They're fine," Feena cooed. "They're just in the other room, eating and napping and learning how to live in a palace."

"'Rella? You 'wake?" a blue and green head poked out from behind the wall beside Marella, and she laughed.

"Yes, I'm awake. Do you need anything? Where's your brother?" Marella winced. She sounded like her mother.

"We eated already. This room big. I swim to top and back by myself. You come see?"

Marella rose from the lounger and stretched. She paused and stretched again. Nothing hurt. She rotated her shoulder in a full circle and took the deepest breath she could manage. No pain.

"Yes, I'm coming." She swam toward the dragon and tried to ignore Feena's gentle hand tugging her back.

"Miss, you need to eat. You needed a lot of healing, and you need food for that to take. Miss, please?"

Marella ignored Feena's pleading and followed Hakkan into the adjoining room. As the dragon had said, it was an enormous space, extending all the way to the pitched roof and down for at least ten floors. Curved walls kept the space enclosed, but windows at many levels admitted so much light it felt like noon in the room.

As she watched, both dragons tumbled and wheeled in the open space. They giggled and laughed, and Marella couldn't help joining their mirth.

"Lookie, 'Rella!" Hakkan swooped low and grabbed something from the floor, spun upwards to the roof, and dropped the thing. It was at least as big as Marella herself, but brown and shaped like a dolphin.

Hakkan dove after the toy and snatched it up before it hit the floor. He laughed and swam back to Marella. "You play, 'Rella?"

Marella smiled. "I certainly will, as soon as I have a bit to eat and get my hair unknotted." Her hand drifted to her head unbidden, and her fingers found exactly what she'd expected: a mess of tangles, sand, twigs, and dirt. She winced.

"I'll help you with that," Feena chirped. She sounded excited by the idea. "It's what I do best. But first, you need to eat."

Marella let the servant lead her back to the table. Heaps of red, yellow, green, and brown seaweed had been piled up to the top of the platter, and Marella ate until she couldn't force another bite down.

"Your mama said you don't eat shrimps or eels or fish or anything that was alive, 'sides plants, so I made sure the kitchen didn't give you anything like that." Feena frowned and shook her head. "It doesn't seem right, though. How can you live on this stuff?" She picked up a brown leaf and examined it. "Never could eat it, myself." She set it back on the platter. "But it's your choice. Now that you're in the dragon flight, you get what you want. I expect the admiral'll be by this afternoon to talk to you about contracts and payments and such, but for now, let's work on that hair."

Marella followed Feena to the vanity and let her mind wander. The girl chattered on about lotions and hair care and what seaweeds would help keep it from tangling, but Marella's mind had stuck on the thing about "contracts and payments and such." What kind of payment could she expect? She fought a tiny wave of excitement. Even the servants in Pharlandzi made enough to use their crig beads for minuscule tasks like timekeeper runes.

How much more does a dragon rider earn? Marella tried to steel herself against acting foolish when the admiral announced her pay. She stuffed down the budding excitement and listened with half an ear to Feena's mindless chatter and the dragons playing in the next room.

"Oh, while I'm thinking of it, I emptied out your pack and put your things away. That yellow mushroom... I, um, you didn't eat that, right? I mean, I understand getting hungry, but you have to tell me if you ate that so I can get the healer back." At Marella's blank stare, Feena added, "It's terribly poisonous. You didn't eat it, right?"

Marella just shook her head, and Feena returned to the task of combing the knots out. While the servant worked her magic on her hair, Marella marveled at what the girl had said. She'd eaten that fungus by the handful and had felt *better* afterwards. The only explanation her mind could come up with was that the poison in the fungus and the dragonaxi poison had somehow cancelled each other out. Which would explain why she couldn't make herself eat any more of it once the dragonaxi poison was out of her system.

Before long, another sound caught Marella's attention. She sat still and strained to make out the noise. It sounded like the roar of many people, but far off. Marella shook herself, unwilling to believe her own ears.

"What's happening in the city today?" She finally asked. "Anything interesting?"

"Oh, yes, miss. There's just today and tomorrow left in the challenge, so most the people in town go down to the gate to see who comes in and what kind of dragons they found."

Marella hesitated, unsure what the customs were around the challenge. "Is that something I should go to? I mean, do the challengers who've already come back go and join the crowd?"

"Oh, yes, miss," Feena repeated. "The others're already down there."

"Well. Do I bring the dragons along? I'd hate to leave them," Marella stared through the doorway and into the tall room where the babies played.

"Oh, no, miss." The servant dragged the brush through Marella's hair again and twisted the bottom section up into an elaborate design. "They're only just babies. You shouldn't take them in a crowd like that until they're trained. I'll watch after them while you go to the gate."

Marella frowned. "I don't know. Should I leave them so soon?" Dyfan's words condemning her for considering allowing someone else to care for her baby echoed in her mind. "It doesn't feel right," she added.

"It's good you're so worried about them. Really, it is. But I can take care of them for a bit."

"How much time have you spent with dragon babies?" Marella watched Feena's expression in the mirror, searching for any hint of unease.

"Oh, I've spent lots of time with new dragonets. My father's a dragon outfitter. I grew up in the stables and only just got promoted to the house this year." Feena beamed, and Marella guessed it must have been a significant promotion.

Feena's reassurance eased Marella's mind, and she let the servant dress her in a simple green tunic that wouldn't stand out in the crowd below.

When she'd been washed and brushed and polished and dressed, Marella let Feena hand her off to another servant, who led her through a dizzying array of passages and tunnels and out onto the wall overlooking the gate.

"Ah, there you are." Admiral Ferroa bowed, and Marella returned the gesture. "I trust you've been healed and fed and well rested?"

Marella nodded.

"Good." He hesitated, and Marella waited, expecting him to start discussing pay. She couldn't wait to hear what the number would be. Instead, he cleared his throat. "I understand you've always dreamed of studying whales. You may find the city less than welcoming to an outsider with a dragon, but I can see that you receive the best zoology training available and will pay you well enough for your trouble that you'll never want for anything. I have two trained riders ready to take care of your dragonets. Just say the word."

Marella couldn't think. "You want me to give up Hakkan? And Deinnu?"

"You must realize how far behind the other students you'll be. There's no way you'll ever catch up. It'll be better for the dragons to have handlers who know what they're doing."

Marella shook her head, numb with shock. He was offering the one thing she'd worked for, dreamed of, and yearned for her entire life. She could join an academy, though certainly not the one she'd failed the exam for back in Kaulo. She could spend the rest of her life pursuing her dream. And she'd have to say goodbye to Hakkan. Forever. A pang of remembered pain shot through her chest, an echo of the loss she'd suffered when Dyfan had stolen the dragons away in the night. And in that moment, her resolve solidified into steel.

"No, I, I can't give them up. We've been through too much."

"Not even for the chance to study whales? You can start next week if you like."

The only dream she'd ever known drifted away on her breath. "No." Her voice came out stronger this time. "No, I won't give them up." She'd have to make a new dream.

The admiral gave a sharp nod and turned back to the wall. "Very well. We start training the day after tomorrow. Until then, you can wait here with us to see who else will join our ranks." He gestured to a line of at least fifty men and women, all dressed in pristine dragon riders' uniforms, with the exception of three others. Marella recognized the three faces from the beginning of the challenge, but since they'd all been in the second group to leave the palace, she didn't know any of their names.

She considered introducing herself, but since no one

had paid the slightest bit of attention to her arrival, she joined the others at the chest-high wall and peered out onto the empty hills beyond the city.

A pod of porpoises frolicked on the horizon, and Marella wondered if they were the same ones that Dyfan had tried to travel with the day she'd found him. She pressed her lips into a line at the memory and wondered if he'd actually met the animals he'd claimed, or if he'd been beaten by his teammates instead.

She tore her gaze away from the porpoises, unwilling to let them lead her mind down that path. It didn't matter. A school of brilliant yellow fish moved slowly past the gate. They moved as one creature, all moving the same direction at the same time, but never in one direction for more than a few lengths. Their movements soothed something deep inside Marella, and she sighed and rested her weight on the palace wall. Nothing that could have been a dragon or a supaerisi moved within her line of sight.

Between the hours spent staring out into the sea, Marella tried to learn the faces of the people around her. She wondered if they were all dragon riders (there were so many!) or if they were others who worked closely with the dragon teams.

A shout echoed off the wall, startling Marella back to the watch. A tiny spec approached from the far left, and for the first time, it looked big enough to be a challenger. And a dragon. Marella's breath caught in her throat. A tiny knot of fear clenched in her gut. She remembered Lilit's desperation in the cave and hoped she hadn't found a new target.

What if she did? What if she comes back here? The admiral's warning echoed in her mind. What had he meant that the city wouldn't welcome her?

Marella shoved the worry away, though it took more

effort than she expected. The other teams would have to approach from a different direction, and Lilit wouldn't know where to intercept them. That thought reassured her a little, and she strained her eyes for a glimpse of the new dragon and challenger. It felt like hours passed before the speck on the horizon grew large enough to identify, and when it did, Marella wilted in relief. She couldn't remember the girl's name, but she knew that face as the girl she'd spent the evening with at the banquet, who'd welcomed her into their group and let her join their game of stones.

"It's Taline!" Someone shouted below, and the name reverberated through Marella's mind. Yes, that had been the girl's name.

The thought of having such a friendly face on the dragon riders with her soothed Marella enough that she gave a genuine smile.

Taline swam up to the gates beside her dragon in a stately, almost regal, procession, and Marella wondered at what she must have looked like arriving the day before. She'd been beaten and bruised and disheveled, where Taline looked like a princess returning from an afternoon swim. She'd spent time on an ornate hairstyle, her clothes looked fresh and clean, and she had a happy glow in her cheeks that Marella envied.

The crowd surged into the walls of people Marella had seen the day before, but this time, she joined in. Taline waved and smiled at the crowd, and again Marella wondered at the stark contrast between this lovely, graceful creature's appearance and her own victory march the previous day.

"Well, I'd never seen this before, so I didn't know how I was supposed to look," Marella muttered under her breath, more to herself than to anyone around her.

The man beside her thumped her on the back hard enough to knock the breath out of her and laughed. "Don't you worry none about it. You set everyone to talking with your double victory. I never seen anything like it. My papa said he hasn't either. Nope, don't worry none about how you looked. You did something special, and don't you forget it."

Tears stung Marella's eyes, but she blinked them away. "Thank you." She gave the man a brilliant smile and turned her attention back to Taline, but this time, she stood a little straighter and held herself with a little more confidence.

Taline vanished inside the palace, and Marella let the crowd carry her back to the wall. She waited there until the daylight faded, and she could return to her rooms and her dragons. She'd missed them through the long day and couldn't wait to spend more time with them. She hoped Feena had been with them through her absence, so they wouldn't get lonely. Her parents sat perched on the edge of the lounger when she strolled through the door, their backs ramrod straight and their faces pale and wide-eyed with fear.

Marella froze. "What's wrong? Did something happen to the babies? Where are they? Are they all right?"

"You're worried about them?" Yeva's voice pitched higher with every word, and the last one was little more than a squeak. "They could have killed us! I won't allow you to stay in the same room as those creatures. I won't have it."

"Now, Madam Kapat, like I said, she has to stay with them." Feena fussed over Yeva and settled a blanket around the frightened woman's shoulders. "She's basically their mother now. They can't be moved away from her. They'll die if you try."

"I care far more about my daughter's safety than some wild animals she dragged in from the trench."

Marella smiled. "It's all right, Mama. They'd never hurt me, and they'll do anything to protect me."

"I can see that for myself!" Her father rose off the lounger and swam across the room and back several times. "I'm inclined to agree with your mother this time, Marella. We came in here to wait for you, and the smaller one nearly killed us both." He drew a shaky breath and met Marella's confused gaze. "It charged at us with claws out and teeth bared. I've never been so scared in all my life. I just don't know that they're safe to have around."

"You're right. They're not." Feena circled around to face Marella's parents.

Marella froze, ready to argue, but Feena continued. "Yet. They need to be trained. That process begins the day after tomorrow, and until then, they stay in here where I can keep them safe from themselves and from anyone who would harm them."

Yeva opened her mouth to protest, but Feena cut her off. "Marella's perfectly safe with them. They're already bonded."

"Mama—"

"Don't you 'Mama' me! I've made up my mind and I'm not changing it."

The door swung open, and Marella stiffened. The admiral entered with a handful of soldiers in the red dragon riders' uniforms.

"I hear there's been a problem with the dragonets?" The admiral's voice was low and dangerous, and Marella shrank back toward her parents.

"Yes, sir," Feena answered. "Marella's parents entered her room without her, and the bonded dragonet charged."

The admiral's face turned a deeper shade of green, and Feena added, "No one got hurt, though. I got the dragons corralled back in their playroom to wait for Marella."

"Well done. You've proven your worth in the palace more quickly than I'd anticipated. Thank you." He shifted his gaze and glared at Marella's parents. "What would make you do something as stupid as entering the lair of an untrained dragon — or two?"

"I...Well, I..." Marella's father began, stammered, and fell silent.

"That's what I thought. Did you ask Marella if you could wait for her in her room?" The admiral's voice had grown cold enough to freeze the water around him, or so it seemed to Marella.

"Well, no, but I've never asked to enter her room before," Yeva answered with a little more confidence.

"She's a woman grown, and still you make a practice of invading her private sanctuary uninvited?"

"Well, no, she's not quite grown yet, and..." At the admiral's glower, Yeva trailed off.

"She's grown. Quite grown enough to tame not only one, but two wild dragons and get them away from their mother without getting ripped to ribbons in the process. I'd say you owe her the respect due an officer in the King's Dragoni, even if you don't believe she's deserving of a measure of privacy."

"It's not a matter of believing her worthy or deserving of respect or privacy." Marella's father placed an arm around Yeva's shoulders and smiled in Marella's direction. "Of course, we think the world of her and would never slight her in such a way. I believe we've stumbled onto a slight difference in how our different nations handle familial relationships. In the future, we'll find a neutral place to wait for her or make sure we have her permission to enter." He turned to face Marella. "Can you forgive us?"

Marella scanned every face in the room, the tension in the set of every jaw, and the fear and anger seething behind her father's calm demeanor.

"Of course. You meant no harm. May I see the babies now? I've missed them today."

The question released all the tension, and all eyes turned to Marella.

"Yes, I need to see you interact with them," the admiral waved her toward the room Feena had called their play room. "First you'll interact with both, then one at a time."

"I... I'm not bonded to both of them, if that's what you're trying to find out." The soldiers behind the admiral gasped, and Marella hoped she hadn't misspoken again.

"That's exactly what I need to know. How did you come to bring them both with you without bonding them?"

"It's a rather long story, but the gist of it is that I bonded Hakkan and convinced him to come to the city with me, and Deinnu came because he didn't want to be alone." She hesitated, and blurted out, "I never thought to tell him he couldn't. I'm sorry if it was wrong."

The anger and fierceness dissipated, and the admiral gazed at her with kindness and compassion. "Of course it's not wrong. Just a little unusual. I'd like to speak with you in private for a moment, if I could." He gave a meaningful look to every other person present.

"Of course." Feena smiled and bowed and ushered all the others out of the room. The door closed with a quiet click, and Admiral Ferroa waved her into the dragons' room.

"You haven't spent much time around dragons, I gather?" The admiral began.

"'Rella!" Hakkan dropped from the roof and pressed his nose to hers. "You back! Mean people came and said I go 'way, but I not go 'way. I just go find fish."

"That's right, you're not going away." Marella smiled and stroked his chest. "I'm sorry I was gone so long. I'll try to come back a few times tomorrow so it's not such a long time apart." The admiral tapped on her shoulder, and Marella shifted her attention. "Hakkan, this is Admiral Ferroa. He's going to help us learn to work together."

"Exactly right," The admiral said. "I'm happy to meet you, Hakkan." He bowed deeper than anyone she'd seen, and Hakkan rumbled and chirped.

"I happy meet you."

Someone dumped a school of large fish into the room from a window near the roof, and Hakkan rushed off to eat.

"You're certainly bonded to that one. The other? Does he obey you?"

Marella frowned. "I've never told him to do anything. He's followed me, but I'm not sure if that's from loyalty to me or Hakkan."

The admiral nodded. "I see. Come, let's talk." He opened the door and swam back into Marella's sitting room. "I don't know how much you know about dragons, but these are some of the rarest and most difficult to train dragons in the sea. Would you consent to allow me to let one of my more seasoned Dragoni attempt to bond the second one, the one you call Deinnu? If they're successful, you'll be well compensated for your trouble in bringing the dragon here, and I'll team you and your dragonet with him so the brothers can stay together?"

Marella cocked her head to one side, considering what the admiral said. "It wouldn't be easy for me to stay with both, would it?" She considered for a moment and added, "In fact, it would be next to impossible. Yes, I think the best plan would be to allow someone else to try to bond with Deinnu."

"Very good. I think they should begin at once. I don't love the idea of closing a stranger in with dragonets, but I can't find any information on this. It's just never happened before. I think the best way would be for you to stay in with the dragons and the soldier tonight and the first half of tomorrow. Once the babies are comfortable, he can stay alone — if that's all right with you. After a few days, we'll try separating the babies into separate chambers. They won't be able to share this one for long with as fast as they're growing."

Horror struck Marella like a fist in the gut. "Promise me no one will take Hakkan from me? I can't lose him." She'd meant to sound strong, but the words came out in a hoarse, pleading whisper.

"Of course not. You're fully bonded. If anyone else tried to remove him, he'd shred them."

Marella sagged back on the lounger and carefully blocked the scene from the flats out of her mind.

Admiral Ferroa sighed. "I apologize for..." he cleared his throat and started over. "I realize I made an error in judgement earlier with my offer. Can you forgive me?"

"I understand why you did. You're not the first to point out how little I know about dragons. The soldier, I..." Marella stopped and cleared her throat. "You said you want him to sleep in here? With me?"

He nodded.

"All right. If you think that's the best way, we'll give it a try. Can I eat first?" Her stomach growled and punctuated her question.

"Of course." The admiral rose but paused halfway to the door. "You'll have to tell me the whole story — everything that happened out there — and soon. But for now, I just have one more question: was Deinnu fully bonded to someone else?"

Marella thought back to the dragon's interactions with Dyfan and couldn't think of a single time he'd greeted Dyfan with even a fraction of the enthusiasm Hakkan showed when he saw her. She shook her head. "No. I think he started to, but the other challenger died before they could finish the process."

The admiral nodded. "Very well. This should be fairly straightforward, then. Good day."

Soon after the admiral left, Hakkan and Deinnu swam in through the wide door. Deinnu settled into the nest, but Hakkan swam over to Marella, laid on the floor beside her, and rested his head in her lap. He'd grown, even in the few hours she'd been away. His head filled her lap and spilled over her knees. His great copper eyes regarded her, and Marella thought she saw sadness in their depths.

"Is everything all right?" She rubbed a hand down his nose, feeling the bumps and ridges beneath the shimmering blue scales.

"I want my Mama," he whined. "Miss her."

Marella sighed. "I know. I miss her, too. She'll be here in a few days, and then you'll get to see her again."

Hakkan let out a purring rumble and nuzzled closer. "Promise?"

"Absolutely. Even if the admiral says it's not customary, we'll find a way for you to see her, all right? I'll do my absolute best."

A knock at the door interrupted, and Marella called, "Who's there?" She didn't want to see more strangers just yet and prepared to tell the visitor to go away, but her mother's voice answered back, and Marella shouted, "Come on in."

Yeva opened the door and froze halfway through the doorway. "Marella," she said, drawing out every syllable. "Dearest, are you sure that's safe?"

Marella stroked Hakkan's nose again. "Absolutely. I've honestly never been safer. Hakkan would protect me from just about anything, wouldn't you?"

A chirp and rumble were Hakkan's only answer. Marella ran her hand over his head again, and the great, copper eyes drifted closed.

Before he could get all the way to sleep, Marella roused Hakkan and urged him into the nest with his brother. He fell asleep before he'd even finished moving.

Marella returned to the lounger and turned to her parents but hadn't said anything when Feena returned with a platter of seaweed and land fruits. Marella dug in and barely registered Feena's bowing exit. Moments later, the servant returned with an arrangement of edible flowers and decorative seeds.

"The admiral sends his thanks, Miss." Feena drifted over to the nest and stared down at the sleeping dragonets. "They're so beautiful," she whispered.

"They really are," Marella said around a mouthful of some sweet delicacy.

"I'm going to be here to help Illiam bond with Deinnu." Feena flushed and added, "If that's all right with you, of course."

"I'd appreciate the help. I'm new to all this, remember?"

"How did you find them? Challengers almost never

find their nests, which is part of why there's so few in the force, I think." She cocked her head and examined Marella's face.

"Well, we were really looking for any dragons, I think. We drew a grid on the cave wall and marked what we found, or didn't find most of the time, in each block at the end of the day. They were the only dragons we found at all." She tipped her head toward the nest and shoved another bit of bright orange fruit in her mouth.

Marella's mother cleared her throat. "This is all very interesting, but what happens now? What do you think you're going to do with a dragon? Or a pair of dragons? What happens to your dream of studying whales? The exam?"

"Well, I guess that's all on hold for a while, at least. I don't think the whales would tolerate having a dragon around." Marella scratched at her forehead and yawned.

"We're going to let you get some sleep. Come on, Yeva." Marella's father rose and grabbed her mother's arm. "We'll see you in the morning, and we promise we'll never barge in without permission again."

He didn't wait for a response but tugged his wife out into the hall and closed the door behind them. Marella sank back on the lounger but wouldn't allow herself to fall asleep. The admiral had said the soldier would join her with the dragons that night. Marella flushed. She hadn't realized at the time that this arrangement meant having the soldier in her chambers all night.

At least she wouldn't be alone, Marella thought. She meditated and listened to the gentle murmurs the dragons made and was startled out of a near-sleep by a sharp rap on the door.

Since she wasn't sure what the protocol was for this sort

of thing, she rose and opened the door herself. Marella stifled a laugh. Of course, the admiral had said nothing like this had ever happened before, so she supposed there probably wasn't much of a protocol.

A long, lean man hovered in the hall beyond the door. He had deep green skin and matching scales that Marella imagined would vanish easily into the murky green waters around the city. He wore a simple black tunic that flowed around his muscular arms. His copper hair had been clipped quite close to his head, and he regarded her with gentle yellow eyes.

"Marella, I presume?" He bowed low. "I'm Illiam MacNele. Admiral Ferroa said I could meet your dragon?"

His voice held all the hope and excitement of a child at the solstice celebration, eager for the gifts the ocean gods would bring.

"Of course. I've been expecting you. Have you met Feena?"

The servant bowed low and stayed close to the dragons.

"I haven't. I'm pleased to meet you."

"Feena used to work with the dragons, so she's going to help you bond with Deinnu. She knows far more about them than I do."

"Very well. I'm sure I'll appreciate the assistance. It's been a number of years since I've tried to bond a dragon. May I have a look?"

"Of course." Marella led him to the nest and stayed beside him, staring down into the deep bowl. "The larger one is Deinnu. The smaller is Hakkan, but he's bonded to me." The last bit came out faster than she'd intended, and heat filled her cheeks.

"Of course. I'm not going to try to interfere with your dragon, so there's no need to worry about that. It is good that I get the larger one, though, isn't it?" He smiled and Marella's breath caught.

She hadn't expected to like him though she hadn't been sure what exactly to expect.

"I'll stay over here with them if you want to get some sleep." He waved an arm toward the lounger she'd been resting on. "I need a chance to interact with him alone — or as alone as we can manage. I don't really want you to leave until I know he won't attack me as an intruder."

Marella nodded and urged him to let her know if he needed anything. The night and morning passed in relative silence, with only an occasional conversation with Feena when Illiam needed a meal or break.

Somewhere around time for the noon meal, Feena swam over to Marella, who'd passed the time reading the leather scrolls she'd gathered before the challenge.

"I need you to leave the room for a few minutes. I want to see how Deinnu reacts to Illiam if you're not here. But before you go, can you help me put Hakkan in the feeding chamber?"

Marella did as she was asked and in minutes, she left Deinnu, Illiam, and Feena alone in the room. It was noon of the last challenge day, so she followed the path the admiral had led her down the day before and emerged onto the city wall twenty minutes later. The admiral approached before she'd had a chance to get her bearings. He smiled and led her to the side.

"How's it going with Illiam? It must be going well if you're out here already?"

Marella nodded. "I've stayed out of the way, so I don't know for certain, but you're right. They wouldn't have asked me to leave if it wasn't going well."

Without another word, the admiral spun and returned

to watching the horizon. The afternoon passed in much the same way as the day before. Only one more challenger returned with a dragon, and he looked nearly as polished and beautiful as Taline had. Marella's shame grew with the realization that she was likely the only challenger to return in such a mess. She remembered the man's words from Taline's entrance and tried to take solace in the fact that she'd done something no one had ever done before.

The last of the light had faded to a deep violet, and the crowd had dwindled to a bare handful, when someone shouted that a group of supaerisi had been spotted. Marella rushed back to the wall. Four guards had rushed out to meet the three people. Marella couldn't see well enough in the dim light to make out faces, but she knew deep down that Lilit and Dyfan's team had decided to try something fishy.

The guards spoke with the three and returned to the castle. Instead of entering through the gates, they swam up to the admiral at the top of the wall.

"Admiral, sir." The man in front eyed Marella with a suspicious glare but snapped his attention back to the admiral. "The challengers below wish to speak with you. They claim she stole their dragons."

A gasp went through the crowd, and Marella flushed, but straightened her back and prepared to defend herself.

"There's no need," Admiral Ferroa cut the noise with a cold, haughty tone. "I've already gotten the whole story from the dragons. Since dragons are incapable of lying, I have all the information I need."

"I beg your pardon, sir, but you can't mean to exile these three. They've clearly found dragons somewhere, or they wouldn't still be swimming."

"I do not like to repeat myself. The dragons have

explained all, including how they stole Marella's pack —
and the antidote she had stashed inside it — when they
tried to steal both babies. Yes, they're cured, but only
because of Marella. They will be happy to live in exile, or
they can choose to stand trial for violating the terms of the
challenge."

"Yes, sir." The guard bowed and departed, but not
without a nasty look in Marella's direction.

Her blood turned to ice water at the chill in his gaze,
and Marella dropped her head.

"Don't let him get to you. The girl was supposed to
wed his brother, so he's not impartial."

Marella couldn't think of anything else to say on the
matter, so she asked a question instead. "Is it true that
dragons can't lie? And when did you get the story from
them? Don't mistake me, I'm glad you did, but when?"

The admiral shook his head and smiled. "I had Feena
question them yesterday while you were up here. I listened
in with a pair of communication runes."

"Of course." Marella sighed and turned to leave, but a
strong hand on her shoulder stopped her.

"I know you had a terrible time down there, and you
had no one you could trust to help you. Yet you still won.
You still brought back a dragon and an extra." He let out a
short, barking laugh. "There will be rumors for a few days,
but you keep your head up. You won. No one can take that
from you."

"Thank you, sir," Marella mumbled. Her throat ached
from the lump that had risen there, and she swallowed hard
against it. "I need to get back to Hakkan."

She didn't give him another chance to stop her but
rushed back to her room and the young dragon waiting
there.

TWENTY-SEVEN

Healer

When Errebeld woke, the cloudy water made it hard to tell how late it was. He stretched, his muscles stiff and aching from the previous day's exertions. Zaká whimpered when he pressed against her leg, and he shot upright and spun to check on her. She kept her eyes closed but pulled her legs closer to her body and let out another pained whine.

"I'm sorry, sweet." He moved away from her and frowned. Where had the others gone? Their bags lay scattered around the little camp, but no sign remained of which way they'd gone. Errebeld shrugged. Maybe they'd gone for a morning hunt. They wouldn't take him along for that. Or Zaká, now that she was injured.

Satisfied that they'd return, he rested on the ground and dug through his pack. Maybe he had one more crig bead that he'd forgotten about. It wasn't likely, given how expensive they were, but it was worth checking. Ten minutes later, he replaced all his belongings. He'd found no crig, no food, and no daquiona. Only clothes and twine and the little figurine Marella had given him so long ago.

He sighed and settled in to watch Zaká sleep and wait for the others to return.

Less than an hour later, Keird's voice echoed against the sunken ships, coming from every direction at once but carrying no words, and Errebeld brought himself upright. Within moments, his friends swam into view. Each wore a similar relieved smile.

"Good hunting?" He asked, returning their smiles. "You all look happy."

"We are." Soraya smoothed a hand over her flowing travel tunic, though it looked spotless to Errebeld. "There's a town not far from here. We stumbled too close during our morning hunt, but it looks promising."

"My sister asked. They have healer." Keird said. "Maybe healer can help." He waved a hand toward the sleeping dragon.

"Did—" Errebeld choked on the words and cleared his throat to try again. "Did you ask?"

Faize shook her head. "No, we didn't know what to say. You did the healing. You need to talk to the healer."

"That's fair." He swung his pack over his shoulder. "Who's showing me the way, and who's staying with Zaká?"

"I stay." Keird put actions to words when he dropped his pack and settled down against the dragon's side and rubbed a hand over her smooth scales. "She knows I am here."

Satisfied, Errebeld turned to the women. "Well? Let's go. The sooner we find this healer, the sooner she gets better."

Faize swam toward the line of sunken ships, and Errebeld followed without glancing back to see if Soraya had stayed behind. He hoped so. She didn't have the same affection for Zaká that the rest of them did, and she didn't seem to care what happened to the dragon. He'd rather surround himself with people who wanted the best for the youngling. The thought put a crease between his eyebrows. He'd never cared about protecting children before. What was it about that dragon that had gotten under his skin?

To avoid looking too closely, he stopped at the first bed of seaweed he found. He ate several handfuls of scarlet seaweed, stuffed more in his pack, and hurried on.

Faize swam straight toward the town and zagged through several side streets before she stopped in front of a house as tall as three of his parents' homes stacked atop one another.

"Here." She raised a hand to knock, but the door swung open and Faize nearly fell into the young woman in the doorway.

Stunned by her sudden appearance, Errebeld couldn't help staring. She was tall, perhaps even taller than he was, but slender and delicately built. Shining black hair peeked out of intricate braids wound around her head, a stark contrast to her pale blue skin and emerald green scales. Sharp green eyes caught the light and examined him from top to bottom.

"I've been waiting. I thought you weren't coming." The woman peered around Errebeld and Faize and scanned the avenue and her friendly expression melted into pity. "Where's the injured one? Were you too late?"

Faize's eyes opened wide as saucers. "No, not at all! She's, I mean, I didn't—"

"Spit it out. Where is she?" The healer drew a deep breath. "Well, come inside. We'll set people talking if we stay out here all day."

She ushered them into a cozy sitting room. Several

chaise loungers lined the walls, with small tables set between them. A tall cabinet dominated the center of the room, its heavy oak doors marked with intricate longevity runes. Errebeld examined the low ceiling and wondered about the building's apparent height. No openings in the ceiling would allow anyone to swim up to another level.

"Well? I heard you lot were asking around for a healer. Here I am. Who needs healing? I don't got time to sit around waiting all day." The woman opened one of the top doors on the cabinet and rummaged around inside.

"Forgive me, I didn't know you were expecting us. I, well, the injured supaerisi isn't exactly a supaerisi. She's—"

"A dragon. I knew that much already. Where is she?"

Errebeld drew himself up a bit taller. "She's resting outside the town. She's a haingana, and she's not quite trained. I didn't—"

"Ooh, how'd you manage ta get close enough to a wounded haingana without losin' yer head?" The woman's careful diction evaporated into a rougher dialect with her excitement, and Errebeld relaxed. He could talk to a woman who spoke that way much easier.

"It's a long story, but we, I mean my companion and I, he's still with her. Anyway, we found her as a newborn. A bultier killed her mother and her clutch mates and wounded her, but I healed her with a bit of crig and we fed her and taught her to hunt and we've been trying to train her, but that isn't going very well." It all came out in a single, rushed breath, and Errebeld had to pause for a moment when he finished.

"My, that is a tale. And now she's injured again?" Her formal diction had returned, and Errebeld felt as if he were speaking to one of the tutors his mother had kept for him.

"It must be quite severe if you managed to heal her from the bultier poison but came looking for me this time."

"It is." Errebeld knotted his fingers at his waist and visualized the deep wounds and broken bones that still marred the dragonet. "I did what I could, but I didn't have enough crig to heal her without killing myself in the process."

"And can you promise that she won't kill me the instant I've healed her?"

That brought Errebeld up short. The image of Zaká crunching down the harnesser flashed through his mind, and he had to swallow hard to keep from losing his breakfast.

"I thought not. Very well. I'll go with you, and we'll bring her here. I can't do what I need to out in the flats." Without another word, she spun and swam out the door, leaving Errebeld and Faize to trail behind.

At the edge of town, the woman stopped. Faize swam past, but Errebeld hesitated.

"I'm sorry. I haven't introduced myself. I—"

"Oh, you're right. I am Younette." She paused to tuck an errant strand of black hair behind her ear. "Younette Le Barge. Sorry. Din't think about—" Her diction slipped, and Errebeld's smile cut her off.

"You have nothing to apologize for. We showed up on your doorstep unannounced. I'm Errebeld, and that's Faize." She'd gotten so far ahead she'd nearly vanished into the murk.

"Well, let's go before she completely leaves us behind. You know where you're going?"

Errebeld nodded and hurried after Faize as fast as he could swim. He checked once to make sure Younette had kept up. She swam a hair's breadth behind him and gave no sign that the pace strained her in any way, so he raced onward toward the line of ships and his poor, broken Zaká.

They arrived half an hour later, and Errebeld thought it must not quite be lunchtime yet, though the dim, murky light made it hard to know for sure.

"Oh, the poor thing. She's just an infant." Younette swam to Zaká and pressed a hand to her broken foreleg, drawing a quiet whimper from the dragon. "You didn't tell me she's a baby."

"I—" Errebeld struggled for the words, but Younette waved him off.

"Let's go. We need to get her back to my place. She's in pain." The healer positioned herself under one wing, and Errebeld took the other. "Let's go," she repeated.

Younette tired out before they even reached the line of ships, and Keird took her place. They followed her around the town and through several narrow, abandoned alleys until the healer pressed a stone on the barren back of a building and opened a door wide enough to admit a fully-grown dragon.

Before they'd even settled the dragonet on the smooth floor, Younette tapped a stone and closed the door behind them, leaving unbroken brick walls on all four sides of the room. Errebeld longed to examine the other walls, looking for signs of hidden doors, but he turned his attention to laying Zaká on the floor without causing her any more pain.

The healer opened a narrow doorway in the floor and vanished below, reappearing moments later with a vial of crigoresi beads large enough to make Errebeld's eyes pop. He'd never seen so much wealth in one place before, and she was about to use that on his dragon. This time, the words didn't cause even the slightest hitch in his thinking. Of course she was his dragon. He'd saved her twice now.

She trusted him enough to let him carry her hundreds of miles after she'd been badly injured, even when every movement had to cause pain in her broken bones.

"Stay close to her. All of you. Your presence calms her." Younette waved them in closer and pulled out a wax pencil.

When they'd all found a spot touching the dragon, the healer drew a series of complex runes on Zaká's scales and swallowed a handful of the mineral beads. Errebeld choked at the sight of such lavish use of the rare mineral.

Blinding violet light flared, reflecting off the unbroken stone walls and hitting his eyes from every direction. Zaká stiffened and whined, and Errebeld ran a hand over her shoulder.

"It's all right," he murmured as close to her head as he could reach. "It's almost over now. You made it through the hard part already."

He kept talking until the light faded and the healer collapsed in an exhausted heap on the floor.

Darkness fell in the room, and Errebeld leaned closer to the dragon. Her breathing evened out, and all the tension leached out of her. "You're all right," he whispered. "It's over now."

She tucked herself into a tight little ball and let out a soft snore. Errebeld smiled and rubbed her shoulder. An eternity passed in darkness and silence before subtle vibrations told him someone had moved. An orb light in the corner blazed to life, blinding him all over again.

When his eyes adjusted to the light, the healer had vanished, likely through the opening in the floor, and the friends all leaned close to the dragon as if to hold her together.

~

Several hours later, Younette returned to the dragon's healing room to find the friends all still gathered there.

"Gracious. I'm sorry I left you like that. She needed more than I anticipated, and I quite ran myself dry. Come down below and get yourselves something to eat. I have someone hunting for the baby already."

Errebeld stretched and pressed a hand to Zaká's newly healed leg for a long moment before releasing her and following the healer below. Only Faize remained longer, and she exited the narrow opening only a few moments behind him.

"I'm afraid I only have seaweed and land fruits. I don't eat Dalphein's creatures, so I don't keep any on hand." Younette flushed a deep purple as she plopped a tray of peaches, oranges, and multicolored seaweed on one of the small tables.

"I don't either. This is perfect." Errebeld flashed a reassuring smile and grabbed one of the peaches. They only lasted a few days under the water, which made them a rare treat he enjoyed whenever he got the chance.

When he'd finished the peach, he straightened. "She'll be all right now, then?"

Younette's hands fell to her sides. "She will, but I'm not quite done. It'll probably take me two more sessions to heal all her breaks and cuts. It's a miracle she lasted so long, even with the little bit you healed."

"But she will be all right? She's going to live?"

The healer nodded. "Yes. She'll live. It'll be a couple of weeks before she has her strength back, though."

"Praise Dalphein," Errebeld whispered. His legs felt weak at the wash of relief.

"Younette, I have different question." Keird smiled at Errebeld and waited for the healer to turn her attention to him. "Is true an outsider joined Dragon challenge? Any news of stranger?"

The healer laughed, a sound more joyful than anything Errebeld had heard in weeks. "Yes, it's true. She showed up here, insulted the king, joined the Dragonaxi Challenge, and somehow, she did it! She's even the first supaerisi ever to return with two dragons. Everyone's all in an uproar over it all."

Actual weakness drove Errebeld down onto one of the chaise lounges. Blackness fringed his vision, and he took several slow, deep breaths to keep from passing out. The thought made him smile, and he imagined Gallien laughing at him fainting like a delicate maiden. Now that he'd made it to Pharlandzi, he'd have to figure out where to find Gallien. He couldn't be far away.

TWENTY-EIGHT

Unwelcome

The next morning, a small rolled-up square of leather accompanied Marella's breakfast. She frowned at it for only an instant before she grabbed it and scanned its contents.

Marella del Kapat,

Here is a list of the supplies you'll need to begin your training. I urge you to also consider a gift for Hakkan, which is customary, but not required. At the bottom of the sheet is your payment account number, which I have opened for you and for all the new trainees. Please purchase all the supplies today.

Tonight, at two hours before twilight, we will hold a banquet to celebrate all the successful challengers. Training begins at sunrise tomorrow.

Very Respectfully,
Commander Loncio Egea,
Dragon Training and Acclimatization Officer

The list that followed held precious few items Marella could pronounce, let alone define, and a crushing sense of loneliness and desperation filled her. Maybe Dyfan had been right. Maybe she wasn't the best one to care for Hakkan.

She picked at her breakfast and sent Feena to ask her mother and Coline to accompany her on the shopping trip. She'd barely seen her tutor since arriving in Pharlandzi, and she'd dearly missed the older woman's calm, no nonsense manner.

"Would you like me to come along?" Illiam asked. "You look like you could use a bit of help."

Marella turned to face him. She'd forgotten he was there since he so rarely spoke to her. "Would you mind? I mean, I know you're working hard to bond with Deinnu."

"The bond is growing, and I think it's strong enough now that I can leave him for a few hours to help you. I'd prefer to make sure you get the best quality rigging, and I doubt you know how to choose."

Heat flushed her cheeks. "Am I that obvious?"

"No, but you're not from here, and you've said several times that there's no dragons where you're from, so it follows that you wouldn't know what they need."

"Of course. I'd appreciate the help." Marella bowed slightly and moved toward the dressing room.

Feena had arranged for servants to put in a second heavy door, closing the dressing room in entirely so Marella could have privacy when she changed clothes. She ducked behind the door, closed it behind her, and leaned back against it. Excitement and fear mingled in her mind. She'd really done it! And now it was time to purchase the supplies she needed. The idea of the banquet sent a shiver down her spine. The last one had been disastrous.

This time, she vowed, *I'll remember the courtesies and won't offend the royals.*

When she'd dressed and let Feena style her hair, Marella and her small group met outside her room to head out on the shopping trip. Marella had begged Feena to come along, but the girl had refused and said her job was to care for the dragons in her absence. Marella had no argument for that, so the conversation had dropped.

Marella struggled to keep up with her mother and Coline and marveled at how quickly her life had changed. Just a few weeks before, she'd been disappointed with her exam results again and prepared to study even harder to pursue her dream of entering the academy as an apprentice biologist. Instead, she was going shopping to purchase the supplies she needed to train as a dragon rider.

Distracted as she was, she barely noticed when they left the palace and swam out into the market. They'd traveled less than a block before the sheer scale of the market caught her eye and left her feeling completely overwhelmed. And tiny. The buildings went up four or five floors with stores packed close together on every level. Supaerisi drifted in and out of stores selling every manner of wares imaginable, and some that Marella had never seen or heard of before.

The growing distance between her and her group alarmed her for a heartbeat, but she stopped to stare at a stunning gown in a shop window instead of rushing to catch up. The current fluttered the wispy red fabric — which would look amazing against her bronze skin, she thought — and tiny beads glittered across the bodice and upper arms. Gauzy fabric hung in layers and swept around the mannequin when she passed it on her way into the store.

Ornate gowns in every color shimmered in every inch of space above and beneath and to either side of the narrow aisle. Several brushed Marella's face and arms when she moved through the store.

"Can I help you with something?" The unfriendliness in the woman's voice brought Marella to a standstill.

"Oh, I'm just looking for something for tonight's banquet." Marella tried to ignore the way the woman's face twisted but didn't quite manage it. "How much is the red one up front?"

"I'm afraid it's not for sale." The woman glared at Marella, who fought the urge to shrink under the woman's rage.

Marella stared back and fought the wave of bewilderment and shame. Finally, she decided to try to smooth things over. "Have I offended you?"

"Your presence is offensive. What makes you think you can waltz in here as an outsider, somehow trick the panel into putting you in the challenge, steal a dragon from a rightful challenger, and then drift in here like you haven't a care in the world? Why should I sell anything to you?"

Frozen in place by the woman's vitriol, Marella gaped.

"Well, what do you have to say for yourself, girl?"

Marella jolted into motion, darting for the door. "I–I'm sorry. I'll see myself out." She rushed out into the market-place before the woman could say another word.

The experience left her baffled and hurt, and she hurried off in the direction her mother had gone. She needed the safety of her friends around her. She couldn't find them on the street, so she hurried along, checking the windows of each store for any sign of them. Her mother's bronze skin would stand out in the crowd as much as hers did, so Marella searched for that.

She considered calling out, shouting for her mother or for Coline, but couldn't stomach the idea that she might be ridiculed for that at the banquet. No, she'd have to either find them or find a way to purchase the items she needed. After an endless minute, she spotted Coline's copper skin and blue hair through a shop window and rushed inside.

Her mother, Coline, and Illiam had gathered around a young man demonstrating some sort of harness, and Marella slipped in between her mother and her tutor. As soon as the man noticed her, his demeanor changed. His enthusiasm evaporated and his voice turned cold.

"Are you with her?" He asked Illiam with a sneer.

"No, she's with me." The dragon rider squared his shoulders and adopted a military bearing that would have cowed the most determined naysayer.

"Oh, well, in that case, will you be buying? Or are you finished browsing?"

Illiam eyed the man with an uneasy glare. "We'll buy two of each. I have a new dragon I need to outfit."

A sly smile crossed the merchant's face, but he reigned it in and replaced it with a friendlier grin. "Excellent. And which of the new dragons is yours, good sir?"

"That hasn't been decided yet," Illiam snapped. "Make them both exactly the same."

They finalized the transaction and Illiam hurried out of the shop, his chin up and his back ramrod straight.

Marella caught up to him in the alley. "Thank you for that. How do I pay you for mine?"

"We'll head over to Maleril's. Have you been there yet?"

Marella shook her head.

"It's Pharlandzi's main bank. Admiral Ferroa arranges

the payments directly into accounts there, so he's not having to distribute coins every week. It's easy to move a bit from one account to another. You have your account number?"

Marella checked her pocket, felt the rolled-up bit of canvas, and nodded.

"Good. Let's go." He took off at a pace she had to work hard to match.

Two dozen blocks of shops and colors whizzed by in a blur, and he stopped in front of a narrow door. No windows showed either above or below the level of the door, and Marella frowned at the imposing building. It had to be at least double the height of her uncle's palace. A solid stone wall extended up toward the surface and unbroken by any adornment, windows, or additional doors.

Illiam yanked the door open and entered in the same hurry he'd shown in the market, and Marella did her best to keep up.

She didn't know what she'd expected, but the bare stone walls and unadorned floors weren't it. A single row of windows opened at the far end of the mostly-empty room, and a few supaerisi milled about in the center of the barren space. Illiam moved into position beside a tall man in a red soldier's uniform and crossed his arms over his chest. Marella stayed close, but no one either looked or spoke to her.

The line moved quickly, and before long, the woman behind the far-left window beckoned them to approach.

Illiam explained the situation, and the woman took down both their account numbers and entered them into a ledger beside her window.

"All done. Is there anything else I can help you with?" The woman chirped.

Illiam shook his head and swam to the door, but Marella lingered. "Can you tell me how much is in my account? I'm new to all this."

"Of course, dear." The woman flipped through a separate ledger. "You have a thousand silver pieces. Nine hundred and eighty-eight after the transfer."

Marella's mouth went dry. "Thank you." She hurried after Illiam, trying to process that much money. She'd never had so much, had never dreamed of having such a sum without decades of experience and work.

The rest of the shopping went smoothly. Marella purchased everything on her list, and though the shopkeepers weren't as hateful as the first had been, they weren't exactly friendly, either. The admiral's warning that she might not be welcome in the city rang true with every encounter.

"I'll meet you back at the palace. I have to meet someone." Illiam grinned and a hint of color touched his cheeks. "I'll be back soon."

Marella wondered about who he was meeting but didn't think about it for more than a heartbeat. When she turned back to the alley, her mother and Coline had vanished. Marella searched every window, her heart pounding in her ears. She wouldn't brave any store without someone else by her side, not after the first experience she'd had that day.

Instead of searching, Marella turned toward the palace and swam hard from corner to corner. She hurried toward the safety waiting in her chambers and the comfort of her dragon's proximity. She distracted herself with the mental image of Hakkan's copper eyes and worked to ignore the prickle on the back of her neck that warned her she was being watched. The sensation didn't lessen when she sped up, or when she turned a corner to escape the busiest street. She checked the alley behind her and saw nothing out of the ordinary, but unease left her queasy, and her heart raced against her ribs.

She turned another corner to align herself with the palace's main approach, but a small group of green-skinned women blocked the path. Each wore an elaborate gown, as if they'd already dressed for the evening's festivities, and their tightly braided hair shimmered with gemstones and pearls. Marella dropped to a lower depth and moved to pass them, but they mirrored her maneuver and blocked her again.

"Where you going?" One woman asked.

"What's the rush?" another chimed in. "Off to steal another dragon?"

"That's right, we know all about your little secret." This woman wore a gown without the sparkle the others had, though the cut and fabric shimmered and flowed with the current. "Did you really think Lilit would let you get away with it?"

"I didn't steal anything," Marella ground out through clenched teeth. She thought she could outrun them if she could break through the group. Their heavy gowns and jewelry would slow them down. She waited for an opening and tried to block their words.

"Right, like a little princess like you could manage to bond a dragon. We're really supposed to believe that?" The woman spat at her, but the distance dissolved the disgusting plug of mucus in the sea water.

Marella shifted backward.

"And you think we'll believe that you managed it when someone who trained her whole life for this challenge, who knew all the different breeds of dragon and their behavioral patterns, who knew the dangers lurking in the gorge, and who knew how to hunt for food — instead of foraging like an insect... You think *she* failed when you succeeded?" The woman with the bright pink hair laughed.

Marella searched for a way around the group, but they'd spread out, so two women stayed above and below, and three blocked her direct path. The pink-haired woman spoke again.

"No, I don't think so. You'll get yours; don't you worry. Lilit lived to tell everyone about your treachery. You won't get away with it for long. Just wait until Admiral Ferroa hears what you did. He won't tolerate it."

Marella longed to scream that Admiral Ferroa already knew the whole story, the truth, but she bit her tongue. Nothing she said would make an impression on these women. Instead, she dropped her chin to her chest and tried to look contrite. When one of the women grabbed her shoulder, Marella elbowed her in the gut and rushed past her and the group. She swam as hard as she could until she reached the palace gates.

She didn't let herself think about what had happened until she'd made it safely to her room and closed the door behind her. There, she sank onto her lounger and let the fear, frustration, and anger out in hot tears and noisy sobs.

A nose pressed against her cheek, and Marella sniffled.

Hakkan pressed closer. "You sick? I help?"

Marella couldn't fight the smile, and she leaned her head against his. "No, I'm not sick. I didn't have a very good morning, but I'll be all right."

"What happen?"

Marella shook her head. "It's too much to explain. I'm not sick, and I'm not hurt. I'll be all right." Desperate to escape his innocent questions, Marella changed the subject. "What did you do while I was gone?"

"I eated." Hakkan grinned. "Feena give me big fishes, and I eated them all. I not have to share with Deinnu today."

"Oh? Why not?" Marella rubbed a hand down his nose.

"Feena say he move in with Illiam. He stay across cord."

Marella cocked her head and tried to decipher the dragonet's meaning. "Across the cord? Oh! Across the corridor?"

"Yes, that word. Feena say I see him every day, whenever I want." Hakkan lowered his head to her lap and rumbled. "I eat big food."

"I'm glad." Marella stroked his head and nose and pressed her forehead to his. "Are you happy here?"

"Happy? What is happy?" The dragon eyed her with his coppery gaze and Marella flushed.

"Well, it means..." She frowned, trying to come up with a suitable explanation. She came up empty handed. Instead, she asked, "Are you sorry you came here with me?"

"No, why be sorry? Feena nice. Illiam nice. 'Rella nice. Food very nice. I not sorry."

Marella nodded and let silence fall between them. She breathed deep and leaned against him, happy to have him there with her. She hoped she'd be allowed to take him with her to the banquet, so she wouldn't have to worry about women like the ones who had cornered her in the city. She fought back a wave of guilt at the thought. He didn't need that kind of pressure. Still, she remembered how he'd protected her from Dyfan's attack and knew she'd be safe whenever he was near. She couldn't manage to feel as ashamed as she thought she should for hoping he'd be allowed to go.

TWENTY-NINE

Rescue

Several hours later, Marella sat still in front of the vanity while Feena braided and wound her hair into an intricate pattern. She'd chosen a shimmering silver gown that offset her bronze skin and gold-toned scales. Feena wove white and silver beads into her hair and hung more silver and white gems from her ears and throat. The effect left Marella breathless. Her yellow eyes glowed in the light from the orb lamps on the wall and her clothes and hair sparkled with every breath.

She grinned back at her reflection and spun to hug Feena. "You're a magician! Thank you so much!"

"You look amazing! You'll be the most beautiful woman inducted into the Dragoni tonight." Feena hugged her tight enough to squeeze the water from her chest and knock the breath out of her.

Her experience in the market flooded her mind, and she asked the question she'd thought of when she'd first returned to her room. "Can... I mean, can Hakkan go with me? I'm a little nervous, and I think I'd feel better if he was there, too."

"You'll do fine. You've got nothing to be nervous about." Feena smiled and held her at arm's length. "You look incredible. Prince Avak will certainly want to dance with you again."

Marella grinned and remembered the rush of dancing with the prince but broke down and told Feena all about her shopping trip and how she'd been treated.

"Oh, you poor dear." Feena fussed at Marella's neckline and sleeves. "Yes, I can see why you'd be nervous, all right."

With a deep sigh, Marella shifted away from the maid. "Is it time to go yet? And can Hakkan join me there later?"

"Do you really think that's a good idea? After what happened with Dyfan? What if he decides you need protecting at the banquet?"

Marella winced. "Good point. All right, but if things go bad, I'm leaving. They can't make me stay there, can they?"

"No. No one will make you do anything. It's supposed to be fun. And you said you made friends with Taline, right? Maybe you two can stay close together and enjoy the party."

"All right. I'll try to have fun." Marella's stomach did a painful flip, and her smile slipped to a grimace.

She said good night to Hakkan and swam out to meet her parents. They traversed the halls together, chatting about the city and the parties and the immense amounts of food required to support such a large number of people.

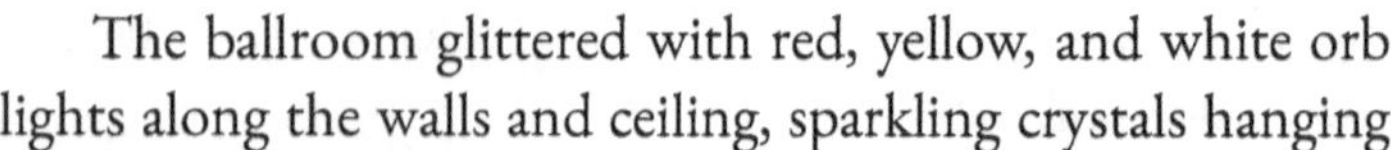

The ballroom glittered with red, yellow, and white orb lights along the walls and ceiling, sparkling crystals hanging every few feet into the water above the dance area, and great waving clusters of decorative sea plants. Musicians in a corner played a soft melody on trumpets and tiny drums, and Marella worked to keep the awe off her face. She couldn't look like the stunned country bumpkin again.

Taline approached as soon as they entered the ballroom with an excited grin that shone brighter than all the gems in her hair. "I'm so glad you made it! I was so worried for you. We had so much fun at the selection dinner, and now we get to train together."

Unable to hold back an answering grin, Marella nodded. "I was so happy to see you return, too! It's wonderful to see a friendly face around here."

"What do you mean? Everyone here is friendly. That's one of the reasons people flock to this city." Taline waved a hand at the crowd. "Oh, my sister just arrived. I have to go say hello."

She rushed off, waving and calling to a very pregnant woman who had just entered beside a finely dressed man.

Marella clung to her mother's side throughout the announcements and never strayed more than a length until the drums sounded the call for dinner. When they arrived in the dining hall, Marella's heart sank. The dragon riders had been assigned seats at a separate table from the politicians and ambassadors. Other guests had seats assigned at the other tables throughout the room. She found her chair between two challengers she didn't know, though Taline sat across the table and one seat to her right.

Anxious flutters filled her stomach, and Marella sent a prayer to Dalphein for a vegetarian option. She didn't think she'd be able to force any slimy dead creatures into her already-queasy stomach.

"Are you all right? You're looking a bit green, and I

don't think that's your normal color." The young man to her right shot her a charming smile.

Marella flushed and dropped her gaze. "I'm just a little nervous. I'm not used to events like this."

"I thought you were supposed to be royalty? The king's cousin, or something like that." The young man smiled again, and Marella hoped this wasn't a trap.

"I'm the Kaulo king's niece, but we never had events like this back home. Our area has tremors and strong currents that knock tall buildings down all the time, so even the palace is a fraction of the size of this room."

"I forget how different life must be in different landscapes. Do you like it there? I've heard great things about the scientists and artists in that region."

Marella smiled. "Of course I love it. Who doesn't love their homeland?" she considered her words and added, "And yes, we have some amazing scientists and incredible artists. When I was little, I dreamed of studying under the experts near my home, but of course all the children there do."

A flood of servants interrupted the conversation with a display of platters, plates, and dishes that made Marella's eyes pop. Brilliantly colored fruits and vegetables from the shore decorated the more neutral seaweeds and creatures Marella had expected to dominate the table.

She wished she'd been able to stay close to her mother but decided to begin as she meant to proceed as Coline had always advised her. She selected several fruits, vegetables, and seaweeds, but refused every offer of fish, eel, and shrimp.

"You really don't eat meat?" The man beside her asked. "I thought that was just a rumor."

Marella smiled and weighed her words. "No, where I'm

from almost no one eats things like that. I'd never tried eel or shrimp until the first banquet I attended here. It was an interesting experience."

The man laughed. "I can only imagine. I'm Demir Tan. You must be Marella." He bowed low without rising from his seat, and Marella worried he'd press his nose into the loaded plate in front of him.

"I am." Marella returned the bow but made sure to keep her necklaces and glittering fringe out of her plate. "It's good to meet you. I guess we'll be training together?"

He smiled. "You bet." He turned his attention to his meal and ate fish, eel, and shrimp with just as much enthusiasm as the vegetables and fruits.

Marella swallowed against the flutters in her stomach and ate as many different fruits, vegetables, and seaweeds as she could manage. She didn't know much about their various nutrient contents, but Coline had always said variety was better than a limited diet.

Taline and the others made friendly conversation, and Marella tried to relax into the meal.

She kept her eyes on her plate while she talked, enjoying the more flavorful fruit and barely tasting the rest. Before she felt full, the drums sounded again, calling an end to the meal.

Another series of drum and trumpet sounds announced the beginning of the dancing, and Marella hung back as everyone else rushed out of the dining hall. She didn't think she could manage dancing with her current anxiety level, so she'd try to stay out of sight while the first couples paired up.

The band struck a chord and launched into an energetic tune, and Marella decided it must be safe to leave the dining hall.

"There you are!" Demir grinned at her as soon as she entered the ballroom. "I thought you were right behind me. Care to dance? I'm not very good, but it might be a fun way to get to know each other." His bright smile almost hid the flush on his cheeks.

"All right. That sounds fun." Marella let him lead her onto the dance area, where they stayed after the song ended.

After the fourth song, Marella laughed and held up her hands. "I need to catch my breath!"

Demir led her toward the snack table. She grabbed a few fruits and nibbled, and he bowed and swam off. She guessed he was searching for more entertaining partners.

"Are you having a good time?" The sneer in the unfamiliar voice shot a dagger of fear into Marella's gut. She took her time selecting a few more pieces of fruit before turning to face the stranger.

"I asked you a question, kidai. I said, are you having fun?"

Marella squared her shoulders and raised her chin. She'd heard that slur enough from travelers in the markets back home, she knew how to control the anger it sparked within her. "I am. Are you?"

The short, stocky woman narrowed her eyes and leaned closer to Marella. "You think I could have fun?" Her voice pitched higher with each word. "You killed my son and stole his dragon, and you think I'm having fun?"

Marella blanched at the woman's fury and pain but held her ground and kept her voice even and low. "I didn't kill anyone. And I certainly didn't steal a dragon. Such a thing isn't even possible. They're big enough to choose who they travel with."

"You lie! I know you killed him. I've talked to the others you stole from and heard the whole truth already! You want people to believe you're so smart and wonderful, but we can see right through that little act. You're a liar and a murderer."

A crowd had gathered, and Marella searched for a friendly face. Seeing none, she lowered her eyes. "I'm sorry for your loss, madam, but I had nothing to do with it. The others were hiding in a cave when he died, so they have no idea what happened. You've already decided what to believe, so I don't think I can change your mind. Good day." She shoved her way past the woman and swam up and over the assembled crowd, but a group of men stopped her before she could reach the door.

"Going somewhere? You just called my daughter a liar, and now you think you're just going to run away like a slug?"

Marella's heart sank. Several more people lined up behind the man, and the crowd she'd just escaped closed in around her.

"What's going on here? Disperse! I order you to disperse!" Prince Avak shoved his way through the crowd and waved them away. He grabbed Marella's arm and led her away from the crowd and through a door in the grand hall's far wall. "What happened? Are you all right?"

Marella blinked and swallowed against the lump in her throat. "I'm all right. I don't know how to respond to this. I swear I didn't kill anyone. And I didn't steal a dragon. And..."

"I know. I've already spoken with Admiral Ferroa. He assures me he's gotten the whole story from the dragons, and you're innocent."

"Thank you." Marella sighed. "Is it too early for me to go back to my rooms? I've had enough, and I miss Hakkan."

The prince smiled. "I've heard it's amazing to bond with a dragon. I'm hoping my parents let me attempt the challenge next year, when I'm old enough to enter."

Marella winced at the last part. She hadn't been old enough, according to the rules, but she hadn't entered, either. "How can I find out who put my name on the list?"

"I don't know what you mean." Avak scowled. "The only way to sign up is in person. Even parents can't put their children on the list unless the challenger is also present." He spoke as if reciting from a rule book, and Marella shook her head.

"But I didn't. I didn't know anything about this thing before that night."

"Well, if you make an announcement that you didn't enter yourself, you'll forfeit your win — and your dragon — and then you can have the future your parents say you'd planned for. They won't even exile you from the city since you succeeded in the gorge. Will that work?" He smiled.

Marella's heart sank. The admiral had made the same offer, but she didn't think anyone else knew that. "No. I don't want to lose Hakkan. He's a friend. I won't, can't, just give him away."

"Well, I guess that's settled, then. If that's really how you got into the challenge, I'd keep it to yourself."

A single drum beat out a simple rhythm behind him, and Marella raised her eyes to the ceiling.

"Oh, good. They're starting. You can stay without worrying about them." He hitched a thumb toward the crowd he'd rescued her from. "They can't bother you once things get rolling."

Marella shifted to see around him, and he ducked down and swam around beside her. More drums joined the first. A brilliant yellow dragon carrying a scarlet-clad rider burst through a door near the ceiling, and the crowd below cheered.

A red dragon followed, and then a green one. Marella searched for one with markings like Hakkan's but none came. A dozen dragons circled the ceiling, moving their tails in time with the drums. Anticipation built in her stomach.

Admiral Ferroa rose out of the crowd to a spot halfway between the crowd and the circling dragons and raised his arms over his head. The drums stopped and the crowd fell silent.

"Our new inductees will spend the next four months in intensive training with their dragons and their new teams. Challenge winners, you won't see your families during that time, so say your goodbyes now." He paused and made a show of searching the crowd below for the winners.

Marella dropped her gaze to the crowd. She hadn't seen her parents since before the meal. There had been too many unknowns going into the night, she decided. Her mother's bronze skin gleamed in the light of a blue orb lamp to Marella's left, and Marella rushed over to her. Without a word, her mother wrapped her in a crushing embrace, and Marella laid her cheek against her mother's shoulder.

"Stay safe," Yeva whispered after a long moment.

Marella blinked and nodded. "I will." She squeezed her mother once and pulled back. "Where's Papa?"

"He was talking to another emissary last time I saw him. We didn't know you'd leave tonight."

"Challenge winners, please line up in front of me." The admiral waved an arm at the empty water between him and the far wall.

"Me, neither." Marella whispered to her mother. "Tell him I love him."

She waited a heartbeat longer, making sure at least a

couple other challengers had left the crowd before she followed.

She had no idea what to expect but gathered with the other challengers under the admiral's gaze, she felt safer than she had since she'd arrived in Pharlandzi. Hope filled her chest that the other Dragoni could help her figure out how she'd gotten into the challenge, and without putting Hakkan at risk. And maybe, just maybe she'd finally find a new normal with her team.

To be continued...

Acknowledgments

So many people helped me make this book a reality. I'm truly thankful for each and every one of you.

My editor, Elizabeth Prybylski, first and foremost. Your support has meant the world to me while I've struggled with this story. My sisters, Rose, Angel, and Jamie, thank you for listening as I agonized over minute details, and thank you for your advice that went a long way towards making the story what it is today. My beta readers (in no particular order): Connie Powell, Karen Grove, Alun Seymore, Joyce Margosiak, Kristine Fintoski, Angel DeJarnett, April Tippett, Jamie Cifaldi, Rose Lewis, Teagan Hunter, Margena Holmes, Ilana Pratt, Jonathan Goodman, and Michael Leason. Each of you gave me feedback that helped me grow this story from a lump of coal into the shining jewel of my imagination.

Thank you all.

Get Updates

If you enjoyed The Dragonaxi Challenge and want to stay in the loop about upcoming books and receive free short stories, sneak peeks, and inside looks at the life of the author, sign up today at https://mailchi.mp/8a48e1a464e9/untitled-page and get Captured, a short story prequel to The Dragonaxi Challenge FREE.

www.ingramcontent.com/pod-product-compliance
Lightning Source LLC
Chambersburg PA
CBHW061053190726
48286CB00006B/1733